JESSICA'S WIFE

"On-target! A bright-eyed novel that tackles just about every topic going today."
Detroit Free Press

Marriage
Group Sex
Women's Lib
Parenthood
Gay Lib

And One Woman's
Spirited Quest
To Make Her
Wildest Fantasy
Come True

"An X-rated, liberated romp."
Kirkus Reviews

"Good, clean fun. She makes you smile . . . she makes you think."
The New York Post

D1453367

JESSICA'S WIFE

HESTER MUNDIS

AVON
PUBLISHERS OF BARD, CAMELOT, DISCUS, EQUINOX AND FLARE BOOKS

AVON BOOKS
A division of
The Hearst Corporation
959 Eighth Avenue
New York, New York 10019

First Avon Printing, May, 1976

AVON TRADEMARK REG. U.S. PAT. OFF. AND
FOREIGN COUNTRIES, REGISTERED TRADEMARK—
MARCA REGISTRADA, HECHO EN CHICAGO, U.S.A.

Printed in the U.S.A.

For my extraordinary husband Jerry

and

Germaine, Simone, Kate, Gloria, Shulamith, Betty,
Robin, Letty, Joan, Joy, Susan, Carolyn, Shelli, Nicky,
Milly, Claire, Pat, Selma, Harriet, Gerda, Sondra,
Nina, Geraldine, Elaine, Julie, Marjorie, Judy, Iva, Joyce,
Beverly, Carole, Libby, Sheryl, Sheila, Hope, Janie,
Spivy, Bunny, Lucy, Fredi, Laura, Phyllis, Wendy, Pam,
Sharon, Donna, Dolly, Rita, Shirley, Abby, Saki, Wilma,
Peggy, Kathie, Barbara, Marcy, Cathy, Nancy, Debby,
Royce, Holly, Brenda, Emily, Jackie, Helen, Kitty, Rose,
Dianne, Ruthie, Valerie . . . and Grandma Nachamie

CHAPTER 1

Jessica had a perfect marriage.

She'd decided this sometime after asking for the divorce and before the baby had been born. It was, and she knew it, an outrageous presumption—particularly since she'd thought the same of her first marriage—but it was instantly a Jessica Truth of Life. A tenet of her personalized faith, as founded in reality as the Tooth Fairy, as comfortingly irrefutable as the stars. It gave her strength for every argument she and Victor had, succored her during their second near-split last Christmas, and raised, on occasion, little Aaron's toilet training to an act of existential beatitude. But like the tenets of all great faiths, Jessica Truths of Life were, at different times, under various circumstances, by other people, subject to interpretation. Celia Remson, just last week, had called Jessica's perfect marriage a crock of shit.

"You don't understand," Jessica had protested. "I mean perfect for *me*."

"I understand that you've become successfully conditioned to your role as Victor's wife, that's what I understand," Celia said. "If you only understood what I understand, Jess, you'd know that too. You're a

7

prisoner in your own home, in your own head. No matter how happy you think you are."

"But I am happy."

"That's your opinion."

"It's my marriage."

"It's a crock of shit."

The Priors' brownstone was one of a row of narrow fraternal buildings that lined the sunny side of West Eighty-seventh Street. Like many of the others on the block, it had three stories above a basement level, a set of stone stairs leading up to the main entrance, and another curving down to a separate apartment. Unlike any of the others, it was painted yellow (a mistake that Jessica would never admit to Victor—who had been against it from the start—or to herself). Jessica's brother, in an unprecedented attempt at humor, called it a gabled banana.

In sunlight the house looked particularly festive. Jessica squinted as she put Aaron into his stroller. She reached into the bag hanging from the carriage for his toy school bus. It too was yellow. She put it on the small plastic tray in front of him. Someone called her name and she looked up. Celia was across the street, waving; her two daughters (Tweedle-dee and Tweedle-dum, Victor called them) sat tandem in an old English pram and flapped their mittens at Jessica.

"Ambush," Jessica told Aaron. She sighed and crossed the street.

By no stretch of a friendship was Celia Remson attractive. She was pudgy and sallow-skinned, given to blotches, chapped lips, and excruciatingly long earrings. Though none of her features was particularly bad, neither was any particularly good. Her short hair

8

was curly but thin, her long eyebrows shapely but hairy. What by itself would have been a beautiful nose jarred in context of her face. She wore contact lenses—though she looked amazingly better in glasses—and from late September to early June she enshrouded herself in a long, dark, woolen poncho with two small orange-and-chartreuse cockatoos embroidered on the side. Jessica had met Celia two years ago in the vest-pocket park on the corner of Columbus Avenue. With Aaron just six weeks old, Jessica had been feeling detached and incapable of relating to her postpartum peers, to detailed recapitulations of pregnancies and labors, to discussions of whether or not Dr. Mark should have his bitchy wife and three beautiful children to marry the lusty ex-nun he'd impregnated on *Life Glides By,* when Celia, looking like someone out of an Italian Western, sat down beside her and opened up with prison reform. Celia was, Jessica soon discovered, her neighbor, mercifully bright, a Phi Beta Kappa from Columbia, and always so intensely involved with a Cause that, like boycotting nonunion vegetables and scooping up after your dog, simply being her friend seemed morally right. Jessica enjoyed being morally right as long as it didn't conflict with her sex life, her perfect marriage, or her Tuesday-night exercise class at the Y. Unfortunately, Celia did.

"You really should have been at the block meeting last night." Celia wagged her head disapprovingly.

"Couldn't. Hi, Naomi. Hi, Ruth." Jessica patted first the two-year old, then the three-year-old. They giggled; Ruth punched her younger sister in the back. "I had class."

"You're coming tonight, aren't you?"

"Tonight?" Jessica hesitated. "Oh tonight. How could

I forget?" Celia had done everything short of stamping the date across her forehead to remind her. "Sure."

"Sure?"

"For godsake, Celia, Do you want it in writing?" It was a rhetorical question. Celia was obsessive about "getting it on paper"—apologies, dreams, ideas, promises. She had a drawer stuffed with purchase receipts dating back to the sixties. Any argument, she'd told Jessica, and she'd have the bastards on paper.

"Jess, it's not for me that I want you to come. It's for you, the real you, the"—she clenched her fist, clawed for a word—"the you *you!*" She opened her hand slowly. "Do you understand?"

"Celia, I—"

"I'm not a pusher, Jess. I don't push. I care. If I didn't care, I wouldn't care, you know what I mean? I can't tell you how unhappy and unfulfilled you really are. I can only hold the candle and hope you see it for yourself."

Celia had been brandishing her candle in an agressive campaign to "Light the Lamp of Liberation" for Jessica since last November, when Jessica had unwittingly agreed to help with a publicity release for Phyllis Oberon, a militant feminist running for district representative. Jessica had suggested deleting Ms. Oberon's more radical sentiments—capital punishment for male chauvinist employers who had degraded the minds of females with years of heavy dictation and endless pencil sharpening, and compulsory castration for rapists—which drove Celia, to say nothing of Ms. Oberon, into a proselytizing frenzy. Jessica's consciousness needed more than raising: It needed excavation. Not that Jessica believed this, but going to a rap session with Celia seemed the only way to prove it.

It was also the only way to get Celia to lend Jessica her car.

Celia had a thing about her car.

Celia, who snatched ice-cream cones from her daughters' mouths for any lean member of a minority group, who gave up her cultured pearls to stop the war, and donated her husband's golf clubs to fight sickle cell anemia, was as defiantly possessive of her car as an old maid was of her cherry. She'd bought the automobile second-hand from an uncle for three hundred dollars and enshrined it for fifty a month in a small, dingy garage between Broadway and West End Avenue. The garagemen thought it was a Mafia hit car—it was moved so infrequently—and were sure Celia was a front. Celia only used it for weekend trips to Woodstock, where the Remsons had a summer house. When Jessica had mentioned a few days ago that she had to rent a car this Sunday, Celia had offered hers on the condition that Jessica attend the rap session. Tit for tat, not to mention Jessica's own good, she said. Blackmail, Jessica knew, but certainly cheaper than Avis.

They walked down Eighty-seventh Street and turned south on Broadway toward Sloan's supermarket. Celia passed the entrance and went instead directly to a bridge table positioned near the window, picked up a flyer without looking at it, and dropped a quarter into a painted coffee can. Two midgets, a man and a woman, were sitting on stools behind the table. They peered into the coffee can, then thanked her. The man raised a tiny plump fist in salute. Celia did the same. She said, "Power to the Little People."

The electric eye that automated the supermarket's In door was out of order; Aaron's stroller bumped against

the glass. He laughed. Jessica cursed, braced the door
with her foot, and with difficulty wheeled Aaron into
the store. When he spied the familiar wire grocery
wagons he squealed and pounded the stroller tray with
his metal school bus. The left fender caught him on the
chin. He blared into tears.

A checkout clerk moaned across her cash register.
"Ohmygod. I can't take another screamer in here today."

"He's not a screamer, you old weed," Jessica muttered as she lifted Aaron into her arms. "Do you want
Mommy to hit the bad bus, honey?" Aaron nodded.
"You're a bad bus." Jessica smacked the roof of the
toy. "Don't you ever hit Aaron again!"

Satisfied with his mother's vengeance, Aaron ges-
tured excitedly toward the shopping carts. Jessica se-
lected one with a seat and sat him in it.

An old woman in a man's long gray overcoat was
hunched over the freezer chest picking up packages of
peas, shaking them and putting them back. The sleeves
of her coat were encrusted with cat hair. Each time she
rattled a box, fur flurried. Jessica reached quickly for
two packages of spinach—but not quickly enough. The
woman gripped her forearm.

"Is that your little girl?" She pointed at Aaron. "I
had a little girl like that once."

Jessica pulled her arm gently away. "He's a boy."

"She's two, isn't she?" The woman touched Aaron's
face. "You're a happy baby, aren't you, honey?"

Jessica moved the cart forward. "He's two and he's
happy. Say bye-bye Aaron." Aaron waved, lurching as
his mother pushed the wagon down the aisle. Why
were the weirdos always waiting to put their paws on
Aaron? The kid seemed to fascinate the aging flotsam

of Broadway who frequented Sloan's. They were never nice little-old-grandmother types. Always weirdos, draped in scroungy coats, even in summertime, their faces pitted and pocked by time and boils, ravaged by unpronounceable diseases, waiting for Aaron, hands ready. How had Albert Schweitzer done it? Jessica never left Sloan's without feeling vaguely queasy and inconsolably guilty.

Outside, Celia was leaning over the bridge table talking to the midgets. Her daughter Ruth had scrambled out of the carriage and was pulling at the man's arm, screaming that she wanted him. Celia told her that he was not a toy, kissed her on the forehead, and sent her back to her sister. She apologized to the man for the chocolate on his sleeve. She advised him to keep up the fight and admitted that raising societal consciousness was a tall order. She handed him a crumpled Kleenex from her pocket as she left.

"I think I'd die without Kleenex," she confided when she reached Jessica. She drew another from her pocket and wiped the girls' mouths. "These two"—she rolled her eyes toward the carriage—"are so oral. God knows what they'll be like when they're older."

God might or might not, but Jessica did. The vision of pubescent Ruth and Naomi Remson was thoroughly unpleasant. Ruth would probably ripen early enough to give hand-jobs for bubble gum and Naomi would remain sour even after being plucked. It was a depressing foresight. Jessica flushed it away.

A slim man in his late twenties and a plaid Cardin overcoat was shaking his fist in the air and walking toward them. He wore sunglasses, earmuffs, gloves, and a camel's hair muffler drawn over his mouth. His only exposed sense organ was his nose. It was red.

"Hi, Ralph," Jessica said.

The man lowered his fist. "Did you see that—pardon me—sonofabitch cab come at me! He could have killed me, maimed me for life. *Whackkobam* and whoops: Ralph, the human vegetable." He drew down his muffler and took a deep breath. "That man should not be allowed behind the wheel of anything outside a penny arcade!" He removed his glasses and brushed his knuckles gently beneath his eyes. "Please forgive me. I have a tendency to overreact when death is near."

"Don't we all," Celia said.

"Oh, excuse me." Jessica turned. "Celia, you know Ralph Asbell, my tenant, don't you?"

Celia smiled politely.

Ralph offered sugarless gum.

Celia told Ralph about a taxicab she'd seen sideswipe a wheelchair, and Ralph said he wasn't surprised—he'd seen one plow into a drummer after the St. Patrick's Day parade. They swapped atrocity stories about New York cabs until Celia's tale of a well-tipped rapist was one-upped by Ralph's about a driver who ran a bizarre service for the handicapped. Celia said she felt sick and Ralph said he felt he ought not to have said what he had and said good-bye. Aaron waved. Little Ruth patted the back of Ralph's Cardin coat with a lollipop.

When Ralph was out of earshot, Celia asked, "Is he a fag?"

Jessica shrugged. "How should I know?" She deplored Celia's dedication to excavating people's sexuality. The woman would turn every social encounter into a sort of Krafft-Ebing dig. At parties she pulled Jessica into the kitchen to give her the Remson Rundown of new discoveries: *You know Harvey Callis, the guy*

*with the black turtleneck? Queer as a three-dollar bill.
Did you see the one in the red dress? I think she's a
dike. Peter Avrams is a closet case. Do you think
Larry Walker is straight?* Celebrities were her favorites,
alive or dead, and her golden roster of inverts boasted
Greta Garbo, Mae West, Rock Hudson, Marlon
Brando, Teddy Kennedy, Bobby Fischer, and Charles
DeGaulle. Ralph Asbell, by his own admission one
hung-over New Year's Day, *was* a homosexual, but
Jessica would be damned if she'd nail his name to
Celia's list.

"I think he's queer, Jess," Celia said, a doctor giving
the family the old man's biopsy report.

"Who cares? He pays his rent on time and he's a
nice guy."

Celia bristled. "I never said he *wasn't* a nice guy.
Homosexuals are nice. Very nice. I know quite a few
really warm and giving, wonderful people who just
happen to be . . . slightly twisted, sexually. I mean, you
certainly don't have to worry about having him in your
house with Aaron around. Child molesters are a whole
different breed."

Celia's confidence suggested that she had a list of
child molesters too. Jessica began to tune her out, plan
dinner. She wondered if she had enough breadcrumbs
for fried chicken.

"I just think people should be honest about what
they are," Celia said. "If you're Jewish, you're Jewish.
If you're black, you're black. If you're queer, you're
queer. I mean if that's what you are, that's what you
are. I respect people who are what they are. The two
girls who are having the session tonight are gay. That's
what they are and they admit it. Let me tell you, I respect them a lot more, a *lot* more, than other people. I

even went to a Gay Lib rally with them. They're terrific. You'll love them. . . ."

Jessica wondered if she should stop at the bakery and buy some éclairs. Victor loved éclairs and she hadn't brought any home for months. It would be a lovely surprise. Maybe it would take his mind off the blue whale. She was just about to start walking toward Ninety-third Street when she realized that Celia was still talking.

"—you'll love them, Jess." Celia touched her arm. "Pick me up at eight. We'll go together."

The Rubicon office was an old surgical-supply store that only a month ago had been scoured of its last vestigial tie with the past (a reassuring legend on the window: TRUSSES SINCE 1918) and become a fully renovated city-subsidized drug information and rehabilitation center. It had operated for more than a year with a peeling ceiling and primitive plumbing, orange crates for desk chairs (the three desks had been castoffs from a Russian dance school in the East Twenties that had been bombed by the JDL) and brightly painted bedpans for incoming and outgoing mail. Jessica had liked the office that way; every time she went there it had made her feel creative, important. Now, with its city-issued green metal furniture and union-lettered RUBICON sign, she often felt like a civil service paraprofessional—functional. It depressed her to think of herself as functional.

Jessica preferred to think of herself as simply terrific. It was a private assertive self-image that had surfaced in her teens, gone down for the deep six months of guilt after her first marriage, and then had risen again in analysis as easily as a cake of Ivory in the bathtub. Mike Halprin had called her simply terrific when she'd first walked into the vivisected surgical-supply store, and then again when she'd asked if they needed volunteers. She had always responded well to people who saw her as she saw herself, and she instantly committed her spare time to saving the addicts of New York.

She wrote fund-raising releases at home, and in six months she'd managed to turn a band of junkies into the Junk Band, a methadone-maintenance group that bad-mouthed drugs and played anti-acid rock. She'd got them a manager, a solid six-city tour, two spots on the *Tonight* show, and a record contract with Columbia. It wasn't the same as bringing forth a new nation conceived in liberty, which in her pre-motherhood days as a high-priced public relations princess, she had actually done. Almost single-handedly she had metamorphosed the tiny and impoverished African kingdom of Ugasha—a nonemergeable nation if there ever was one—into a bastion of democracy and a chic jet-set playground with a party for three Hilton Hotel executives and a well-planned, never-to-be-expected civil war that pressured the Foreign Aid Committee to hefty benevolence. The President of Ugasha had presented her with his father's knobkerrie as a token of appreciation.

But her work at Rubicon was rewarding, and it did, after all, help them win a city subsidy. Mike had asked her then to work full-time (as he continued to ask her), but it was out of the question. Not that the idea didn't appeal to her. But responsibilities were responsibilities. There was Aaron, the house, her perfect marriage . . . and that was all there was to it.

Jessica rolled Aaron's stroller into the office. A tall

girl with a mandarin mane of black hair was sitting on one of the desks, surrounded by folders, filing her nails. She yelped when she saw the stroller and raced across the room, dropped to her knees in front of it, and kissed Aaron on the nose.

Aaron sneezed.

The girl laughed and nuzzled his cheek. "It was good for me, too."

"He's getting hung up on you, Abby. He'll never be happy with anyone else."

"Why should he be? I'm going to wait for him. Do you hear that, Aaron? Just hold your Pampers 'cause I'm going to wait for you. And when you're big and strong we'll fly away to the land of chocolate milk and honey where the only thing you can ever shoot up on is a star."

"How's Denny making out on the methadone?"

"I haven't seen him in two weeks. Neither has anyone at the clinic. As far as I'm concerned, he got hit by a truck. I'm living with his ex-therapist now. It's a groove. We throw up every morning."

"Throw up?"

"You know"—she held her stomach, leaned over, and made a gargling sound—"throw up. Purifies you. Gets out the garbage. Gives you a fresh start every day. I've never been more together."

"I'm glad," Jessica said, and meant it. Abby Osterman was a nineteen-year-old waif with a body created for a centerfold and a life that ran to disaster as casually as a matron to fat. The luckiest break she ever had, she'd told Jessica, was, at sixteen, when a steel girder cracked loose from a building on Fifty-seventh Street. It had saved her from pregnancy and Bellevue by quashing her stepfather—by transforming him into a smudge.

"Mike left some papers for you. They're on his desk. He said to call him at home if you had any questions."

A large brown envelope with "Sica" handwritten across it lay atop a half-eaten English muffin. "Sica" was Mike's own abbreviation of her name. He called her that because no one else did, and because he knew that she knew no one else did. And because both of them knew that it was the closest they'd ever come to fucking. Sometimes she wondered if they both didn't know too much.

She put the envelope behind Aaron in the stroller. "I hate to break this up, Juliet, but Romeo has to take his nap."

Abby gave Aaron's nose a final kiss. "I dig your kid, Jess. Anytime you need a sitter, just ask."

"I don't know if I trust you two."

"Not to worry. I'm cool." She winked at Aaron "Besides, I'm on the pill."

Jessica stopped at a bakery on Ninetieth Street to buy the éclairs. The woman behind the counter was a pale, underleavened matron with a white braid coiled like a cruller on her head. She told Jessica that the last two éclairs had just been sold. She suggested napoleons and began folding a flat piece of cardboard into a small box.

There was something too eager about the woman, too defeated about the napoleons. Jessica pointed to a thin apple strudel. The woman made a face as she lifted it to the counter. She reached for a larger piece of cardboard and began putting together a new box. Jessica asked if she could have a cookie for Aaron.

The woman held out a small flat one with a green fruit chip on top. "Ten cents," she said sourly.

"That's a lot for one cookie, isn't it?"

"You want bargains, go to the A & P. Ernshweiger's cookies aren't social tea biscuits." She put it back. "Let me tell you something." She stretched her arm across the counter. "You think it's fun back there with those ovens? Sometimes it gets so hot I think I'm going to faint right in the middle of a pumpernickel. But I don't. You know why?"

"No."

"Because I'm a pro, that's why. A pro—*professional*. Twenty years ago I tried to work my way up in Hostess Cupcakes, but they kept me down. I was married, a bad risk. I couldn't get further than cream fillings. When my son was born I made up my mind that I wasn't going to slave behind a stove all day while my husband was out climbing telephone poles. No siree. Not Lilly Ernshweiger. I wanted a career, and I got it. Believe me, cookies aren't something I *bake,* they're something I *am*. If I was to give one away to every runny-nosed kid that pushed a finger against this case"—she thumped the glass with her forearm—"you know what that would make me?"

Jessica shook her head. "Uh-uh."

Lilly Ernshweiger snorted. "A grandmother."

"A grandmother?"

"A grandmother. A freebee cookie machine."

Aaron began to cry.

Jessica put a dime on the counter. "I'll take one of those chocolate ones."

"That'll be another nickle."

"I thought you said ten cents?"

"You want bargains, go to the A & P. Ernshweiger's fudgies aren't Oreos, lady."

Aaron's fudgie fell to the pavement, half-eaten, three houses from home. Jessica was about to kick it to the side when she saw the dog. She stopped. Mauser was relieving himself in the gutter about ten feet away. Anyone who knew Mauser would not consider that clearance.

Mauser was the Moby Dick of West Eighty-seventh Street. At first glance he looked like an average black and tan German shepherd, except for an oddly curled tail, but no one ever mistook him for one of the other twenty or so German shepherds on the block. Completely unbiased and totally berserk, he lunged for everything and everyone that moved. Jessica had seen him disembowel an out-of-bounds football—and never forgot it. His owner was a young writer who lived across the street, talked to few people, and kept his hair tied back in a ponytail. Everytime Mauser lunged the owner would shout, "No!" or "Out!" with a ferocity that equaled the dog's. Many a night Jessica would hear the click-click of heels on the pavement, the sudden bone-chilling growl, and the sharp "Out!" of the man with the ponytail. Celia said that she'd heard the dog was part wolverine, and Gino at the Martinizing store said the dog was fed ground rats and assorted entrails. Victor, for some perverse reason—most likely the same one that had drawn him to the blue whale— liked the dog. On the other hand, Victor was one of the few people Mauser never lunged for.

The man with the ponytail saw Jessica, nodded, and hauled the dog to the other side of the street.

Jessica smiled. It was what one did when Mauser went to the other side of the street.

"Nice doggie," Aaron said, pointing. "Nice doggie."

Jessica hadn't the heart to correct him. It would only confuse him. Besides, it would probably screw up his toilet training. Everything else did.

Aaron's toilet training, like Celia's dialogues on women's liberation and Victor's on the blue whale, had, over the past four months, become the litany of Jessica's life. Her responses to all three were automatic and inconsequential. Victor really didn't give a damn whether she ever learned the difference between a humpback and a sei whale and Celia slalomed around Jessica's pointed liberation rebuffs like a champ. Aaron, whom she brought to the bathroom after each meal and every glass of juice, inevitably wet his pants afterward with the happy mindlessness of a puppy. Jessica was secretly secure that if she applied herself she could out-rorqual Victor and probably trip up Celia, but Aaron's toilet training was something else.

It was frustrating.

It was particularly frustrating since she had devised a master plan for it during her second trimester. It was entitled *Down with Diapers,* a guide for mothers that she had written for packaging, with every pair of Todd-laurent Training pants. It had put Toddlaurent on the Big Board and earned her a TTP Gold Seat Award—a pair of bronzed training pants usually given to TTP's top salesman of the year. The award disappeared three days after she got it, along with her stereo and an imitation lynx jacket. She knew the disadvantages of starting too early (they were italicized), the dangers of sitting too long (boldface), the disaster of flushing too soon (all bold caps). In fact, she had approached the whole problem of Aaron's training with more preparedness than she'd ever tackled anything in her life. (Her only research before pushing Ugasha to the brink of civil war was a quick reading of *The Red Badge of Courage*.)

Her notable lack of success confounded her. *She* was doing everything right, why wasn't Aaron?

She'd moved into action at Aaron's first sign of readiness. It wasn't much of a sign, more of a grunt, but a soiled diaper coupled with a look of discomfort was a Go! signal according to her own pamphlet, and to Dr. Spock and Dr. Zimkin too. (Dr. Zimkin was Aaron's pediatrician, a boyishly wizened man who said the same things Dr. Spock did, but charged fifteen dollars for listening.) Regularly, Jessica would place Aaron on his firmly secured Toidy Seat. She would sit on the edge of the bathtub and enthrall him with visions of being a big boy who could wear pants instead of diapers, rhapsodize the vistas open to such boys. She cheered his every success, and, even in the face of overwhelming evidence to the contrary, she expressed sublime confidence in his eventual ability to do it like Mommy and Daddy.

After four months her sublime confidence had withered to a faint hope.

Mechanically she put the bag of groceries on the kitchen table, put the strudel on the counter, and her work from Rubicon on top of the refrigerator. She took off Aaron's coat and carried him without delusion into the bathroom. As she sat on the edge of the tub she comforted herself with thoughts, thoughts of her TTP Gold Seat Award, thoughts of her knobkerrie, thoughts of Aaron never having to go into the army. She lit a cigarette and blew a perfect smoke ring at the mirror. Aaron began to fiddle with his penis.

At seven thirty that evening Jessica was again sitting on the edge of the bathtub. Aaron was asleep in his crib. Jessica held a cigarette in one hand and Victor's unfinished piece of apple strudel in the other.

Victor was shaving.

Jessica enjoyed watching him shave. She felt it was a marital intimacy that couples too rarely shared. Sometimes, on weekends, she would encourage him to shave just so they could feel close. Everytime the chrome razor plowed off the cream it was like seeing his face for the first time.

Actually, the first time Jessica had seen Victor's face it was her own that had been covered with cream.

She and Ira had been divorced for about two years then, and she was living alone on East Seventy-seventh Street. It was a Thursday night in March, rainy, perfect for self-pity, old records, and a facial. She had just slid into Helena Rubinstein's foam mask when Victor knocked on her door asking for Valerie.

To this day she did not know why she let him in.

And to this day, whenever she and Victor had an argument, he would always ask her why she had let him in.

She had no answer. But every time Victor would ask, she would counter with a question about Valerie, and the subject would be dropped. Victor never said anything about Valerie. Jessica was glad. It lent him an air of mystery that she enjoyed almost as much as watching him shave.

Victor had told her his life story, exclusive of Valerie, that rainy March night.

He'd been born six hours after the bombing of Pearl Harbor in a little town about 8,000 miles away: Elcho, Wisconsin. He was the son of an itinerant bank guard and a horticulturist. Since there wasn't enough money in Elcho to support even a Christmas Club, his father traveled often to find work.

Most of Victor's early education came from long days of cross-pollinating tulips followed by quiet evenings with his mother and a Gideon Bible. It was this Bible and the miracle it wrought, he told Jessica, that set him firmly on the course of his life. It happened when he was seven.

His mother had just finished reading the Twenty-Third Psalm, and, as usual, had been moved to weeping. She clutched the Bible to her breast as she wiped her eyes. At that precise moment, a bullet from a neighbor's .22 rifle sped toward her heart. It hit the Bible, pierced Genesis, and stopped, miraculously, at the Twenty-Third Psalm. Victor knew then that there were only two paths to his destiny. One was religion, the other publishing. Aware of the limitations of the former, he opted for the latter. Now, twenty-five years later, he was senior editor of Ecopress.

Jessica beamed as he brought the razor carefully down his jaw. It was a strong jaw, a classically handsome jaw.

Jessica's mother told people that he looked like a young Abe Lincoln.

"It's the same old shit, again," Victor said through the corner of his mouth. "George just about groveled at Faraday's feet at the meeting today. Whining—I mean it—*whining* about his frigging swans."

George Wiffet was the other senior editor at Ecopress. He was a sallow, sharp-faced man in his middle thirties who, according to Victor, drank sweet whiskey sours and whined a lot. He lived in New Jersey with a wife and three blackbirds. In his spare time he wrote vignettes about the birds, occasionally selling a piece to a local paper and *Scholastic* magazine. Victor told her that George had once candidly admitted, after two sweet whiskey sours, that apart from a quaint and ardent courtship dance, blackbirds had very little distinction among *Aves*.

Both George and Victor worked directly under Avril Faraday, Publisher, President, Editor-in-chief of Ecopress. Since the company released only sixteen books a year, both men vied constantly for Faraday's favor, and, concomitantly, publication priority for their respective books. George's projects were usually related to birds, reptiles, and crustaceans. Victor handled mammals, amphibians, and fishes. The rest of the animal kingdom was divided by phyla unequally between Mindy Anoplura, a giant redhead who slept with Faraday at book publisher's conventions and spent her afternoons lunching with agents, and Ruth Maitland, a former Boston debutante who could read thirty-six manuscripts a day, and often did. All other ecological areas were up for grabs.

"Swans?" Jessica said.

"Swans," Victor said again. "A slick, hack, swanbook by Boris O'Hara writing under the name of Cord Erikkson, PhD."

"Can he do that?"

"He's done it. *The Last Song: Taps for the Trumpeter Swan!* The whole thing's a tear-jerking sham. George knows it, too. The trumpeter swan has been out of danger for a year now, but George is planning to keep the new conservation statistics a secret until after publication so he can attribute the trumpeter's salvation to his book."

"No!" Jessica was appalled.

"Yes. You should have seen George today, whining to Faraday about how we have to rush it into the June schedule. Whining about how it will be the death of the fairy tale if we don't get behind swans the way we got behind vasectomies."

Victor was referring to *Short Cut To Happiness: The Truth About Vasectomies, Laparoscopies, and Sin* by Myron Cummings, DD. It was a sleeper brought in by Ruth Maitland. It won a National Book Award and was mentioned in *Newsweek* as a peripheral factor in lowering the birthrate for the year.

"Isn't June when your blue whale book is coming out?" Jessica asked.

"Was coming out," Victor said.

"What happened?"

"What happened? What always happens? What's been happening for months? The blue whale gets the shaft again." He jammed his razor into the air.

Tufts of shaving cream spattered on Jessica's slacks. "Victor, be careful." Jessica stood up. "I have to leave in a few minutes."

Victor took the strudel and handed her a towel. "But you"—he pointed—"you will be back. When the *blue whale* goes—next week, next month, next year—it will be gone forever. If that book doesn't come out in June it'll never sell a copy. People won't give a damn about the blue whale any more than they give a damn about the brontosaurus. It will be too late."

"It's never too late," Jessica said kindly.

"Tell that to the blue whale," Victor said. "Goddamn George and his frigging birds."

Jessica took a last drag on her cigarette, blew a smoke ring, and flushed the butt down the toilet. "I hate to leave, hon, but I promised Celia."

"Frigging birds," Victor said. Then he swung his arm around her waist, bent her backward, and kissed her roughly on the mouth. "You're a lot of woman, Jess. A helluvalot."

"Would you call me liberated?" she asked.

"I'd call you by your maiden name if it made you happy."

"That's ridiculous."

Jessica's maiden name was Siskandinowstein. It had been the scourge of her early school years, the verbal acne of her adolescence. It was one of the reasons, which came out in analysis, she had married her first husband. Ira's last name had only four letters: Cohn. When Jessica's brother Howard had graduated from dental school, a year after her wedding, her parents had shortened the name to Siskand. They gave him a wooden sign with his new name and DDS after it as a present.

Victor kissed her again.

She pushed him away gently. "Please, hon, I don't have time."

"I thought you said it was never too late."

"A woman's entitled to change her mind."

"You're a helluva woman, Jess," Victor said.

Jessica smiled. She wiped a dab of shaving cream from his earlobe and left.

Victor bit down hard on the strudel. "Frigging birds," he muttered.

CHAPTER 2

Celia jabbered like a parrot in heat all the way to Riverside Drive. She repeated how Jessica would love gay but honest Bert and Sharon. She repeated how ridiculous it would be for Jessica to feel self-conscious among sisters. She repeated how happy she was to be holding her candle. Celia believed that if something was worth saying, it was worth repeating.

And Celia believed in the worth of everything she said.

She also believed in punctuating her sentiments with an elbow in the ribs.

By the time they arrived, Jessica's side felt as if it had been worked over by a spastic masseuse. She resolved to try Hertz the next time she needed a car.

The living room of Bert and Sharon's apartment had about it an aura of studied fanaticism: the kind most often associated with freshman dorms and German beer halls. On one wall was a six-foot-high poster of Wonder Woman. Her right fist was raised and her left smacked against her upper arm in classic Italo-American defiance. The bubble above her crown said: "... You too, Steve." Next to it, one atop the other, hung two dayglo bumper stickers: SEXISM IS SHIT! and: LIB

29

IS NEVER HAVING TO SAY YOU CAME! On another wall, a small gold-on-green petit-point sampler framed in rosewood and under nonreflective glass said simply GAY IS GAY.

The bookcases, built by Bert, Celia said, from old seltzer crates, went sporadically from floor to ceiling across the side of the room. It was a honeycomb of feminist literature except for three floor-level cubicles which contained home repair manuals, the Golden Book Encyclopedia and the complete works of Charles Dickens. The bookcase was painted antique white. It was peeling.

Celia slipped out of her poncho with a veronica befitting El Cordobes. "Take off your coat," she told Jessica. "You've arrived."

Jessica sidestepped to avoid Celia's eblow. She unbuttoned her jacket.

Three young women in dungarees and loose sweaters sat on a transparent inflatable couch at the far end of the room. They were speaking loudly and with animation of acupuncture. They quieted abruptly when Celia shouted a hearty "Right on!"

The three waved, smiled, immediately focused on Jessica.

Jessica raised her hand, smiled and immediately focused on an older woman standing near the bookcase. She had her back to Jessica, but her sugar-white hair, braided and coiled like a cruller on top of her head, was familiar. It was the Shylock of cookiedom: Lilly Ernshweiger.

Jessica whispered to Celia, "I know that woman."

"You know them all," Celia said.

"I do?"

"They're all your sisters," Celia said. She swung her

elbow into Jessica's ribs. "Come on, I want you to meet Bert and Sharon first. You'll love them."

In the kitchen, the two sisters Jessica was to love were mixing peanuts and raisins and distributing them evenly into four brightly colored cups made from truncated milk cartons. They were snarling at each other.

Celia coughed.

The sisters stopped. A few peanuts skittered across the floor.

"Roberta, Sharon," Celia said "I'd like you to meet my friend Jessica. A Jeannie-come-lately, but here at last."

Roberta and Sharon wiped their palms on their jeans as if they were drawing pistols. They shook Jessica's hand in turn. Bert was short, cublike, and in her early twenties. She had the curly black hair of a Persian lamb, dimples, and a prominent Adam's apple. She wore a necklace of aluminum flip-tops and a good grin. Sharon, a tall blonde with the warmth of a stiletto, had the charm of an assassin. Her smile was a cross between a sneer and a menstrual grimace. They both said hello.

"I like your apartment," Jessica said.

"Thanks," Sharon said. She grabbed two of the sawed off milk cartons, crunched a peanut underfoot. "Bert, get these nuts cleaned up, will you." She kicked one to the side and walked out.

"Fuck you," Bert said sweetly. She picked up the remaining containers and followed Sharon.

"Aren't they terrific?" Celia asked. "Don't you just love them?"

Going back down the narrow hall, Celia and Jessica were blocked by an attractive girl with persimmon-colored hair. She was standing in front of a small mirror flicking at her eyelashes with her pinky.

"*Uno momento,*" she said. She puckered her lips toward the glass and applied some gloss. "*Bene!*" She clicked her purse shut.

"Lisa," Celia said. "This is my friend Jessica—"

"Super." Lisa flashed a wide smile. Then she turned and went into the living room.

"She looks like—" Jessica began.

"Modess," Celia said softly.

"Modess?"

"Modess and Tiparillos. She's a model. Lisa Lee. Great girl." Celia took Jessica's arm. "They're all great girls."

In the living room the smallest of the great girls lifted a tiny bare foot and pointed it at an empty bridge chair, nodded to Jessica. Jessica sat and thanked her.

"Don't mention it. Around here it's drop ass and raise consciousness," the girl said happily.

"Right on," Celia said and plomped to the floor beside Jessica.

The girl was a blonde with hyperthyroid hazel eyes and a nose no larger nor more appealing than a goober. "Sandy Felgus," she said.

"Jessica Prior," Jessica said.

"Used to sleep with Douglas Fairbanks, Jr.," Celia whispered to Jessica when Sandy turned to answer a question.

Jessica nodded knowingly. She lit a cigarette. Neatly folded flyers were stacked on a small coffee table to her right. She took one. It was a two-page promotional pamphlet for a book—*The New Movement Guide to Masturbation: A complete Handbook of Autoerotism*

For and By Women. There was a photograph of a woman masturbating in silhouette.

Someone suggested mobilizing an elite cadre of radicals for the off-year elections.

Jessica began to read the pamphlet.

Celia gave Jessica's foot a disapproving tap. Jessica slipped the pamphlet into her purse. The voices of the great girls rose angrily.

"It won't be good for our political offensive," shouted a girl named Gloria, whom everyone called Kiki.

"What's good for some is good for all," Sharon shouted back. "That's sisterhood."

"That's aristocracy," Jessica corrected.

"Bullshit," Sharon said. "That's sisterhood."

"But—"

Celia pinched Jessica's ankle.

Lilly Ernshweiger stood up to speak. She hesitantly raised a wraithlike arm and the room quieted. The effect of her powder-pale hair, her doughy skin, her white space shoes, was nearly spectral. When she spoke her voice quavered with earnestness and glottal stops:

"Sisters, I am new to the Movement but old to the game. What I'm telling you now, I'm telling from the heart. An old heart. A many-times-broken heart. If there is one thing I know, it's that ... we ... must ... knead ... together. If we let ourselves be drawn apart, what are we? Little sweet cakes. But if we knead together we won't have to settle for our fair share of the pie—we can and will *be* the pie."

The Off-Year Elections were forgotten; Lilly held the room in thrall.

She recounted the whole painful story of her struggle

up from Hostess cream fillings, detailed the invidious ways that pasty-faced bastards at another corporate bakery humiliated her when she begged for a chance to work the ovens. They had laughed, she said, at her aspirations. Nervously clutching her braid, she told how, swallowing her pride, she had to perform fellatio on a potbellied union organizer just for the right to make it in a man's world.

"I never owned to that before," Lilly said passionately. "I was so ashamed. But"—she twirled her finger in the air—"dollars to doughnuts if I hadn't done it when I did I wouldn't have my career. In those days if a girl didn't give she didn't get anything but a husband. Thank God women don't have to do that anymore. Thank God for sisterhood." Lilly covered her face with her hands and wept.

One of the girls on the inflatable couch stood up. The plastic farted. Everyone including Jessica looked at the floor. The girl put her arms around Lilly Ernshweiger's shoulders. "It's better to have gotten it out, Lilly. You're not alone. We all understand. We've all gone through so much of the same thing."

Lilly kept her hands over her face. She did not move. Heads nodded.

Sandy Felgus explained quietly to Jessica that conversion, full embracement of sisterhood, did that to some women. It was almost a religious experience, she said, the closest to orgasm a lot of women ever came.

"I see," Jessica said, and stared at Lilly; at the moment she looked more like Lot's wife than a liberated women.

"I had to go down on three photographers before I did my first Modess ad," Lisa Lee said encouragingly.

Lilly still did not look up.

The sisters rallied. Testimonies of oral sex under duress were fired from every corner of the room with evangelical alacrity. One sister confessed having to do it for her husband if she wanted to watch a different TV program than he did; another to having had to do it to a policeman who had arrested her for having done it to her boyfriend; another to having had to do it to her brother in order to play with his trains. Each candid ejaculation stimulated another, until, finally, Lilly Ernshweiger's lone blow-job was lost in a fellatic maelstrom of sisterhood.

Jessica rifled her conscience for a worthy anecdote to shoot into the fray, but none—on quick perusal—seemed significantly humiliating.

Kiki began a chant, and the others joined her.

> *We don't have to fake it!*
> *We don't have to take it!*
> *We don't have to make it*
> *just for THEM anymore!*

They stomped their feet, raised their fists, lifted their voices. The floor trembled and quaked like a grandstand before the final kickoff.

> *We don't have to fake it!*
> *We don't have to take it!*
> *We don't have to make it*
> *just for THEM anymore!*

Jessica felt excluded.

She felt as sisterly as Harriet Tubman to the Daughters of the Confederacy, as sisterly as Golda Meir to

Eva Braun, as sisterly as Debbie Reynolds to Elizabeth Taylor.

She felt unreasonably hostile.

When the chanting subsided to the murmur of a few lone singsongers, she said quietly, "What's wrong with just getting a husband—with being a housewife?" and with that hushed the room as baldly as a drunk shouting obscenities from the back of a church.

Even Lilly Ernshweiger looked up.

"We don't say housewife anymore," Celia told Jessica quietly. "It's like saying *colored*."

"Colored?"

"Instead of *black*." Celia stared into her lap, obviously embarrassed by Jessica's gaucherie, clearly wishing she hadn't earlier proclaimed their friendship so emphatically.

Jessica smiled. "Well, what do you call a woman who's married and doesn't have a career? Just 'wife?' "

"*Wife* is acceptable in some circles," Celia said. "But it's comparable to *Negro*. *Married person* is preferred."

"*Required* by Hippolyte Green," said Kiki.

Hippolyte Green, despite her constant protestations to the contrary, was the aurora borealis of feminism. She had risen years back from the sororital ranks in two quantum leaps which put her on the covers of *Newsweek* and *Time*. First, she had successfully converted six Playboy Bunnies and had convinced them to burn their costumes in front of the New York Club on Easter Sunday; and second, she'd had her abortion televised live on public TV. Her book, *The Feministo*, had topped *The New York Times* best-seller list for thirteen weeks. Celia had given Jessica a copy months ago, and Jessica had promptly lost it, after reading only the introduction, on the crosstown bus.

"Well, then," said Jessica. "Is there anything wrong with loving your home, your husband, your kids, having stimulating outside interests? You know, being a happy wife—a happy married person."

Kiki jumped to her feet. "Aha, there's a difference! The happy wife is like the vaginal orgasm."

Jessica crossed her legs. "Oh? How's that?"

"They're both myths," Kiki said.

"Fakes," Sharon added.

"Cunts," shouted someone from the inflatable couch.

"A wife," Celia said, with resuscitated confidence, "could be a married person, but a married person would never be a wife. They're the same yet completely different, if you know what I mean."

"No," Jessica said.

"A married person is a total *woman*. She's sexually free, politically aware, and domestically unencumbered. A wife, as even my two girls know, is a loving *slave*." Celia cleared her throat. "In the words of *The New Women's Dictionary: Wife,* derogatory noun, someone who does the shopping, cleaning, child-raising, cooking, caring—semicolon—an overworked, underpaid laundress, nurse, seamstress, comparison shopper, bedmaker, waitress, floor washer, dog walker, nose wiper, messenger—" Celia ran through the firmly established litany with skip-rope rhythm in one long breath which expired with "—and a cheap fuck!"

"Tell it, sister!"

"Screw McPig!"

Jessica barely heard the shouts. Striking into her head with the sudden clarity and the absolute happenstance of divine vision had come a single thought. A simple thought, as simple as civil war in Ugasha.

It was: No home should be without one.

Instantly it was a Jessica Truth of Life.

"Can you see it—see the difference?" Celia asked.

Jessica blinked her eyes. Blanked.

"You need to read *The Feministo*," Sandy Felgus said.

"You need to affirm your priorities," Kiki said.

Jessica said nothing. How could she? She knew what she needed. She knew what she never knew she needed before. She needed a wife.

For the rest of the evening Jessica was lost in the enormity of her revelation, stunned by the simplicity of it. It was like discovering that putting one foot in front of the other was walking. It was the perfect way to maintain the perfect marriage. Her mind toppled into glorious streams of fantasy, splashed through pools of self-fulfillment, floated as free as an unfettered buoy in guiltless seas of indulgence. Her silence was misconstrued for conversion and when she put on her coat to leave, Celia was beaming. Bert said that she was glad, really glad, to have met her, hoped to see her again. They shook hands.

Jessica could have sworn Bert's fingers scratched her palm.

The lights were on in Victor's den when Jessica arrived home. And a woman was laughing.

It was an affected laugh. It was the laugh of a woman laughing to please a man. It was Beverly Davis' laugh.

One of the things Jessica loathed about Beverly

Davis was her laugh. The other was her habit of trying to commit suicide every six months. Biannually she would swallow six tins of Midol, call Victor, and be waiting for him in a black nightgown, raincoat ready for the cab ride to St. Vincent's. An intern who had been on hand for two of these occasions told Victor that the emergency staff had named the stomach pump after her.

Beverly Davis was twenty-two years old and a latent nymphomaniac. She was also a virgin. Being a virgin helped keep her nymphomania latent. Her fantasy, which she repeatedly revealed to Victor on rides to St. Vincent's, was to excite Norman Mailer to premature ejaculation.

Beverly Davis wanted to be a writer.

Dick Rofhard, a friend of Beverly's, wanted to be a writer too.

Victor had rejected both their manuscripts, which were virtually identical, on the same day, and had written each of them about the suspiciously coincidental similarities of the works. The following week Beverly and Dick appeared at the office, each claiming to be the originator of the communally rejected manuscript—an hour-by-hour report of the marathon recycling drive in Astoria, Queens. (Beverly's was titled: *Play It Again Uncle Sam.* Dick's was simply: *Ditto.*) Beverly accused Dick of plagiarism. Dick accused Beverly of copying. Victor took them both to lunch and talked them into collaboration. Two and a half months later, Beverly and Dick, with Victor as mentor and master editor, became Rowena Westcott, the widely successful paperback Gothic writer. (*Echo the Winds of Fear* had already gone into a fourth printing, and *Publishers Weekly* had dubbed *House On Satan's Hill* a "chillbinding terror-ama!") Beverly and Dick wrote the novels. Victor rewrote, edited, and added the soft, subtle nonsequiturs which were the "Rowena Westcott touch." Beverly and Dick believed firmly in writing about what they knew. All their books were set in a remote section of Queens and no heroine entertained more sexual involvement than a cloistered nun.

Jessica walked into the den and said, "Hi."

"Hey, guess what?" Victor said. "We've another Westcott chillbinder *sur le tapis.*"

As the *coeur* of Rowena Westcott, Victor had cultivated the habit, in front of Beverly and Dick, of garnishing his conversation with French. It impressed Beverly; embarrassed the hell out of Jessica.

"Swell," Jessica said.

Dick held the arms of his chair with both hands and pushed himself politely up. He said hello, then sat down quickly and began to gnaw the stem of his pipe.

Beverly smiled and told Jessica that she had a pair of shoes just like the ones Jessica was wearing. She added that she'd bought them in Albany, that it certainly was a small world.

"Isn't it, though," Jessica said.

"Sure is," said Beverly enthusiastically.

"Sure is," said Dick.

"Petite monde," Victor said.

Jessica told them to carry on.

Upstairs Jessica sat crosslegged and naked on the bed. She reached into her purse for a cigarette and lit one. Then she took out the pamphlet and opened it:

THE BOOK THAT PUTS YOU IN
THE DRIVER'S SEAT!

THE NEW MOVEMENT GUIDE TO
MASTURBATION:
A COMPLETE HANDBOOK OF AUTOEROTISM
FOR AND BY WOMEN

Whether you're single, married, gay or straight, here at last is a book that tells you how to achieve ultimate sexual pleasure anytime, anywhere, without any body but your own.

INCLUDES SUCH FEATURES AS:
- Step-by-step to the multiple orgasm
- The importance of self-love
- Autoerotic foreplay
- Understanding your clitoris
- Mirror eroticism
- Simple pleasure devices you can make at home

PLUS! Over 100 easy-to-learn fantasies, masturbation secrets of Movement women, dozens of illustrations, and much, much more . . . .

On the facing page was a quote from Germaine Greer:

Lady, love your cunt. Because nobody else is going to . . . daily masturbating no hands is the easiest way to develop muscles of the pubococcygeal region. Think of something nice and contract the buttocks rhythmically. . . . You can even focus your attention on some member of your immediate environment and circumvent the essential egocen-

tricity of common forms of masturbation. . . .
Cunt is beautiful. So suck it and see. If you're not
so supple that you can suck your own, put your
finger gently in, withdraw and smell, and suck.
There. How odd it is that the most expensive
gourmet foods taste like cunt. Or is it? Squat over
a mirror or lie on your back with your legs apart
and the sun shining in, with a mirror. Learn it.
Study its expressions. Keep it soft, warm, clean.
Don't rub soap into it. Don't dredge it with
talc. . . . Give it your own loving names.

We must regain the power of the cunt.

Jessica reread the last sentence. It had the simple eloquence of a Jessica Truth of Life. It had pizzazz.

On the back was a coupon to cut out and send away
with eight dollars. It guaranteed the book in a week,
success in ten days, or your money back. There were
also testimonials from three smiling women.

The first was Colleen Fixel, coed, Oskaloosa, Iowa.
Poor offsetting lent her the look of a cornered raccoon.
She said:

Before I heard about THE NEW MOVEMENT
GUIDE TO MASTURBATION I was putting out
for creeps just to clear up my complexion. Now I
can make it with any guy I want in the privacy of
my own room or right in class and my skin is as
clean as my reputation.

The second was a handsome woman in her thirties,
Monica Lewis, married person, Dayton, Ohio. She
said:

*My husband is a career officer in the Navy, and a
very poor letter writer. I only get to see him a few
times a year, but thanks to THE NEW MOVE-
MENT GUIDE TO MASTURBATION I get to
see him every night and our marriage is better than
ever.*

The last, Fiona Krepps, caused Jessica to move
closer to the bed lamp. Fiona Krepps was a grandmother from Pulaski, Tennessee. Even allowing for
poor offsetting, the woman could not have been a day
under eighty. Her statement was simple, poignant:

I ain't never been happier.

Jessica dropped the pamphlet back into her purse
and scratched herself abstractedly. She had never given
any real thought to her vagina. Natural childbirth class
had taught her a lot about her cervix—compared it to
the neck of a very tight turtleneck sweater—and more
about her uterus than she certainly needed to know.
But her vagina, for all its intrinsic reproductive stature,
was simply: the Birth Canal. Functional.

Jessica recalled once having attempted to sort out
her labia majora from the labia minora and pinpoint
her clitoris by comparing herself to a drawing in an
anatomy book, and giving up. She had to confess that
the penis, hanging out in all its streamlined splendor,
did strike her as esthetically more pleasing than the
damp, labyrinthian folds of the vagina.

Maybe Greer was right, when you came down to it.
Jessica had never named her primary sex organ, while
a lot of the men she'd known had appellations for
theirs. Thinking back, there was a "Bernard," skinny,

with an annoying proclivity for impotence; a "Marvin," short fat, and inflated with indomitable chutzpah; several "Peters" with no distinctions other than the commonness of their name. There had been a one-night stand with a "King Kong," a misnomer if there ever was one, and another with an "Attila," whose barbaric spirochetes had stormed her vaginal tract and battled with savage tenacity against massive doses of penicillin. For all the nomenclature, Victor's "Randolph" was in appearance, performance, endurance, and ingenuity, without peer.

She snuffed out her cigarette, pulled a hand mirror from her purse.

Resolutely, as if it were a homework assignment, she lowered her head and spread her legs.

That was it, all right.

She studied the reflection in the mirror.

It might be the font of her womanhood, but how gynecologists turned on for their wives at night would always be one of the inscrutable mysteries of life.

She parted her pubic hair, inserted a finger, then withdrew it.

How odd it is that the most expensive gourmet foods taste like cunt. . . .

Jessica sniffed, hesitated. She recalled one of her brother's more inspired bromides—"Don't knock it if you haven't tried it"—and did.

She'd stick to veal *cordon bleu*.

She turned off the light and lay back on the bed.

She thought about Fiona Krepps. She wondered what Fiona Krepps had named her vagina. She wondered what Germaine Greer had named hers.

She thought about a name for her vagina, for Celia's, for her mother's, for Mamie Eisenhower's, for

Helen Keller's, for Marie Curie's, for Lucretia Borgia's, for Princess Margaret's, and was on the verge of laughing when she realized that her hands were between her thighs and that she was playing with herself.

Her first response was surprise—surprise that even after years of abstinence it came back to you like swimming.

Her next response was automatic, with a touch her body slid into motion.

Her mind-screen flashed a muscular Con Ed workman. His shirt was opened at the neck, a black jungle bouquet sprouted from the V. His pants were tight and grease-stained, menacingly bulged. He advanced on her slowly, confidently, helmet glaring. A toothpick was spiked between his teeth; a jackhammer was in his hand. Smiling, he snapped the pick between his thumb and forefinger and lowered the jackhammer to the floor. He unbuckled his pants. She stepped backward, but his arm snaked around her waist, wrung her. His hands were on her buttocks, arching her toward him, when she heard the soft click of the doorknob.

Breath caught in her throat, a small guttural sound escaped. Her arms shot to her sides. Victor entered and flicked on the light. Jessica yawned as casually as she could without fainting from the pounding in her chest. The brightness gave her an excuse to cover her eyes. She ignored the throbbing of her outraged clitoris.

"Waiting for someone, or just posing for a calendar?" Victor asked. Jessica stretched. "Everyone asks me that." She sat up. "Did they go home?"

"Just left." Victor began unbuttoning his shirt.

"Any progress?"

"Except for a few details we have *Dark Triumph*

45

peu pres parfait," Victor said. He unbuckled his trousers.

Jessica did not look up. "Such as?"

"Such as how to get the heroine out of the house for about eight hours without anyone, including her husband, missing her."

"Hmmmm," said Jessica.

"Any ideas?"

"One," said Jessica.

"Give."

"It won't work for the book," said Jessica.

"Oh." Victor sat on the edge of the bed and carefully took off his socks. They were a gift from the author of *America's Bright Tomorrow*. They were wool, biodegradable, were supposed to break down and return to the soil at the same rate as a leaf. They ran in the washing machine and Jessica hated them.

"How was your meeting?"

"Interesting," Jessica said, immediately adding, "I mean really interesting." *Interesting* was her mother's euphemism for anything dull, ugly, or obscene. Anytime Jessica used the word she compulsively modified it.

"Oh?"

Jessica smiled. "And I had a brainstorm."

"How much is it going to cost me?" Victor asked.

"What a rotten thing to say."

"Rotten? What's rotten? Your last brainstorm cost me two thousand dollars, or have you forgotten?"

Jessica had not forgotten. She had convinced Victor, against his better judgment, to invest in her uncle Henry's last business enterprise. It had sounded like a sure money-maker: a hair lengthener and restorer that truly worked. Uncle Henry had come to their house and poured the stuff on a billiard ball and two hours later the thing looked like a peach. Unfortunately, the formula's filamentous intensity had not been fully researched. It grew hair on everything—the gloves used to apply it, the sink—and before Henry could put it on the market, the FDA padlocked his factory. A photograph of one of his vats appeared in *The Daily News*. It looked like something out of a Japanese horror film. The whole family dropped a bundle.

Jessica studied her knees.

"I'm sorry," Victor said. He ruffled her hair. "I didn't mean to bring up Uncle Henry."

"You never do—mean to, that is."

"Two thousand dollars is two thousand dollars."

"It's only money," Jessica said.

"If it were jellybeans, I wouldn't give a shit," Victor said. "Honest."

"Hmmmph."

"Come on," Victor said gently. "What was your brainstorm?"

Jessica folded her arms, grinned. "You'd never guess in a million years."

"I'd never guess in a million years." Victor conceded.

"A wife," she said happily. "For me."

Victor shook his head and stared. "For you?"

"Well," Jessica said petulantly, "if you want to be technical about it, okay—for us."

"You're right," Victor said. "I'd never have guessed in a million years."

CHAPTER 3

"Look at it this way," Jessica said. "With a wife we could both work full-time and fulfill ourselves. Aaron would be happy because he'd have a mother around, not someone who was wiping his nose and goofing with him just for the money, but someone who really cared. And she'd do all the shopping, the laundry, the cleaning, the babysitting, the—"

"I hate to be a heavy," Victor said. "But may I ask one question?"

"Certainly."

"Why would someone want to do all this?"

"For love, of course."

"Of course."

"And security."

"Naturally."

"Well?" Jessica asked. "What do you think?"

"I think you need a vacation."

"Come on."

"Bigamy is a crime."

"Don't be technical. Come on, what do you really think?"

"Actually"— Victor clasped his hands behind his

head and lay back against the pillows—"I think it's terrific."

Jessica leaned over and hugged him.

Victor's arms encircled her back. His fingers thrummed her spine. "It's a good thing we have a king-sized bed."

"Ummm," she said. She nuzzled his neck, burrowed her nose behind his earlobe. Then, slowly she unburrowed her nose, halted her nuzzling, and sat up.

"Hey." Victor reached for her. "What's the matter?"

"Why did you say that—about the bed?"

"Why not?"

"Not why not—why?"

"Well, for godsake, a standard double would be ridiculous for three."

"Oh." Jessica bit her lip. "I haven't really thought about *that part.*"

Victor grinned. "I have."

Jessica lit a cigarette, blew a smoke ring. A sideglance at Victor told her that he had indeed thought about *that part,* was in fact still thinking about it, was conspicuously aroused by it.

And it rankled her.

Drove a Samurai blade to her gut.

Made her want to smash him in the mouth.

Also, and startlingly, it animated her recently bereaved libido.

This befuddled Jessica. Ordinarily that would not have bothered her. She often reacted to situations and things in ways, had she analyzed them, that would have baffled her, so therefore she was prone to just plowing ahead, simply accepting it all comfortably, as comfortably as a teacher did apples.

But this was a whole new bushel of apples.

She'd thought about women competitively (her analyst had told her it was healthy), companionably (her mother had told her it was necessary), but never sexually. Not that the idea repelled her, but it was so alien she'd never considered it. It was like considering flamingos sexually.

And, it was one thing to put the make on a flamingo, but quite another to share your husband with it.

Some bushel of apples.

Jessica pursed her lips and exhaled. She envisioned herself on the phone at Rubicon, wheeling and dealing with the mayor and saving addicts, she saw herself coming home to warm dinners, scrubbed floors, and vacuumed rugs. She saw herself walking *past* Sloan's supermarket, *past* the Chinese laundry, *past* the playground.

It was a whole new bushel of apples, all right. She had no intention of tipping the cart.

Jessica snuffed her cigarette. "She'll have to have the right qualifications, of course." "And the right proportions," Victor added.

"Victor! We're not talking about some kinky freelance pussy," Jessica said hotly. "What I want is a wife."

"What's wrong with a wife with nice proportions?" Victor ran his hand up Jessica's side. "You're a wife, you have nice proportions. Very nice."

"I need something to write on," Jessica said. She went to the bureau and returned with a lined yellow legal pad and a ballpoint. The pen was a souvenir of her mother's last love crusade in the Catskills. It said: *Kitchner's Castle. Where sun shines and Cupid reigns.* Two weeks at Kitchner's had netted her mother a button manufacturer, a case of ringworm, and the pen.

The ringworm disappeared about the same time as the button manufacturer, and the pen leaked.

Jessica put the pad in her lap, wrapped a tissue around the pen. *Qualifications*, she wrote at the top, and underscored it. She put the numbers 1 through 10 down the side of the page. "Must like children," she said, and wrote it next to number 1. She tapped the pen against her teeth, then began writing again. She finished the list, added a sweeping paraph, and handed the pad to Victor. He read aloud:

"One. Must like children. Two. Good cook. Three. Good housekeeper. Four. Good reputation." He stopped. "Good reputation?"

"We don't want a slutty type living with us. After all, she'll have to take Aaron for walks and—"

"Oh. Sure." Victor shook his head. "Five. Good personality. Six. Frugal. Seven. Friendly. Eight. Funny— funny?"

Jessica shrugged. "I like girls with a sense of humor."

"Nine. Must iron. Ten. Must sew." Victor looked up. "Is that it?"

"You have something to add?"

"What about sex—about being good in bed?"

Jessica snatched the pad from him. She scrawled *sex* at the bottom of the list. "Are you happy now?"

Victor laughed. "You're a helluva woman, Jess."

"What?"

"Let's fuck."

Later, lying in the darkness, lying entwined in Victor's arms, Jessica said, "Victor? How are we going to find a wife?"

"I don't know. Same way everyone else does, I suspect."

"How's that?"

"Shop around." Victor yawned. "You certainly don't want to marry the first girl you go to bed with."

That was Tuesday night.

On Wednesday morning neither Victor nor Jessica mentioned the discussion. The household routine was so normal, so oppressively normal, that it was significantly unusual. There was not even the most mundane ripple. No cap was missing from the toothpaste, no manuscript had been misplaced. Victor had clean underwear, did not forget to kiss her, was not running late. Aaron didn't so much as bump a knee.

In five years of marriage this had only happened twice. The first time was the morning after an Ecopress Christmas party. Rose the bookkeeper and Joe Monsonnato the mail clerk worked most of the day decorating Avril Faraday's office and by four thirty the room was cancerous with the spirit of Christmas. Pleated bells, balls, and potbellied Santa had metastasized across the ceiling. "Merry Christmas" in shiny green and red cardboard letters spanned from a pole lamp halfway across the room to a corner of the bookcase. A small silver tree, wearied with ornaments, balanced precariously on the desk between photographs of Avril Faraday's children: Hansel Scott and Gretel Lorrie. Hansel Scott's acne had been air-brushed out, his lips painted gentian violet. Gretel Lorrie was on a lawn in a communion dress. You could hardly see her face. The snapshot was six years old.

Streamers were draped over everything—scotch bottles, cold cuts, corn chips, pretzels. Rose, who thought the streamers were festive, had twined them through her Dynel wig. She'd also wrapped some around the ball of Mr. Faraday's Selectric typewriter, which was partly responsible for her dismissal on New Year's eve.

Jessica arrived at five thirty, an hour after everyone had begun to drink, half an hour after Joe Monsonnato had done his impression of Mindy Anoplura combing her hair, and just in time to see Victor and Ruth Maitland play pass the pickle. She drank four paper cups of scotch to catch up and in less time than it had taken her to taxi across town she bit George Wiffet's ear, soul-kissed Avril Faraday, passed out in the ladies' toilet. Mindy Anoplura carried her back into the office and put her on Faraday's Naugahyde recliner. She remained there, unnoticed, until eight thirty when Victor announced to his co-workers that he was going to haul her home to take advantage of her. She woke up long enough to see Joe Monsonnato in a raincoat, flapping a pickle at her obscenely.

The second time was the morning after she had confessed her rape fantasy to Victor. She'd told him that she saw herself in brassiere and panties, bound and blindfolded by an intruder who looked like Charlie Bronson, who smelled of clean sweat. He would hurl her to the bed, savagely fondle her, rip off her brassiere with his teeth. Then, fully clothed, he would violate her. Victor thought it was a terrific fantasy and took to the Bronson part like a wild boar to a truffle. Jessica thought it was corny, wretchedly uninspired, a discredit to her natural creativity, to their mutual sexual imaginativeness—and a waste of two good Vassarette bras. The household routine the following morning was unerringly normal.

*

Only after Victor had gone to the office did Jessica begin to think of a wife again. The perfection of the idea overwhelmed her. Every so often she would rush to Aaron, pick him up, and squeeze him. She hummed as she put the breakfast dishes into the dishwasher. She hummed *I Want a Girl—Just Like the Girl That Married Dear Old Dad.* But she stopped halfway through. There was no way that she wanted a wife like her mother. Florence Siskand was a good woman, a great Mah-jongg player, a mean cha-cha dancer, an enthralling coloratura soprano who could sing the "Bell Song" from *Lakmé* in three languages. But that was it. She neither sewed nor ironed. She abstained from housecleaning with Brahminic piety, and she spent money like a call girl. Cooking was her forte—and at its best it was vile.

Florence Siskand prided herself on her culinary prowess. She spent hours, sometimes days, preparing gourmet dishes with prime meat, exotic spices, expensive wine. The results were always the same. Vile. No one ever went to Florence's for dinner without eating first. She prepared a five-course meal for every family gathering, and each course would return to the kitchen slightly rearranged, but gram for gram intact. She never seemed to notice and beamed like Julia Child from fruit cup to mousse. The only one Jessica had known who had ever eaten, and actually enjoyed, her mother's cooking was her father. He had died ten years ago, a healthy, as her mother said, and a happy man.

Wednesday evening Victor came home depressed. The blue whale was definitely out for June and George Wiffet's trumpeter swan was in. Victor was inconsolable. He was cranky. He snapped at Jessica and picked at his food. When she offered him chocolate pudding, he refused.

She poured his coffee in silence, then sat down at the table.

She told him that she'd thought of a possible wife.

Victor looked up. The blue whale submerged. "Suzanne," she said.

"Suzanne Heddon?" Victor grimaced. "No way."

"She likes Aaron and has a nice figure," Jessica said. "She sews all her own clothes and she's always talking about settling down."

"She never shuts up. She has opinions about everything—doors, light bulbs, Flair pens, book matches. Book matches! How can anyone have an opinion about book matches? She once went on at me for ten minutes: they're dangerous, they explode in your hand, your kid will eat them and go blind. God, Jess, that girl is an unqualified nut."

"She's a buyer at Bloomingdale's," Jessica said.

"She's a nut," Victor said. "A nut."

The blue whale surfaced.

On Thursday Jessica suggested:

"Bobbie Silvers."

"Hmmmmm," Victor said.

"She's cute and she loves to try new things," Jessica said. "Remember when she ordered those snake glands or whatever they were at the Balinese restaurant?"

"Yeah," Victor said slowly. "And she went to that nudist camp."

"Won the volleyball contest," Jessica reminded him.

"Yep." Victor nodded thoughtfully. "But what about Harry?"

"What about him?" Jessica asked.

"They're practically married," Victor said.

"We *are* married," Jessica said.

"Nah, Harry's a nice guy. He lent me his tape recorder."

"Maybe he'll lend us his girl?"

"Uh-uh," Victor said.

"Shit," said Jessica.

On Friday Jessica suggested:

"The nurse in Doctor Jacklin's office."

"You're kidding," Victor said.

"No," Jessica said. "I'm serious. She's very pretty and—"

"Beautiful," Victor said. "But we don't even know her name."

"Dr. Jacklin calls her Miss T."

"I like when she bends over me to fill the rinse cup and lower the chair," Victor sighed.

"Actually," Jessica admitted, "my strongest image of her is stuffing cotton in my mouth."

"Your problem," Victor said.

Jessica looked distressed.

"We'll work it out," Victor assured her. "Go on."

"I thought we could—well, she knows my brother is a dentist, and I thought we could say that he's coming for dinner and invite her over. Howard wouldn't be here, of course, but you and I could keep the conversation going about plaque and caries, mastication, root canals, and stuff while she drank her martinis—"

"How do you know she drinks martinis?" Victor asked.

"For godsake, Victor. So she'll drink scotch, bourbon, screwdrivers, what do we care?"

"We're out of bourbon, you know." Victor said.

"Victor!"

"Go on," he said.

"Well"—Jessica took a deep breath—"as soon as she's . . . you know, sort of receptive, we could broach the subject. She might . . . it might . . . you know, you never know about these things."

"I know," Victor said. "It won't work. We'd end up having to find another dentist."

"Pessimist," Jessica said.

"Just because I see her going back and telling Jacklin everything that happened? Jacklin, who's probably secretly in love with her? Pessimist, ha! You won't call me a pessimist when he sinks that high-speed drill through my lower lip."

"No?" Jessica asked.

"No." Victor said.

"Damn."

On Friday night Victor suggested his ex-wife and Jessica told him that he wasn't funny.

And on Saturday Jessica suggested:

"Marilyn Kantor."

"Marilyn Kantor?"

"I don't know why I didn't think of her before," Jessica said, though she knew perfectly well why she hadn't.

Jessica hadn't thought of Marilyn Kantor since the April Fool's Day Marilyn had scrawled *"I do it"* and Jessica's phone number in magic marker on billboards in Lexington Avenue stations from Sixty-eighth Street to Pelham Parkway.

Marilyn Kantor was trouble. Marilyn Kantor was an automatic sex drive that shifted from bed to bed as effortlessly as a Mercedes slipped from second to third. Marilyn Kantor had, before the end of her junior year at Hunter, slept with an entire fraternity and the president of two sororities. Marilyn Kantor was perfect.

"Who's Marilyn Kantor?" Victor asked.

"She's a girl I went to Hunter with," Jessica said. "Probably the most sexually liberated female east of Los Angeles. She did everything, anything. She told me about doing things that I *still* haven't read about in books. I heard she was married for about twenty seconds, got divorced, and was living in the Village."

"What's she look like?" Victor asked.

"She was once a Miss Subways," Jessica said.

"Can she sew?" Victor asked.

"What if she can't?" Jessica said defensively. "We're not marrying the first girl we go to bed with."

"What if we want to?" Victor asked.

Jessica shrugged. "Statistically it's a bad risk."

"Find her," he said.

When they made love that night it was more vigorous than usual. Jessica responded enthusiastically several times to Victor's virtuoso performance, but as she furled herself for sleep she began to wonder. She wondered whether Victor has been pleasuring in Marilyn's body and not her own. The thought nettled like grit on the sheet.

"Victor?" she whispered.

There was no answer; he was asleep.

Resentment curdled inside her. Victor was a chronic insomniac. Never, except for the first time they'd gone to bed together, had he fallen asleep before her. It was almost . . . rude.

"Victor," she called softly again.

"Huh?" He started. "What's the matter?"

"Were you thinking of Marilyn when you made love to me?"

"She was terrific," he mumbled sleepily. "Find her."

Jessica stared at him in the darkness, stared at the face she loved to watch him shave. She waited until his breathing was deep and regular for a full five minutes before she spoke.

"Don't forget," she said loudly, fascinated by the way his eyes twitched open. "We have to go to Howard and Sylvia's tomorrow. It's Kim's birthday."

She turned on her side and pushed her head into the pillow.

Victor moaned, sat up. He fumbled for a cigarette.

"I love you," Jessica murmured, and dived into dreamland.

Victor groped in the darkness for a match.

Victor's eyes bleared bloodshot above deep bluish crescents the following morning and Jessica told him to go back to sleep until it was time to leave. They went to DeVica's garage at one thirty to pick up Celia's car. It was a green '69 Pontiac with a bullet-shaped front end and an I STOP FOR ANIMALS sticker on the rear bumper. There were four small indentations on one front fender—Mauser's teeth, aimed for a cat, had missed. The seats were protected by covers of tinted plastic. Celia hadn't used the car for three months, and it took the attendant twenty minutes to work it out from behind the rows. He told Victor that he wished people would notify him ahead of time when they wanted their cars, told him it was a bitch getting the mothers out, told him that working in that garage was like smoking ten packs a day, coughed, spit, and said he was going for X rays next Saturday. Victor gave the keys to Jessica and handed the man a dollar. Jessica thought it was exorbitant. Victor saw it as an ecological reparation and told her how good he felt about it all the way to Teaneck, New Jersey.

Howard and Sylvia Siskand and their daughter Kim lived in a tiny little seventy-thousand dollar Tudor house that looked as if it were being seen through the wrong end of a telescope. It stood on a half acre of Astro-turf, bounded on the left by a thick wall of Scotch pines—which concealed the home of a reputed Mafia attorney—and on the right by Temple Ohevet Shalom. At night the light from Temple Ohevet Shalom's majestic menorah played on the wall of Kim Siskand's bedroom and gave her nightmares.

The house had previously been owned by Maxwell Crane, a slight, whimsical actor who had starred in a TV series in the late fifties. He had sold the house to Howard and Sylvia and moved to Australia after being acquitted of a morals charge. Neither Howard nor Sylvia could recall the name of the TV series, but they knew his morals charge by heart: lewd and lascivious public behavior, sodomy and corruption of a minor. Howard had discovered a stash of photographs of young naked boys and several *Spanking* magazines in the garage. He kept these hidden in his study in a large leather-bound volume on malocclusion which he would pull synaptically from its case whenever Sylvia was out of earshot and a willing viewer within range.

Howard was in his study with Sylvia's cousin when Jessica, Victor, and Aaron arrived. Sylvia and little Kim greeted them at the door.

"Better late than never," Sylvia said gaily. She was a

tall, bony woman in her mid-thirties, with angular features that in certain light made her appear whittled. She was dressed in a mauve pants suit, wore her bituminous hair in a lavishly lacquered upsweep of curls. She placed her glossy lips lightly on their cheeks. Her lipstick smelled like overripe raspberries.

"Are we late?" Victor asked, surprised.

"Oh, just sixteen minutes," she assured him. She nudged her daughter in the small of the back. "Say hello to Aunt Jess and Uncle Vic and baby Aaron."

Little Kim Siskand, who was staring at the package in Victor's hands, stepped forward with catatonic verve. "Hello Aunt Jess and Uncle Vic and baby Aaron," she said. Then she moved solemnly back to her mother's side. "I think they got me a game, Mom," she said tonelessly.

"We'll see when you open your presents, won't we?" Sylvia said. She stepped in front of Kim to help Jessica off with her coat.

"I hope it's not Candy Land," Kim said.

"Kimsee," Sylvia said. "Why don't you run upstairs and get Mommy some more hangers."

"I hope its not Parcheesi," Kim said.

"The hangers," Sylvia said, her voice as tight and sugary as a sourball.

"Okay." Kim turned to Victor. "I hope it's not Good Old Charlie Brown. I got that last year."

"It's not Good Old Charlie Brown," Victor told her.

"Thank God for small favors," she said, and rolled her eyes. She went upstairs for the hangers.

"You'll have to forgive Kim," Sylvia said quietly. "She's very excited today. Usually she's a regular cucumber. So cool, so sophisticated, you wouldn't believe it. Would you believe that last Saturday she had a date with a boy?"

"A date?" Jessica said.

"It was chaperoned, of course," Sylvia said. "Kim goes to the Teaneck Junior Miss Charm School three afternoons a week. They arranged the whole thing. They guarantee that your child will never go through a gawky adolescence. Kim gets sex education, diet lectures, makeup, and modeling tips from professionals. Last week there was a slide show and discussion on how to find a boy and hold him. Isn't that adorable?"

"My God, Sylvia, six is a little young to—" Jessica began.

"The Junior Miss motto is: You're never too young and you're never too old, for charm knows no age. They have adult classes on Wednesday nights. Oh, by the way"—Sylvia lowered her voice, leaned to Jessica—"you didn't bring her a game, did you?"

"No—why? Doesn't she like games?"

"It's the tension," Sylvia said. "She can't take the tension. It makes her throw up."

Across the room, Florence Siskand saw her daughter and grandson and squealed like a winner on a quiz show. She bore down on them with her right hand elevating the hem of her long palazzo pants, her left hand tugging a tall, heavyset man. The tall man's name was Manny Wiesenthal. He was retired furrier who lived in Florida, a cousin of one of Florence's girlfriends. His face was tanned the color of fried steak, his balding pate was freckled and peeling. He laughed like a lecherous Santa Claus with loud, suggestive Ho-Ho-*Ho's*.

Florence made introductions while Manny chucked Aaron under the chin and made faces at him.

"Manny, this is my daughter Jessica," she said.

"And I certainly would have known." He took Jessica's hand. "May I?" Without waiting for a response he kissed it. "Honey," he said, "If you don't mind my saying it, you're almost as lovely as your mother."

"Oh, Manny," Florence said, turning her head away without blushing.

"It's a pleasure," Jessica said. She forced a smile.

"And this must be—" Manny pointed at Victor.

"My son-in-law, the ecologist," Florence said.

"Editor," Victor corrected. He held out his hand. "Victor Prior. Nice to meet you."

Manny gripped Victor's hand and squeezed it, squeezed it hard.

Victor was nonplussed. He squeezed back.

Manny's knuckles grew white. Victor's knuckles grew red. There was a quiet crackle of joints and both men dropped their hands to their sides.

"Not bad, son," Manny said. "Not bad at all. Play any handball?"

"No," Victor said.

"Great sport," Manny said. "Keeps you toned. I'm on the courts every morning. Seven thirty every morning On Collins Avenue I'm known as Bouncing Manny Wiesenthal." He zoomed his right arm into an upswing, shifted his weight from foot to foot. "Guess how old I am?"

"Sixty?" Victor said politely.

Manny guffawed. He turned to Jessica. "Guess how old I am?"

"Sixty-one?" Jessica said.

"Sixty-three," he said. His arm shot up again. "And I have the ticker of a twenty-year-old." He thumped his chest with a fist. "An A-one ticker. A number one.

How many sixty-three-year-old guys do you know that can say that?"

"I don't know any," Victor said.

"None," Jessica said.

"Goddamn right," Manny said.

Howard Siskand and Sylvia's cousin Philip emerged from the study. Howard, who in his youth possessed the lean leathery look of a rebel, had, like leather, softened over the years, stretched out. He had also developed a paunch and a vexing insouciance toward everything except crabgrass, perversion, and teeth. He was wearing a light blue bodyshirt and grinning. Philip, a feather-weight man with shoulders no larger than his hips and arms as muscular as linguini, was hunched in a gray wool suit. His face was pale, his small eyes dilated. He looked as if he had just witnessed the bombnig of Dresden. Howard smacked him on the back and crossed to Jessica and Victor.

"Well, look who's here," he said, stopping near Aaron. He hoisted his nephew and spun him around. When Aaron began to laugh, Howard cradled him in one arm, gently pinched his cheek, and peered into his mouth.

"He's got Siskand teeth, all right," Howard said. "Those lower incisors are as good as fingerprints."

Aaron squirmed, started to gag. Howard put him down and watched him walk to the coffee table and grab a fistful of M&M's.

Jessica kissed her brother on the cheek.

"Keep him brushing," Howard said seriously. "Nothing to worry about right now, but those lower molars are targets—sitting ducks for caries."

"Hi, Howard," Victor said. He extended his hand.

"Victor!" Howard slapped him on the shoulder. "Long time no see. How's the old ecology game?"

Jessica's family, despite repeated admonitions, refused to acknowledge Victor as an editor. Any family could have an editor, an ecologist was a prize.

"Better than ever," Victor said cheerlessly. "How are things with you?"

"Buzzing, really buzzing along," Howard said. "I got a new drill last week and it is a lulu. God, what an instrument. The power in that thing is unbelievable, and the precision . . . jeezus, you would not believe it. You can hardly tell when it's on. I filled a triple surface two days ago and my patient couldn't believe it. From the moment she opened her mouth, she told me, it was nothing but pleasure. I'm telling you, I feel like God or someone with that tool."

"I can imagine," Victor said.

Sylvia signaled to Howard and he excused himself. She whispered something to him, pointed around the room. Howard nodded and began emptying ashtrays and picking up crumpled napkins.

Little Kim stood in front of the table on which her presents were stacked, stood as silent and reverent as a mourner at graveside.

Florence and Manny asked her if she was having a good time and she told them she was. Philip's wife, Carolyn, asked her if she was anxious to open her presents and she said not particularly. Victor asked her how she felt about being six and she told him that gentlemen didn't discuss a lady's age.

Jessica was about to ask her if she wanted to play with Aaron when Sylvia stopped her.

"It takes her time to warm up," Sylvia said.

"Oh." Jessica nodded.

"She's like this in new situations. When we were in St. Thomas last Christmas she hardly said anything for three days. Then"—Sylvia snapped her fingers—"like that she warmed up and had the whole hotel eating out of her hand."

"I thought mother told me that you went to Mexico?" Jessica said.

"We did," Sylvia said. "In February. We're going to San Francisco for Easter."

"It's nice that Howard can get away," Jessica said.

"Nice?" Sylvia snorted softly. "It's essential. I couldn't take it if I didn't get away from here at least four times a year, and Howard knows it."

Jessica bet Howard knew, bet he knew it damn well: Sylvia was a woman of few ambiguities.

She told Jessica she hardly had time to breathe during the week what with half her mornings spent calling repairmen or waiting for some delivery or another. Last Thursday she'd had to wait until two in the afternoon for the man from the dry cleaner's to pick up her clothes. She thanked God that the man ever came. And a matinee or shopping in the city really popped her, especially when it preceded one of the nights she and Howard went out to dinner, which they did three times a week.

"Well, maybe it would be easier just to stay home and cook one of those nights," Jessica offered.

Sylvia's upper lip rose like a chipmunk's. She said the only time she went near a stove was when she was out of matches and wanted to light a cigarette. She thanked God that Howard liked to cook as much as he did, which, she admitted, wasn't really enough anyway. She thanked God for her thyroid and iron pills even though she still came home utterly drained on Mondays and Thursdays after bridge at the club. And Fridays at the beauty parlor were sheer hell; she could never get out in less than three hours. She said she was counting the days to San Francisco. She thanked God for Easter.

Howard took Bouncing Manny Wiesenthal into his study and closed the door. A few moments later there was a loud Ho-Ho-*Ho* from inside. Sylvia's cousin Philip, who was sitting alone on the couch, heard the laughter and flushed embolically. His wife, Carolyn, told him he was drinking too much and walked angrily from the room.

Sylvia led little Kim from her table of presents, gave her a knife, and aimed her at the birthday cake. Little Kim went to it with chilling determination. Howard dimmed the lights, lit the candles. Florence led everyone in singing Happy Birthday. As Kim made her wish, Florence gave a solo rendering of the tune in German. It sounded a lot like the "Bell Song" from *Lakmé*.

Howard snapped his Polaroid when Kim raised her knife. The flash was dazzling. The photograph that appeared one minute later looked like the front page of the *National Enquirer*. The caption might have been: Child Goes Beserk At Birthday Party. Florence showed Aaron the photo and he dropped it into the onion dip.

The party ended abruptly after Kim had opened the last of her presents. Holding a set of Chinese checkers, she stood and faced the room. She curtsied, said thank you, put her fingers to her lips to blow a kiss, then threw up.

Halfway across the George Washington Bridge, Jessica told Victor that she thought he was valiant and

Victor told Jessica that he loved her a lot. They kissed at the toll booth, and, within the confines of their seatbelts and while Aaron slept in the back, they groped each other adolescently all the way home.

After she had put Aaron into his crib, Jessica went downstairs to the hall closet and took out a large cardboard carton, dragged it into the living room, and sat down beside it.

"What's that?" Victor asked.

Jessica began taking out papers, books, photographs, and laying them on the floor. "My past," she said.

"What are you looking for?" he asked.

"I'll tell you when I find it." She picked up a small album, flipped through it. "I've found it."

"What is it?" Victor asked.

"A picture of Marilyn Kantor." Jessica removed the photograph and handed it to Victor.

Victor studied the picture in silence, then gave it back.

"Well, what do you think?" she asked.

"Find her," he said.

Jessica phoned three old friends who she thought might know Marilyn's whereabouts. Each of them said they hadn't heard from her in years, said they wondered whatever happened to her, related at least one crazy Marilyn Kantor story, and suggested a reunion.

Jessica was discouraged.

She dialed information and got the phone numbers of four Marilyn Kantors. The first Marilyn Kantor wasn't home. The second Marilyn Kantor was a recorded message that said, "Hi, this is Marilyn Kantor. I am not in my office at the present time, but please leave your name and number when you hear the bleep and I will call you back." Jessica waited for the bleep and did as the machine had requested. She tried the third Marilyn Kantor and got Gristede's.

The fourth Marilyn Kantor answered the phone on the sixth ring and said a slurred, sleepy "Hello."

"Is this Marilyn Kantor?" Jessica asked.

"You'd better believe it," the voice said. "Who's this?"

"Jessica Prior."

"Who?"

"Jessica Siskandinowstein," Jessica corrected.

"Make up your mind, lady," the fourth Marilyn Kantor said.

"Jessica Siskandinowstein," Jessica said firmly.

There was a long pause. For a moment Jessica thought they had been disconnected; then, when she realized that they hadn't she became embarrassed. She was about to apologize and hang up when a wild whoop broke the silence.

"Jessica Siskandinowstein!" the fourth Marilyn Kantor shouted. "You old Victorian cunt, how the hell are you?"

CHAPTER 4

Marilyn Kantor was coming to dinner on Wednesday night.

Jessica had made the invitation sound casual. She'd told Marilyn that she'd been browsing through old photographs, found her picture, and wondered what she was up to, wondered if she wouldn't like to come to dinner some night that month? There was a fine line between not appearing too anxious and sounding insincere. Marilyn had proposed Wednesday. Jessica had told her that she couldn't have picked a better night.

After she'd hung up the telephone, Jessica stared at it incredulously.

"Well?" Victor asked. "What happened?"

"I did it," Jessica said. "I really did it. She's coming for dinner on Wednesday."

"Great."

"Is that all you can say?" Jessica was amazed.

Victor shrugged his shoulders uncomfortably. He was unused to being pressured for a reaction. He tried "Terrific."

"Don't you know what I've just *done?*" Jessica clutched the receiver.

"Invited Marilyn Kantor for dinner."

70

"I've initiated a seduction, that's what I've done. I've coldbloodedly initiated a seduction." She paused, thought a moment. "I am the person I always distrusted and never went out with again."

"Hon"—Victor put his arm around her shoulders—"you haven't seen the girl in ten years. She'll come to dinner and you'll have a terrific time rehashing your college days and that will probably be it."

"You say that and she thinks that, but I know differently. I was aware of my ulterior motives every moment of the conversation. They weren't even in the back of my mind, they were right up front, making me feel guiltier and guiltier. God, how can men do that all the time! It's awful."

"Awful," Victor agreed. "But think of it this way—your intentions are honorable. You're looking for a wife."

Jessica brightened. "That's right."

The following evening, when Victor returned from the office, Jessica was in high spirits, even though she'd decided to skip her exercise class. After a long harried morning of taking Aaron to the bathroom and thumbing through cookbooks trying to find a recipe for a dish that could easily be prepared beforehand on Wednesday night—something that looked complicated and tasted offbeat enough to be considered gourmet—her mood climbed steadily. Around noon she'd chosen moussaka (the recipe served ten, but she could always freeze the leftovers) and half an hour later Gino's wife, at the Martinizing store, had offered a toilet-training suggestion that so far had given Aaron a three-out-of-five success ratio. She'd told Jessica that before her boys were tall enough to stand and "release themselves," she'd seated them backwards on the toilet seat. Aaron seemed to enjoy the directional change, was fascinated with the flush handle, and managed to move thirty-two gallons of water through the house's new copper pipes with each piss.

Aaron was straddling the toilet, whacking the handle, when Victor walked in.

"What the hell's going on?"

"Shhh." Jessica kissed his cheek. "Don't raise your voice. I think we're onto something that might work. I'm calling it Operation Dry Baby."

"Why is he sitting like that?"

"Holding the tank makes him feel secure. Shhh."

"It looks perverse."

Aaron shook the handle rapidly up and down.

"Hey—he's going to break the toilet. Aaron, no—"

Jessica clamped a hand over Victor's mouth. "Victor, please."

"Do you know that plumbers cost twelve bucks an hour?" Victor whispered loudly.

"Do you know how much Pampers cost?"

"All right, all right. How long does he have to sit there?"

"Well, I guess he can come off now." Jessica lifted Aaron from the seat, stood him barefoot and grinning on the floor. "Watch him while I get his pajamas."

"Sure." Victor hunched down. "How's Daddy's big boy today, huh?" Jessica left them in the bathroom and hurried down the hall. She'd just reached the entrance to Aaron's room when she heard Victor shout.

"What's the matter?" she called.

"Bring a rag back, will you—and another pair of socks for me. Operation Dry Baby is a bust."

Jessica's spirits plummeted.

*

Later, after dinner, Jessica listened with attentive abstraction as Victor recounted the latest George Wiffet outrage, calling it an insidious coup. George had brought one of his blackbirds to the office and neatly managed to disrupt the editorial meeting by uncaging it just when Victor was discussing his books.

"Damn thing flew figure eights right over my head."

"I'm making moussaka Wednesday," Jessica said.

"What's that have to do with Wiffet?"

"Nothing. It has to do with Marilyn Kantor."

"Oh." Victor fell silent. "I was thinking about that a little today."

"Me too," Jessica said offhandedly. "Should be interesting—I mean pleasant, no matter what happens."

"Sure." Victor shook his head. "No matter what happens."

"Do you think something's going to happen?" Jessica asked suddenly, her voice louder than she'd intended.

"Could. Depends on how we handle it, I guess."

"I hope you don't blow it."

"Me? You're the one who started this whole thing. You're the one who wanted a wife."

"You're shouting."

"Sorry."

Silence.

A tiny grin flickered on Victor's face. "Well, I used to be pretty good at pushing a conversation subtly around to sex."

"Maybe you should nudge it around to marriage first. The other way seems so—crude."

"For godsake, Jess. No married man even mentions the word when he's trying to get a woman who's not his wife into bed with him. You don't know anything about getting laid."

"You don't have to rub it in." Jessica was miffed. "Go on."

"Use logic, Jess. That's what it all comes down to. Valid reasoning is the surest way to approach anything sucessfully. I don't know why women can't understand that."

"Who says?"

"Name one great female military tactician. Someone, let's say, to equal Alexander?"

"I can't—offhand."

"See!" Victor stood and paced the room, snapping his fingers the way he did when he worked out a Rowena Westcott plot. "We have to take this step by step. Let's eliminate for a moment the hypothetical and deal with *givens*. First, Marilyn Kantor is coming to dinner. Second, at one point in the evening it is *reasonable* to assume that she will ask me what I do for a living. At that point I will tell her about Ecopress, bring up the blue whale and make some small joke about its mating habits. And from whale sex we go to sex in general, in books, in movies, down to sex in particular, like between different types of people, right smack down to sex and us. Given the givens, and a little booze, and given what you've told me about Marilyn, that should do it." He looked enormously pleased with himself.

Jessica frowned. "No. I don't think it's going to work. I'd better handle it."

"And how do you propose to do that?" Victor's voice was sarcastic.

"I'm not sure, but something tells me I should make the overtures."

"Odd. Something tells me I should," Victor said.

"That so?" said Jessica.

Victor's chin angled defiantly. "That's so. Moreover, it is in accordance with the laws of nature and man." He tweaked her cheek playfully.

"Uh-uh." Jessica held her resolve as tightly as a drumstick in her fist. "I'll do it."

"Why?" Victor asked. "Give me one logical reason."

"Simple," Jessica said. "She's my friend."

"What difference does that make?"

"Would you want me to seduce one of your friends?"

"Of course not," Victor said angrily.

"See?" Jessica picked up his cup. "More coffee?"

"I think I'll take a walk instead," Victor said.

"Whatever you want," Jessica said.

"Ha!"

When Victor returned a half hour later, Jessica was in bed. She had a yellow legal pad in her lap and a number 1 Venus Velvet pencil clamped between her teeth. She was thinking.

"What are you doing?" Victor asked.

"Shopping list," she lied. To tell Victor that she was thinking would only make him more inquisitive. How could she explain that she was trying to remember lines guys had used to get into her pants? Especially when she was trying to recall them for the express purpose of sexually recycling them. Besides, the only one remotely workable that came to mind was; "No other girl has ever turned me on the way you do," and it left a lot to be desired.

"I had a nice talk with that writer across the street. Rick. The one with the dog," Victor said. "Did you know that's not a real guard dog?"

"A Bengal tiger in drag?"

Victor ignored her. "Mauser's just a tough, atavistic shepherd. It took Rick two years to get him under control. Any other owner would have had him put to sleep long ago."

"Says a lot about Rick," said Jessica, who'd always thought the young man a bit strange, and probably prone to fetishes. Leathery things. She began to doodle on the pad.

"I've been thinking, though," Victor said. "I might like a real guard dog." He stood naked in front of the mirror and sucked in his gut, strutted, studied himself. "What do you think?"

"Nice," Jessica said. She wasn't really listening. She was wondering how Victor would look to Marilyn. A good-looking husband would definitely be an asset. Possibly a necessity. Victor's face was handsome enough and he was still basically slim; though appraising him from another woman's point of view she did notice that his belly had softened in the last five years and was broaching a mild tumescence.

"Turn around," Jessica said. "Face me."

Victor walked to the foot of the bed. "Weren't you listening?"

"Of course I was." She tapped the pencil against her teeth, and made contemplative clicking sounds with her tongue.

Victor looked down at his body, up at Jessica. "What are you staring at?"

"Randolph."

Victor covered himself with his hands. "Really!"

"I'm pretending I'm Marilyn and that I'm seeing you for the first time."

Victor drew his hands to his hips, cocked his head to

the side. He lowered his lids to what he referred to as bedroom level, which made him look a little like Robert Mitchum and a lot like someone who's had smoke blown in his eyes. "You've captured my interest. Go on."

"I wondered how you—oh, now there, that's better!" She pointed the pencil at him. "I know how terrific Randolph is, but first impressions are so important. Do you think you could—well, try harder when you get undressed? I mean, just so that he's not—oh, now that's even better still!"

Victor gripped himself with his right hand and sneered. "She'll take one look at me . . . and she'll faint with ecstasy."

"Victor, this isn't a joke. I am seriously planning to embark on a sociological experiment with enormous ramifications, one which will alter our lives, and you—oh, Victor, he's going down," Jessica said, her observation powdered with disappointment. "I certainly hope that won't happen on Wednesday night. I'm really counting on you."

"I'll do my best," he said sullenly. He got into bed and pulled the covers to his chin.

"I have a rough idea of how I'm going to play the evening, but it's still drawing-board stage. I don't want us to come on too strong, but then again, the converse could lead to nothing. I'll give you the cues as soon as I've worked it out." Jessica glanced down at Victor. "Why are you so quiet?"

"I'm wondering whether we'd be better off with a male or female."

"Wife?"

"Guard dog."

*

77

The following day, thirty-one hours and twenty-seven minutes before Marilyn was expected for dinner, Jessica left Aaron with Abby and met her mother for lunch at Wong Lee's on Broadway and Eighty-third Street. They always met at Wong Lee's when Florence was treating. Aside from being inexpensive, Florence Siskand liked the restaurant because the food wasn't too exotic, the waiters spoke articulate English, and the owner always told her she was losing too much weight.

When Jessica arrived, Florence was dipping her pinky into the crumbs of what had been crisp noodles and sipping a daiquiri, trying to look as if she were lost in thought. Except for two Puerto Rican moving men in coveralls at the bar watching a baseball game, the restaurant was empty. Jessica slid into the booth opposite her mother.

"Darling!" Florence cried. "I didn't even see you come in." She crooked a finger at Jessica and pointed to her cheek. Jessica leaned over and kissed her. Florence turned her head and pointed to her other cheek. Jessica obliged. She loved her mother and the first kiss was always genuinely given; the second—an affectation her mother had somehow acquired at Kitchner's Castle—was more often an obligation.

"Tell me, tell me," Florence said, "how's my little Aaron? Victor? What have you been doing?"

"Mom, you just saw us on Sunday," Jessica said.

"Two days ago," her mother said, not the least bit defensively. "People can fly to London in five hours—a lot can happen in two days."

"Everybody's fine," Jessica assured her. "What's happening with you?"

Florence sighed. She put her drink down and ran her fingers up and down the stem of the glass, stared at the circles she'd made on the tablecloth. "I'm glad you asked, Jess."

Jessica knew her mother was glad that she asked, was quite aware that had she not asked, her mother would have had to pose the question herself. *I suppose you're wondering what I've been doing?* Florence Siskand would find an opening for what she wanted to say if she had to swing the whole conversation ajar.

"I have a problem," Florence began. "It concerns a man."

Jessica ordered a Bloody Mary and rested her head back against the red Vinyl upholstery. Ever since her mother had entered widowhood ten years before, she'd had problems concerning men. Mostly the problems were the men themselves. Florence Siskand had a relentless, homing-pigeon instinct for losers: short, pensioned, parsimonious creeps who courted her at afternoon movies where they could use their Over Sixty discount cards, balding leisure-village Lotharios out to prove they could still get it up by selecting women who'd prefer that they didn't, chunky Medicare regulars who couldn't sit down for a meal without bringing up their cholesterol problems, couldn't go past two dates without discussing their prostate. Ten years. A decade of schmucks.

"Whatever you're going to tell me, Mom, I have the feeling that we've gone through it before," Jessica said.

"This is different," Florence said. "I think this is— the real thing."

Jessica sat up. "No kidding?"

"I get butterflies when he phones; migraines when he doesn't. And when he pinches my cheek, I think I am going to drop dead." Florence gripped her daughter's hand. Her 2.7 Tiffany-set diamond, turned palmward so as not to attract muggers, dug into Jessica's knuckles. "You know me. If I didn't believe it was the real thing I'd be sure I had cancer."

Jessica had to concede that such would be the case. Florence Siskand, who'd never been ill as long as Jessica could remember, panicked at the slightest physical variance in her bodily functions. Mild indigestion prompted fears of an ulcer, simple fatigue was a clear indication of leukemia, and everything else, from hiccups to athlete's foot was undoubtedly a late warning sign of cancer. "So," Jessica said, increasingly aware of her impaled knuckles, "who is it?"

"You know," Florence said coyly.

"That guy you brought to Kim's party? Bouncing Manny whatshisname?"

"Weisenthal," Florence said. "That's him."

"He seemed nice," Jessica said. There was very little else she could say.

"A heart of gold," Florence said. "And a personality —like, well you wouldn't believe it. What a personality on that man. Even my friend Blanche Kogan—you know, the one who works for NBC—even she says so."

Blanche Kogan was a fifty-seven-year-old dike who interviewed contestants for a daytime quiz show. She was one of those semi-executives who delighted in discomfitting anyone not responsible for her paycheck. She had a gift for selecting contestants who could publicly humiliate themselves on the air, without reflecting badly on the show itself. Blanche rarely had a kind word for anyone.

"Hmmm," Jessica said. "That is going some for Blanche."

Florence flustered. "Well, she didn't say it in so many words, if you know what I mean. But—"

"I know what you mean," Jessica said. "Anyway, what's the problem?"

"I think we should order first." Florence hid behind the menu.

"Mom," Jessica said. "You're blushing. What is it?"

Florence closed the menu carefully. Raising a finger she signaled one of the waiters, who was sitting with his two co-workers at a table near the rest rooms eating rice. He picked up his pad reluctantly and came over. Florence Siskand had firmly established herself at Wong Lee's as a 15-percent tipper, and the waiters knew it. She ordered wonton soup without the wontons and a number two combination dinner. Jessica asked for spareribs and knew she wouldn't eat them.

When the waiter left, Jessica said, "All right, Mom, tell me."

Florence looked serious a moment, then giggled. When she stopped giggling she grew serious again. "I think I'm going to marry Manny," she said.

"You devil," Jessica said. "When did he ask you?"

"Well—he didn't. Not exactly, that is, but I just know he will. And—" She lifted her chin and took a deep breath, held it.

"And what?"

"And I'm going to go all the way with him." She let out her breath, took a long sip of her daiquiri. Swallowed. "Before."

"Before?" Jessica asked, suddenly very uncomfortable.

"Before."

"You're a big girl, Mom," Jessica said. "I've given you advice for ten years. Sometimes you've followed it and sometimes you haven't, but that's neither here nor there. I can't live your life for you. I've tried to be your friend as well as your daughter. If you love him, do it. If you don't, don't do it. Marriage shouldn't even enter into it."

Florence nearly choked. "Of course it should. It does! Really, Jessica, do you think I'd even consider *that* if I wasn't sure that he was going to marry me?" She paused. "Of course, if I didn't have to work, if your father had provided for my years without him a bit more generously—not that he hadn't wanted to—I probably wouldn't consider *that* at all."

"Mom, what are you saying?"

"Quite candidly, darling," Florence Siskand told her daughter, "sex doesn't run on our side of the family."

At Molfetta's Fruits and Vegetables, gazing at a bin of voluptuous eggplants, Jessica thought about what her mother had said, thought about Marilyn, and felt traitor to her own flesh and blood. It took her nearly half an hour to select what she needed for the moussaka. In fact, she stood unmoving so long in front of the eggplants that Mr. Molfetta, an embittered immigrant who was rarely solicitous, owing to a speech impediment that, coupled with his accent, made him the target of cruel local jokes, actually managed to ask if she were feeling all right. Inordinate, self-defeating time consumption was the emotional extortion demanded by Jessica's unconscious as reparation for small guilts. Once, after frivolously spending thirty-five dollars on a very tiny Pucci scarf, she fell asleep on the subway (her worst fear realized) and woke up in Coney Island. Embarrassed at being caught in her own penance, she hastily snatched the first eggplants that came into her hand—only discovering afterward that one of them was a mango—and hurried on to the butcher.

Al's Prime Meats and Poultry was a narrow shop sandwiched between Norma's Lingerie and Ace Uniforms. The display window of each of the three stores were comparably unappealing. Norma's Lingerie exhibited chipped, truncated torsos encased in pantyhose and torturous-looking spandex girdles that were said to "breathe." Ace Uniforms had one dusty twenties mannequin dressed in a white pants suit, and Al's window was virtually obliterated by "Today Special" posters. Jessica was happy to note that the special that day was lamb.

As she entered the store, which was no wider than two steers nose to nose, she nearly tripped over little Ruth Remson. Celia's three-year-old was happily burying her sister in sawdust while her mother argued about a chicken with Al.

"It was rancid—foul," Celia said loudly.

"Mrs. Remson. I've been in business twenty-two years, and I've never sold a bad chicken. Something must have happened to your refrigerator," Al said.

"Your chicken. That's what happened to my refrigerator," Celia said. "I could have gotten fowl cholera and died!"

"It wasn't my lucky day. I didn't win the lottery either," Al said tiredly.

"I want another chicken," Celia demanded. She saw Jessica and broke into a wide smile. "Hey, I tried to phone you before."

"Lunch with Mom," Jessica said.

Al plopped a chicken on the counter. "There. Take it and let me live without ulcers."

"Are you sure it's fresh?" Celia asked.

"Oy! What do you want? A coroner's report? It's so fresh I'm not even sure it's dead."

"All right. I'll take it."

"Women!" Al muttered. Fortunately, Celia didn't hear him.

Jessica gave her order, then sat down on one of the folding chairs against the wall. Celia joined her, ignoring her daughter Naomi's unintelligible protests about the sawdust.

"They'll have to learn to cope," Celia said. "What are you using all that lamb for?"

"Moussaka. I'm having company tomorrow night."

Celia clutched her poncho. "You can't. There's a session at my house tomorrow night. I told you it would be Wednesday."

"I forgot," Jessica said.

"Jess, you'll fall back to point zero. You can't just launch your consciousness and then deprive it of fuel."

"I'm sorry," Jessica said. "I'll make the next one."

"Being sorry isn't enough," Celia said. "I'm sorry that you don't feel the vibes of the Movement strongly enough to relinquish a solitary social obligation—but what good does it do me?"

"None, I suppose," Jessica said honestly.

"I'm sad," Celia said. "I'd hoped last week meant something to you."

"But it did," Jessica assured her. "You have no idea."

"I consider sisterhood . . . well, almost a religion," Celia said. "I wish you could understand."

"I do," Jessica said. "It's really very intolerant of you not to see that."

"Intolerant!" Celia bridled. The concept, applied to herself, was unthinkable.

"You don't have to go to synagogue or a church to believe," Jessica said. "So——"

"So—what?"

"So I'm raising my consciousness at home tomorrow night," Jessica said. And somewhere in her primal recesses she prayed that God would not strike her dead.

That night Jessica and Victor took turns playing Marilyn, trying out various opening gambits. They rated each other's effectiveness on a scale of ten.

Victor's "I hope this won't shock you, but you've become a star in our sex fantasies," rated a 6.2. His "The majority of American women aren't very good in bed," got a consolation 4.

Jessica's "We have an orthopedic mattress that you have to lie on to believe," garnered a 7.6, and her "Victor gives the greatest back massage in the whole world," championed the evening with a 9.9.

It was tacitly agreed that Jessica would take the initiative.

Victor had insomnia most of the night.

Somewhere around 4 A.M. Jessica thought she was coming down with the flu. By the time Aaron awoke, she was convinced she had a peptic ulcer or an ovarian cyst. Victor told her that she was beginning to sound like her mother and she broke into tears.

She had a piercing headache the rest of the day.

At seven that evening, the doorbell rang. Jessica and Victor froze.

"It's her," Jessica whispered.

"She," Victor corrected. "You'd better let her in."

"She might be fat and ugly. I haven't seen her in a long time," Jessica said.

"Life is a gamble."

"Victor, are we really going to go through with this?" Jessica asked.

The doorbell rang again.

"Not if we don't answer the bell," said Victor.

As Jessica walked down the hall she rubbed the Ugashan knobkerrie for luck.

She took a deep breath and opened the door.

The girl who stood before her was a stranger.

CHAPTER 5

The girl on the stoop was taller than Jessica remembered Marilyn by at least two inches, and slimmer by an easy ten pounds. Her hair was blazing butter yellow, frizzed out in a spectacular Aryan Afro. A leather mail pouch was slung over one shoulder of a World War II aviator jacket.

She wore motorcycle goggles.

"Y-yes?" Jessica said.

"Yes, indeedy!" The girl whipped off her goggles and threw her arms around Jessica; the mail pouch swung against Jessica's thigh with a *thump*. "Siskandinowstein, you haven't changed a pubic inch!"

"Marilyn! My god, I'd never have recognized you. You're taller—"

Marilyn kicked out her foot, pointed to the three-inch platform on her shoe. "Better to intimidate you with, my dear."

"And your hair—" Jessica heard Victor come up behind her. She turned. "Oh, hon, this is—"

Marilyn brushed past Jessica and put her arms around Victor's neck. "I loathe formal introductions," she said, and kissed Victor hard on the lips. "That gets a lot of shit out of the way. If there's one thing I've learned from T groups, it's get that shit right out of the way." She turned to Jessica. "This is the famous Victor, right?"

"Uh—yes," Jessica said.

"I've heard a lot about you," Victor said.

"It's all true," Marilyn said. "I was once Miss Subways." She took off her jacket and flipped it to Victor. She wore a long-sleeved polo shirt with SCHLITZ emblazoned across the front in rhinestones. "Hey, this place is all right." She walked into the living room.

"It's home." Jessica linked her arm through Victor's. "An urban-renewed love nest."

"Love nest, hell," Marilyn said. "You could throw some orgy here."

"How about a drink," Victor said, with some difficulty.

"If that's the best proposition you can make, okay." Marilyn flopped onto the couch, kicked off her shoes, and put her feet up on the cushions. "Vodka, straight. I've got some dynamite Columbian shit for later."

"Pot?" Jessica asked.

"The best. Oh, God, don't tell me you don't smoke."

"We do," Jessica assured her, "but usually only on weekends, or at parties. You know."

"Same old Siskandinowstein." Marilyn took the drink from Victor. "Thanks."

"My pleasure," Victor said.

"I'll get the hors d'oeuvres," said Jessica. She went to the kitchen and returned with a large tray of cheeses and an assortment of imported crackers. The crackers had come in a tin and cost two dollars. They tasted like salty cardboard but impressed guests. She laid a slice of cheese on one and handed it to Marilyn.

Victor was saying, "But on the whole it hasn't been

too bad a March. Even last month wasn't too bad. Our fuel bill was down from what it was last year."

"I didn't know that," Jessica said.

"Didn't I mention it? Considerably lower," Victor said.

"Considerably lower?" Jessica asked, looked surprised and feeling horrifically certain that only a blackout or a bombing would ever bring the conversation around for a shot at seduction. As it turned out, neither a blackout nor a bombing was necessary.

Victor poured himself another drink and launched the blue whale. As he was explaining the difference between a humpback and a sei rorqual, Marilyn interrupted.

"Don't you ever talk about anything but sex?" she asked.

Victor nearly gagged. "What?"

"That's an ice-breaker," Marilyn said. "Sometimes I use ethnic jokes, but I prefer sex. That's something everyone can get into." She tugged the bottom of her polo shirt, pulling it taut across her breasts. "Am I right?"

"*Absolutement!*" Victor said. He thrust up his glass. A few drops of scotch sloshed onto the carpet. He pretended not to notice.

Jessica clamped on an instinct to rush to the kitchen for paper towels. "You always were uninhibited."

"Uninhibited, shit. I was an easy lay." Marilyn looked from Victor to Jessica and broke into laughter. "Hey, I hope I'm not being out of line."

"Oh, no," Jessica and Victor assured her in unison. They were immediately embarrassed.

Marilyn relaxed, made herself more comfortable on the couch. She was secure that she was the star. "Have either of you seen *Nothing By Mouth?* It's a dynamite flick."

"No, we haven't," Victor said. "I've heard it has really fine cinematography and some hilarious satire."

"Piss on the satire," Marilyn Kantor said. "That's good porn. There's one supererotic scene where two Schrafft's ladies come into this big executive's office. While he's munching away on a sweet Danish, one little lady is eating him and the other is doing herself with his dictaphone. It's a real turn-on."

Victor shot Jessica a look that said: This could be your opening.

Jessica cocked her head coyly. "Speaking of that," she said, and suddenly felt her peptic ulcer and/or ovarian cyst grip her guts, "er . . . dinner's ready." A sense of failure swept her.

It was a feeling of having missed opportunity's knock.

It was a feeling of having sinned by omission.

She could not meet Victor's eyes. "We're having moussaka."

"That always sounds obscene," Marilyn said, winking playfully at Victor.

"It's a Greek dish," said Victor.

"No offense, but anything'll be better than these crackers. They taste like salted cardboard."

Victor went unenthusiastically to the table.

The situation looked bleak.

Marilyn began to tell Polish jokes.

Jessica silently rationalized that Marilyn wasn't wife material, and why bother with something that didn't even have potential? She consoled herself with: If this is the way things are working out, then this is the way God wants it. Just as she relaxed, Marilyn passed around a joint and proceeded to recount her more vivid sexual adventures.

"If I ever had time to put them all in a book," she said, "it would be an instant best seller. There must be easily three hundred shrinks who've heard my name." She told them about a Hungarian juggler who kept a tether ball in the air while he made love to her. He bounced it off his spine on the outstroke.

Victor was impressed. "I'm impressed," he said, and rested his chin on his palm. "You've aroused my admiration."

That wasn't all Marilyn had aroused. Jessica knew what Victor's glassy-eyed look meant from experience; Marilyn knew it by instinct.

"Go on," Jessica said. She felt slightly lightheaded and daring. "Don't stop now."

"You're among friends," Victor said. He reached over and patted her knee.

"I feel like a dirty Scheherazade," Marilyn said. She told another about making it with two rock singers who kept a microphone on the pillow and sent her orgasmic shouts through a concert amplifier.

"Too noisy," Jessica said. She made a face, then giggled. *Now*, she said to herself. Now or never. It would all have to be in the delivery. She wouldn't have a second chance. Like Mary Marvel shouting SHA-ZAM! she felt herself calling upon all her old Madison Avenue muses not to fail her. Every word, every nuance, counted. Her poise, her pose, the intensity of her voice would all come into play. The desired effect was to be subliminally coercive. "Marilyn," Jessica said, "have you ever been to bed with a hus—" She caught herself, was appalled by her own stupidity, but then immediately pleased with her recovery, which, had she not been slightly inebriated and resoundingly high would have been equally appalling. "—with a her and a him?" She coughed, and amended: "A male and a female?"

"You mean a couple?" Marilyn asked.

"I guess you could call them that," Jessica said. She nodded her head for longer than she'd intended. When she realized it, she blushed.

"Say. . . ." Marilyn drawled. She folded her arms and looked from Victor to Jessica. Squinted. "Are you two up to what I think you're up to?"

"Well. . . ." Victor said, smirking like a turtle.

"No!" Jessica said.

"What?" said Victor.

"Well, maybe," said Jessica.

"Hold it right there, Siskandinowstein," Marilyn said.

"Prior," Jessica corrected.

"You two are into trios, aren't you? Well, I'll be a monkey's cunt. I wouldn't have believed it."

"I think 'into' is not the appropriate word," Victor said gently.

"Ah-ha. I get it," said Marilyn Kantor, whose extraordinary look of superiority left little doubt she did. "I'm the genital guinea pig. Well, well, well, what do you think of that?"

"What do *you* think of that?" Victor grazened.

"Hmmm." Marilyn's face grew serious. "I think before I answer that we have to go over a few things. You realize, of course, that there are problems with first-timers—especially husbands and wives."

"I never realized that," Jessica said. "Did you, Victor?"

"In all honesty—no."

Marilyn tapped her spoon contemplatively on the table. Then she said, "All right! You know what they say about an ounce of prevention?"

"Worth a pound of cure," Jessica said.

Marilyn nodded approval. "First off, I think you should know that it doesn't always work."

"It doesn't?" said Jessica.

"What doesn't?" said Victor nervously.

"The scene," said Marilyn.

Neither Jessica nor Victor had the courage to ask her to elaborate.

"Secondly, Jess, it's sometimes a shock for a wife to know that her husband is making love to another woman."

"It's not as if he's doing it behind my back," Jessica said.

"Good attitude. Nice," Marilyn said.

Jessica felt as pleased as if she'd just named all the state capitals in alphabetical order.

"And," Marilyn continued, "it's sometimes unnerving for a man to see another woman with his wife." She eyed Victor suspiciously.

Victor furrowed his brow. It was his concentration grimace. Jessica held her breath. Suddenly Victor snapped erect. His eyes were as clear and purposeful as brass buttons. "I am prepared," he said, "for whatever comes."

Jessica exhaled. Victor gripped her hand. She put hers over his and he put his other over hers. Marilyn gripped the bottom of her SCHLITZ polo shirt and hoisted it over her head.

"What the hell," Marilyn said. "Let's go!"

Jessica had a moment of frenzied indecision. Should she ask Marilyn to wait while she put the leftover moussaka into the refrigerator? Or should she risk ruining the moussaka, which served twelve and if carefully frozen would easily stretch for two quick dinners? *Screw the moussaka!*

As they climbed the stairs to the bedroom, Victor stared at Marilyn's breasts. He described them to Jessica later as "pearlescent globes." His mother had had an art nouveau lamp in her bedroom with "pearlescent globes." When he was a boy he painted faces on the globes with his mother's lipstick.

Jessica, too, stared at Marilyn's breasts. Surreptitiously. They reminded her of Forty-second Street novelty beanbags, the right having slightly more beans than the left. Beanbags used to make good potsies. They were for tossing into numbered squares chalked on the sidewalk. Jessica and her brother used to play the game often when they were growing up in Brooklyn. Now she and Victor were going to play with Marilyn's potsies. It was funny how childhood habits stuck with you.

Victor closed the door to the bedroom and the three of them fell silent. They were all instantly very, very sober. Jessica could not look at Victor and Victor could not look at Jessica; neither of them could look at Marilyn, who had begun unzipping her slacks.

"Well?" Marilyn said. "Are we or aren't we?" She stood before them in a pair of paisley bikini underpants.

"We are," Victor said. He unbuttoned his shirt.

Jessica fumbled with the hook and eye at the side of her long hostess skirt. "They're nice panties," Jessica said. "Where'd you get them?"

"Would you believe Bloomingdale's basement?" Marilyn said proudly. She snapped the elastic.

"No kidding?" Jessica stepped out of her skirt.

"They've got some terrific stuff down there," Marilyn said. "You ought to go."

Jessica pulled her turtleneck over her head. "Is it only junior sizes? I wear an eight." She kept her voice casual, trying frantically to surpress a rush of juvenile embarrassment. Though she was not unduly modest and was proud of her breasts, which were still pleasingly curved and uptilted, varying from moderate- to medium-size depending on the time of the month, she was humiliatingly conscious of her unexpectedly taut, raised nipples. She felt as subtle as a flasher."

"I wear an eight too," Marilyn said, unaware of Jessica's nipples. "They have some great sports clothes, and separates."

"I've been hunting all over for a pair of brown slacks," Jessica said.

Victor coughed.

Jessica closed her eyes for an instant and childishly prayed for the whole thing to be over.

Victor was naked. He was trying to look relaxed, and failing. Randolph was semi-erect, waiting on standby for the right signal. Jessica had no idea what that signal was. Fortunately, Marilyn did.

She slid her paisley bikinis down over her hips, stepped from them. She put her hands on her hips, sassily. "Well," she said. "The least one of you could do is kiss me."

Victor took Marilyn into his arms. Randolph left standby like a 747 that had been waiting on a stacked-up runway.

Jessica felt as if Dr. Jacklin had just driven his high-speed drill through her guts.

In bed, Jessica came to her first conclusion about

multiple sex: The reality did not live up to the fantasy. Without a choreographer, three real people on Wamsutta sheets on a king-sized bed in a brownstone on West Eighty-seventh Street on a Wednesday night bore as little titillating resemblance to the sensual photographs she'd seen in *Playboy* as a sneeze did to an orgasm.

From the moment they got into bed, Jessica's brain repeatedly asked: *Is it really happening?* This was very disconcerting. And dumb. *It* was obviously happening. *It* was happening right before Jessica's eyes!

Victor, who always did have a childlike attraction for the new, was utterly fascinated with Marilyn's potsies. He bobbled them, licked them, squeezed them like oranges. Occasionally he'd release one of Marilyn's and fondle one of Jessica's. It was like reassuring an old teddy bear that it was still loved.

Marilyn seemed to sense Victor's preoccupation, and whether it was out of camaraderie for her old school chum or a penchant for diversion or (as Jessica later secretly suspected) a desire to show off, she rolled Victor over on his back, wriggled down him like the stripes on a barber pole, and drew him into her mouth as effectively as an upright Hoover.

Jessica's mother had an upright Hoover. It was powerful enough to depilate a shag rug. It wasn't half as effective as Marilyn. Jessica was impressed. Jealous.

Victor moaned, grasped one of Jessica's breasts. Good old teddy bear.

Marilyn reached up and laid her palm over Jessica's other breast, moved it clockwise in a slow polishing motion. Jessica grew rigid. Marilyn trailed her fingers lazily down across Jessica's belly; her head bobbing between Victor's legs like a well-oiled piston.

Victor moaned again. His moans sounded a lot like an upright Hoover depilating a shag rug. He released Jessica's breast and put both hands on top of Marilyn's head. He stroked her hair in time with her movements.

Thralled and unable to sort out one emotion from another, Jessica felt Marilyn's fingers burrow into the cleft of her thighs. Victor's rhythmic stroking accelerated to a frenzied scalp massage. Jessica thought she should kiss someone's something, squeeze someone's something, touch someone's something, at the very least. But whose? It was as if she were being attacked by a school of piranhas from the inside. Her libido had collapsed into a heap of confused desires. She couldn't decide whether she was sexually excited or murderously jealous and she didn't discount the possibility of both. The only problem was that she couldn't pin down what was exciting her or whom she was jealous of. Was she jealous of Marilyn pleasuring Victor? After all, he was her husband. Jessica had spent five years learning his love signals. (She'd scouted his erogenous zones with a slow but sure hunt-and-peck method that had revealed the inner knee, the Archilles tendon, and, surprisingly, the clavicle and the nose, which were particularly sensitive to rapid successive flicks of the tongue.) Or was she jealous of Victor pleasuring in Marilyn? He'd told Jessica that she was the most sexually stimulating woman he'd ever met. Had he met another?

Victor's moans had turned to "oh's." The "oh's" were slowly going up the diatonic scale. Somewhere between "re" and "mi" Marilyn began to pump against the bed, her buttocks rising and falling like honeydew melons on a trampoline. When Victor's "oh's" reached "fa," she leaped up suddenly, straddled him, pressed his hands against her potsies, and rode him like a Derby jockey coming down the stretch. She crossed the finish line 2.7 seconds after Victor's "la" ... "ti" ... "Do!"

Victor's arms fell to his side.

Marilyn smacked his chest. "Fucking-A-All-right!" she said, and rolled off him with a bulldogger's whoop. She hugged Jessica. "Your husband is terrific. Don't go away. I'll be right back." She danced out to the bathroom.

"There's a girl who doesn't fake 'em," Victor said. He looked quite pleased with himself.

"I don't think you can take credit for that," Jessica said.

"I'm not so sure," Victor said defensively. "I was doing some pretty intricate gyrations on the upward thrust. Besides, you heard her, she said I was terrific."

"She was being polite."

"You're jealous."

"You could have been a banana for all she cared."

"That's sour grapes, Jess," Victor said.

Marilyn came back into the room. Victor pulled her playfully down onto the bed. He began to kiss her neck. Marilyn giggled. Victor made funny noises. They sounded like a harmonica being played through a Turkish towel.

Whether it was Victor's noises or Marilyn's giggles that triggered her, Jessica could not be sure. But she knew she would have to do something and if she wanted a wife she knew she would have to do it sooner or later. And as her brother once said, "There's no time like the present."

The problem was that Jessica really didn't know what to do.

It wasn't a situation where she wanted to wing it, but it was that or resign herself to the endless pilgrimages to Sloan's supermarket, the Chinese laundry, the potty with Aaron. She pretended not to hear the harmonica through the Turkish towel, and concentrated.

Her reference frames were scant. The best she could do was harken back to the few X-rated movies she'd seen. Only one was relevant. It was: *I, A Schoolgirl,* a Danish movie filmed in Burbank, California, about a blind student at a private girls' school who had an affair with the headmistress. The headmistress was a thirtyish blonde with boobs like Phantom-jet nose cones. Her name was Vanessa Clyte, and she'd been the victim of a nameless Nazi sex atrocity. She wore a lorgnette. Vanessa Clyte befriended the blind student—who had been injured in a freak accident at a carnival, and proceeded to use her as a private humping ground for the rest of the film. In the pivotal scene she re-created the trauma of the student's freak accident by whapping her across the face with her boobs, and the blind girl regained her sight.

Jessica knew what she had to do. With a quick shrug of reality she thrust herself into the role of Vanessa Clyte, leaned over, and began floridly licking Marilyn's nipple. She ignored Victor completely.

Marilyn stopped giggling and immediately took on a new appreciation of her old school chum. Within moments the two were pretzeled in an intricate embrace, legs, joggling, tongues darting, fingers probing in narcissistic frenzy. Marilyn's experience gave her the edge. The edge accounted for three of Jessica's orgasms to Marilyn's two. Jessica felt she could have evened the score had she been able to locate Marilyn's clitoris. That gave her a devil of a time. It seemed to be sheer luck every time she found it. Though she knew quite well where her own was, it didn't help in her search for Marilyn's. Every sex manual she'd ever seen had pointed out the importance of stimulating the clitoris, but not one had offered any suggestions on how to find it. It was tucked in the folds somewhere, but you needed sonar to pin it down.

Jessica hunted and pecked. She was rewarded by a lucky streak.

Three-up.

Victor joined in with renewed vigor. Foreplay had been reduced to a token stroke and Marilyn was turning into chopped liver.

Victor climbed Marilyn with Mauser-like gusto. Jessica resented the fact that he didn't have to find her clitoris. All he had to do was elementary hip moving and he was home free. Nature had a way of playing favorites. Heterosex was nature's favorite.

Suddenly Jessica saw that Victor and nature were in trouble. Could Randolph the indomitable be . . . faltering? Mixed emotions flooded Jessica. One part of her filled with compassion for her husband's all-too-obvious predicament. Another part filled with strictly social embarrassment. (Marilyn was their guest; it was terribly impolite.) And then there was another part—a part that felt more than mildly superior. A part that felt maliciously triumphant.

It was this last part that stoked Jessica's guilt and fragmented her libido into unpleasant niggling doubts. She didn't even noice that Victor and Randolph had rallied; that Marilyn was savaging the pillow with her teeth. *My God*, she thought, ignoring Marilyn's muffled scream, *I'm a lesbian!*

Victor had gotten up and brought cigarettes back to

the bed. Marilyn was brushing her hair. Jessica lay on her back, arms crossed over her chest. She looked like her grandmother had looked the last time Jessica had seen her.

The last time Jessica had seen her grandmother had been at the Riverside Memorial Chapel. Nana Meltzer was in a box lined with mauve satin. Her face was like newspaper that had lain too long in the sun. A cosmetologist had rouged her cheeks "Living Pink." All the relatives at the chapel told each other that it was "better" that she died the way she had, "better" that she didn't suffer. All the relatives were, of course, lying. Nana Meltzer had lived to suffer. The doctors told Florence Siskand that her mother had died without pain, had passed on "like that" in her sleep. It was the unkindest cut of all. Jessica wondered if her grandmother had ever enjoyed suffering with the thought that she was a lesbian.

Victor asked Jessica why she was so quiet. She told him. He said that she was about as much a lesbian as Jane Fonda. It was little comfort to Jessica. Celia had Fonda's name on her list.

Marilyn told Jessica to think of it this way: If men made love to women, why couldn't women make love to women? Equal rights, and all that.

"Don't be dumb," Marilyn said. "Didn't you ever hear of women's lib?"

Jessica uncrossed her arms, relaxed. What Marilyn said had the ring of a Jessica Truth of Life. She felt much better and rolled over to go to sleep.

Victor asked Marilyn if she had a lipstick in her purse; he wanted to draw faces on her "pearlescent globes."

Marilyn told him affectionately to fuck off, mumbled

a wish that she'd brought her Water Pik, and then promptly and sanely passed out.

Jessica speculated on how she would politely get rid of Marilyn in the morning.

CHAPTER 6

Victor was dressed and ready to leave for work the next morning even before Aaron shouted "Pee-pee."

Jessica couldn't believe it. "Pee-pee" was Aaron's personal cock-a-doodle-doo. Usually he stood in his crib and bellowed it Teutonically down the hall, experience having taught him that no other sound brought his mother as rapidly to his side, except gagging, but he'd only done that once—when he'd swallowed his teddy bear's nose. Jessica hadn't used an alarm clock since she'd begun the toilet training. Aaron's 7:30 "Pee-pee" was as regular as the bells of St. Mary's. Neither Jessica nor Victor ever stirred from bed before it.

Victor blew her a kiss and quietly closed the bedroom door before she was awake enough to say a word.

She sat up and rubbed her eyes. *What the hell had gotten into*—Something moved beside her in the bed. Marilyn! It all came back, like soapsuds in a clogged drain.

"Holy fuckin' shit," Marilyn said sleepily. "What time is it?"

"Shh. It's only seven twenty. Aaron's still sleeping."

"Lucky Aaron," Marilyn said, bounding up. "But this little chickie has to get her ass in gear and hustle it on down to work. Is there deodorant in the bathroom?"

"In the medicine cabinet. But—"

"Swell," Marilyn said. She dashed down the hall. A few minutes later there was the whine of water running through the shower pipes.

Jessica dropped her head to her chest and waited. Spent.

"Pee-pee!" Aaron shouted. "Pee-pee, pee-pee, pee-pee!"

Aaron was standing in his crib, rocking it back and forth against the wall. Jessica hugged him and as inconspicuously as possible probed his overnight Pamper with her finger. She couldn't believe it. He was dry.

"Good boy!" she said lifting him from the crib. "Good boy. Now we—" She stopped. Marilyn was in the bathroom, in the shower. She knocked on the bathroom door, but Marilyn didn't hear her. The door was locked.

"Pee-pee," Aaron said. He pointed at his diaper.

Jessica felt sick. If she allowed Aaron to wet now it would ruin everything. She was going to have to try for the downstairs bathroom. With Aaron tight in her arms, she raced down the staircase, into the hall, through the kitchen to the small first-floor half-bath that had become the repository for the household's ailing plants because of its large, steam-puffing radiator. Quickly she removed the rhododendron from the toilet seat and pulled down Aaron's pajamas. She lifted him under the arms and held him in front of the toilet. "Good boy," she said encouragingly.

Aaron began to cry.

Oh, no, she thought. It's going to be a trauma. Dr.

Zimkin had warned her about "the pressure to perform." So had Dr. Spock. She tried singing "The Eency-Weency Spider" to distract him. He cried louder.

"Please, Aaron?" she said softly. And, miraculously, he did. Both of them were equally relieved.

Jessica put up a pot of coffee and waited for Marilyn. She averted her eyes from the dining room where the wasted remains of last night's moussaka glared at her, reminded her that somewhere in Cambodia a child was starving.

Aaron was stuffing his mouth with a piece of toast when Marilyn entered.

"Well, isn't he cute." She said it as if he were a lhasa apso, and poured herself some coffee. After two sips she put down the cup. "Must run." She glanced into the dining room. "Yech. What a mess. I don't envy you. There's nothing I hate more than cleaning up the morning after." She slung her mail pouch over her shoulder and kissed Jessica's cheek. "It was really great seeing you again. Let's not be strangers, huh?"

"Sure," Jessica said.

Marilyn patted Aaron as she left. "Nice kid," she said.

When the door slammed, Aaron cocked his head quizzically at his mother.

"Don't worry," Jessica said. "Not on a bet!"

Celia stopped by later that afternoon to tell Jessica she'd missed a terrific session, and that there was going to be a rally that night at the VFW Hall on Seventy-fourth Street. Hippolyte Green had arranged the rally to blast off a nationwide campaign designed to press as many women as possible into politics. The thrust was to convince women that no matter how unqualified they thought they were, no matter how uninterested in the political process, it was their moral duty to run for office, or, at the very least, to put aside all party and personal convictions and support a female candidate.

Celia handed Jessica a hastily Xeroxed flyer:

REMEMBER IN NOVEMBER—
If there's a woman running—follow her!

Underneath were step-by-step instructions on how to run for public office. They were printed in English and Spanish.

"Great, huh?" Celia asked.

"Are you planning to be a candidate?" Jessica asked.

"I'd love to, but my folks' fiftieth anniversary is in November. We're making a party for them at the Americana and I'll have my hands full. But, believe me, I'll be running in spirit. Will you come?"

Jessica was too guilty about last night not to. She told Celia to pick her up at seven thirty.

"You're doing the right thing, Jess," Celia said.

Victor phoned somewhere around three to tell Jessica that he'd be a little late coming home; he was going to enroll at the gym. Jessica told him about the rally. The only reference to the evening before, to Marilyn, came at the very end of the conversation. It came from Victor, as an afterthought.

"By the way," he said. "Your friend Marilyn gave me a hickey."

Jessica pulled her scarf tightly around her neck as she pushed Aaron's stroller up Broadway toward Rubicon. She felt changed, as if she had become her own stranger. She found herself noticing people and reflecting on them in ways she never had before, particularly females.

Ordinarily, when Jessica noticed women they were either unusually attractive or unnaturally bizarre, and even then she did not give them any real thought. But today she found herself scrutinizing those she passed, analyzing them. She wondered if a cheerful-looking girl in a navy pea jacket who was walking her collie liked children. The girl tugged the collie's leash impatiently, and Jessica lost interest. Anyone that short-fused with a dog would be no good for Aaron. She refocused, running each female who caught her eye through the checklist: did she like to cook? Could she clean and sew and iron? Had she a sense of humor? Almost, but not quite, frivolously, she also wondered what each would be like in bed. This disturbed her. It disturbed her almost as much as Victor's hickey.

She stopped outside the Rubicon office and pretended to fuss with Aaron's stroller for several minutes before she entered.

Mike Halprin immediately waved her over. He was talking on the telephone, but Jessica had his attention. It felt good.

Abby carried Aaron to a corner. She gave him a box of paper clips and he began happily dropping them into a paper cup, becoming distressed only when she stopped him from drinking them.

Jessica sat on the corner of Mike's desk. She crossed her legs and tweaked the phone cord with her finger. Mike reached out and grabbed her hand, squeezed.

"Ouch!" Jessica made a face.

Mike signaled her to be quiet. He scribbled "Important" on a piece of paper, turned it toward her.

Jessica took the pencil and wrote: "More important than me?" She pushed the paper back to him. He looked up and smiled. He scrawled, "Never!"

Jessica crunched the note and tossed it over her shoulder into the waste basket. Mike nodded admiringly.

Mike Halprin was a big, good-looking guy in his late thirties; one of those men who'd reached puberty through divorce. It was hard to believe that he'd once been an obediently monogamous insurance salesman whose driving ambition was to sell a million dollars' worth of policies. Three years ago he had given up his Long Island commuter ticket—along with a wife who believed that male facial hair was the mark of degeneracy, and sex more than twice a week unnatural—and come to Manhattan to work with addicts. His mustache, an elegantly cultivated secondary sex characteristic, was one statement of his liberation; selective promiscuity was another.

He hung up the phone and leaned back, folded his arms behind his head. He held Jessica with his eyes for a long moment. "That's nice stuff," he said wistfully.

Jessica shrugged, flattered.

"Guess you can't win 'em all," Mike said. Sometimes he reminded Jessica of her brother.

"Don't be greedy," she said.

"Spoilsport." Mike tousled her hair. "Okay. Let's see what you've got."

"Er, I haven't finished the release yet."

"Holy Christ, Sica, you've had the stuff for over a week. I was counting on you—"

"I know. I'm really sorry. I'll get it to you on Monday. I promise."

"Shit!" Mike riffled through the papers on his desk. "I told the printer we'd have copy for him tomorrow. Now I have to work out a new schedule, call those idiots over at Ace, get Frank to hold off on the mailers—"

"I'm sorry, Mike."

Mike stopped riffling the papers, leaned back again in his chair. "I know, I know. You have the baby and the shopping and the house. Damn it, though, I wish you could figure out a way to work here full time. I'd hire someone else tomorrow if you weren't so fucking good. Can't you get a babysitter for Aaron, a nursery school, or something?"

"I'm working on it," Jessica said.

Mike's head jerked up. "Really?"

"You wouldn't believe how I'm working on it," Jessica said. "Not in a million years."

Celia was at the house before Victor came home that evening. She was nervous about being late and checked her watch at two-minute intervals like a primipara monitoring contractions. When Victor finally arrived, Jessica told him quickly that Aaron was asleep and that dinner was in the oven. He just had time to show her his new gym shorts and jockstrap.

The VFW Hall was one flight up from His 'n Hers, a unisex beauty salon. A sign on the window proclaimed that Mr. Leslie from Miami's Eden Roc Hotel was with them. The shop, according to Celia, was a hangout for dikes and drag queens.

The hall itself was a long, brownish-red room that looked, with its bare-bulb lighting, like the inside of a

giant wound. At the far end was a raised plywood platform, flanked on one side by a faded American flag
and on the other by a shimmering VFW banner.
Wooden folding chairs had been set up in wavering
rows. All the chairs had been taken by the time Celia
and Jessica arrived. They were told this at the door by
a spiderishly slim girl who was so thin that Jessica experienced a brief resurgence of guilt about her wasted
moussaka.

"Cash for clout, sisters," the girl said. She held up a
cigar box filled with dollar bills.

Celia and Jessica dutifully dropped in their money.

"November." The girl raised her arm and made a
fist, then turned away to greet more new arrivals.

Inside, those without seats were milling and jockey-
ing for vantage along the walls, and the room pulsed
with anticipatory noise.

"Over there." Celia pointed.

Bert and Sharon were staunchly guarding a niche
near a steam pipe. Bert waved.

"I thought you'd never make it to us," Bert said
when they did. "Look at the size of this crowd. Doesn't
it give you goosebumps? What a turnout." She smiled
at Jessica. "We missed you Wednesday. It was one of
the most exhilarating raps we've ever had."

"I'm sorry I couldn't make it," Jessica said. "It was
just one of those things."

"Did Celia tell you about Lilly Ernshweiger?"

Jessica said that she hadn't.

Bert shook her head. "Just fantastic. That woman is
one goddam sharp cookie. I'm not one for making pre-
dictions, but believe me, I'm sure we've got a winner."

"Oh? What's Lilly running for?"

"She hasn't decided yet. Either the House or the

Senate—or maybe just the State Assembly. Whatever. She can't miss. She's not a celebrity, not a blueblood. She's nothing but a plain old lady who'll be taken seriously. I'm telling you: no looks, no connections, she's got what it takes to go the distance."

Jessica admitted that it sounded so. She stepped back, out of the line of conversation.

Two girls on the platform were tapping the microphone and whispering "Testing . . . testing." A woman stood behind them. Watching.

The woman was tall and in her mid-thirties, hypnotically humorless, with gray-flecked bronze hair parted in the center that hung straight to her shoulders, as if its ends had been weighted. She wore modified army fatigues with a Pucci scarf tied in a poet's bow around her neck. As the girls adjusted the microphone, she tapped her foot with the impatience of someone waiting for a bathroom. She was definitely not wife material.

"That's Hippolyte Green," Celia said. There was reverence in her voice. "She's done more for women sexually, emotionally, and politically than vibrators, Quaaludes, and Elizabeth Cady Stanton combined."

Jessica felt it imprudent to dispute the fact. She also felt, though not too strongly, that it might be incorrect. It was another one of those things she preferred not to think about.

There was a cannonade of handclaps, shouts, whistles, and foot stomps as Hippolyte Green stepped to the microphone. She waited for the room to quiet before she said, "Welcome, sisters," which brought on another barrage of cheers. She stood by the microphone, unsmiling, and tapped her foot.

"Sisters, we all know why we're here," Hippolyte

Green said, "and we all know where we're going—and we're not going to quit until we get there. We've come a long way since our first march, but there's a lot more marching to do."

A woman in the rear shouted: "Fuck the marching. Storm the locker rooms!"

Shouts of "Clout now!" mixed with "Ssshhh," and a curious tension knotted the room. The schism in the Movement between the radical left—who wanted nothing less than matriarchy—and the radical right—who wanted nothing more than equal pay for equal jobs— had chasmed over the past months. According to Celia, Hippolyte Green's liberal radicalism, which was supported by the majority of concerned feminists, had grown too mild for the activist left and too radical for the reactionary right. Hippolyte Green appeared unruffled. She continued.

"By *marching* I mean *running,* and running means going for every political office available, and every political office means from dogcatcher right on up to the top, and you *know* what that means. So, when I say we've a lot more marching to do—"

A loud "Booo!" broke from the rear of the room. "No more marching!" someone shouted.

"Douche the bastards out!"

A woman in the third row stood and yelled to the back of the room: "Terrorist tactics lose votes."

"Shit, I say," the heckler in the rear shouted. "You're afraid to let go of your own apron strings. It's pansy-asses like you who keep us carrying coffee at conventions."

"Who are you calling pansy-assed?" A fat woman in a blue beret, sitting next to the woman in the third row and obviously of similar Movement persuasion, stood up. She began edging out into the aisle.

Hippolyte Green shouted for order.

The rear of the room shouted for the President's balls.

Two other women in the third row, which was now conspicuously the conservative bastion, got up and followed the fat woman in the blue beret down the aisle.

"Who you calling pansy-assed?" the fat woman bellowed as she made her way toward the rear.

"You!" a voice shouted. It came from the other side of the room. Obviously a troublemaker.

The fat woman whirled. "Who said that?"

There was a sudden scraping of chairs and a flurry of exclamations near the VFW banner. A woman with the body of the Hindenburg and the hair style of Adolph Hitler erupted from the throng. "Me, fattie," she said, coldly oblivious to their immense similarity. "Wanna make something of it?"

Hippolyte Green tapped her foot, tapped the microphone. "Sisters! Please!" she cried.

The Blue Beret lumbered toward the Hindenburg. Those in aisle seats moved quickly, trampling toes as they scrambled into the rows for safety.

"Uh-oh," Bert said. "It's hitting the fan."

The two behemoths had started slugging it out.

Hippolyte Green stood rigidly by the microphone, working the zipper of her modified fatigues nervously. Two of her retinue, spindly dedicated ingenues, flanked her, forming a tenuous phalanx. Though they remained motionless, their eyes surveyed the room for the fastest exit.

Jessica was thrown back against the wall. Intermittent squabbles flared into open combat around her, and she had an instant image of Scarlett O'Hara fleeing Atlanta. She called Celia's name, but was drowned out in the din. Screw it. She started for the door.

A girl in a demin jacket spun around. "Hey, watch it, sister!"

"I'm sorry. I—" Someone shoved Jessica from behind. She lurched forward, knocked the girl in the denim jacket to the floor. Before she could apologize, the girl shouted, "Bitch!" and sank her teeth into Jessica's shin.

Without thinking, Jessica swatted her hard across the ear.

The room had been transformed into an Amazonian circus with several main events occurring simultaneously. Near the podium, the behemoths were hurling their masses of flesh against each other to no discernible effect, while in the center of another ring of onlookers, two wiry girls—one of whom Jessica recognized as the checkout clerk at Sloan's—were savagely stalemated, gripping each other's hands to ward off hair-pulls.

As she approached the door, Jessica heard odd, crisp shouts coming from the center of still another circle. "Oo-ee!" "Ai-ai!" "Ai-oo!" They sounded like Oriental gasps of orgasm. Over the heads of the crowd she saw something round and white and coiled like a cruller bobbing up and down.

Lilly Ernshweiger, her white apron tied about her waist and folded over like a long breechcloth, her legs planted firmly apart, stood facing a formidable-looking matron with tightly drawn back hair and psoriasis scabs on her forehead. Lilly circled the woman, then jumped and rent the room with a splitting "HIEEEE!"

She chopped at the air. The matron's lips quivered. She was about to cry.

"You'll never get out this way." A short girl with glasses tapped Jessica's arm. "Follow me."

The girl, whom Jessica had never seen before, led her to a fire exit at the other end of the hall. The EXIT sign had been covered by a banner that said WELCOME SISTERS. Jessica wondered how the girl had known about it. When the two of them reached the street, Jessica asked her.

"I rented the place for tonight," the girl said tiredly. She introduced herself as Eleanore, and before Jessica could say more than her own name, Eleanore had hailed a taxi and was beckoning Jessica to hop in.

"I don't really live that far—" Jessica began.

"Don't be foolish. Hippolyte owes us something after that fiasco."

Jessica got in and Eleanore gave the driver an address on East Eightieth Street, off Park Avenue. "You don't have to get home right away, do you?" Eleanore asked.

"Well, no—"

"Relax, then. Have you ever been to Hippolyte's place?"

"Is that where we're going?" Jessica was surprised and more than slightly intrigued.

"Unfortunately, yes." Eleanore dropped her head back against the seat, stretched her legs out. "I work for her."

"Really? What do you do!" Jessica asked.

"Everything but her bodily functions," Eleanore said. "Euphemistically it's called public relations."

"Oh. I used to be with Mason and Oakun," Jessica said.

"Very impressive," Eleanore said, meaning it. "Where are you now?"

"Uh . . . between jobs," Jessica said.

"Anyone who's worked for Mason and Oakun shouldn't have any trouble landing something good. I wish I worked there. I could use the money."

"You'd never get what you deserved," Jessica said. "Wayne Mason still pays according to genitals."

"So what else is new?" The cab stopped and Eleanore pushed Jessica's hand away when she tried to offer money. "Hippolyte picks up the tab for all her less fortunate sisters whenever she can. Haven't you read that?"

"Is that true?" Jessica asked.

"Are you kidding? I gave that quote to *Newsweek*. She loved it. It got me a small but honest-to-God expense account." Eleanore leaned closer to Jessica. "Just between us, Hippolyte Green is cheap. Get her away from the press and it's separate checks—even at Howard Johnson's."

Riding up in the elevator, Jessica wondered why Eleanore was revealing these things about Hippolyte to her—a stranger.

"I suppose," Eleanore said, "you're wondering why I'm telling these things about Hippolyte to you—a stranger. Well, what the hell difference does it make? Sometimes it's easier talking to a stranger, right? I'm tired of this game. Burned out. Besides, I saw where your sisterly feelings were when you swatted that babe across the ears."

"She bit my leg," Jessica said.

"Bitches," Eleanore muttered. "Hung-up bitches, the lot of 'em."

Jessica was truly stunned. Here was Hippolyte

Green's right arm severing herself from the Movement! She wanted to hear what else Eleanore had to say, but the door opened and two anxious girls squealing that Hippolyte was "frantic and going bananas" pulled Eleanore away. Tossing a resigned "excuse me," over her shoulder, Eleanore disappeared into the throng of bodies that packed the apartment.

Most of the bodies were female. The ones that were not belonged to reporters who were, they told Jessica as they shook her hand, "political sympathizers." Jessica asked one, a freckled-face, spongey-palmed young man named Geordie, what that meant.

"We take you chicks seriously. We don't make puns in our copy, you know what I mean?" He didn't wait for Jessica to answer. "None of that 'Girls flip their lib' stuff, or 'Lib and let lib,' or 'Lib me alone,' or any of that Ms. stuff like *ms*take, *ms*fire, *ms*—"

Jessica told Geordie that she understood.

"Gets us interviews with Hippolyte, too. She's usually pretty down on media males. But for Christ's sake, what's the difference between men and women, *really*. We're all born, we all die, we all go to the bathroom."

"No argument there," Jessica said. She squeezed a smile and started to move away.

"Christ," Geordie said to her back, "I know broads who can run rings around me."

"I'd imagine," Jessica said. She edged past him before he could say more.

Hippolyte Green's apartment was spacious and expensively decorated in green cheeks. The green-checked curtains were the same green-checked fabric as the cushions on the neo-country wicker chairs, and the same green checked design on the foyer-, bathroom-, and dining-room wallpaper. The living room was white and striated with climbing, clinging, drooping, and wandering green plants. They hung from the ceiling, sprang from large ceramic planters, tendriled up on lattice that covered one whole wall. So vast and overwhelming was the greenery that one vacillated between feeling like a beetle and feeling nauseous.

Right now Jessica was feeling slightly queasy and claustrophobic. Someone handed her a drink. Someone else pinched her ass. She saw Hippolyte stretched out on a green chaise longue at the far end of the room talking to the press. She looked as if she'd just retired to her chamber with the vapors. Jessica downed her drink and made her way back to the door. Eleanore stopped her.

"Sorry about setting you adrift like that," she said. She led Jessica down a tubelike hall away from the crowd. "Hippolyte got herself in a bind with the media. I had to bail her out. That one can't say 'excuse me' without a prepared statement."

They entered a small library and Eleanore closed the door. The room's only distinctions were—other than the paucity of books—the absence of plants and the presence of three tiny poodles wearing green-checked collars. The dogs yipped berserkly while Eleanore searched for their chew-toys. She explained that Hippolyte was freaky about the dogs, kept them away from strangers because she was paranoid about someone feeding them poison. Eleanore tossed them their playthings and they settled down. Their chew-toys were hard rubber dildoes.

Jessica sat on the couch. "I just have time for a cigarette and then I'd better be getting on home."

Eleanore sighed. "I don't blame you. You're married, aren't you?" Jessica nodded. "Any kids?"

"A two-year-old. Boy."

Eleanore shook her head, approvingly.

Jessica looked intently at Eleanore. Good skin: healthy, olive-toned. Teeth nicely even, capped possibly, but a good dentist. Clean hair, clean nails. Good health habits evident. Interesting. Very interesting.

"You like children?" Jessica asked.

"Sure, they're great."

"Interesting," Jessica said, not meaning to have said it out loud.

"Not particularly," Eleanore said.

"I mean it's interesting considering Hippolyte's feeling."

"You're referring to the *Times* article?" Eleanore asked.

"I'll confess it made me sick. I guess I'm old-fashioned. I think kids need mothers."

"Made *you* sick!" Eleanore said. "I had to write that garbage. Think how I feel."

"Why did you do it?" Jessica asked.

"Thrust," Eleanore said.

"Thrust?"

"What's a movement without thrust? A club. Girl Scouts are a club. They make lousy copy. They were all right when Baden-Powell's old lady got them started, but they petered out. They never learned about keeping up the provocatives. If they suddenly started giving merit badges for making IUD's instead of lanyards they'd be back in the ball game. Doing PR for the Movement isn't easy. Manipulating minds is a dirty little business. You have to learn how to pass in Garfield Heights, Ohio, as well as in Harlem, have to know how to bring tears of recognition to an audience *before* the question and answer period. Writing 'Dump the

Kids and Run' was just another part of the job." She sighed again. "A dirty little business. Someday I'm going to get out."

"Tell me," Jessica said, "do you like to cook."

CHAPTER 7

"And she likes to cook," Jessica said.

She leaned over the side of the bed and looked down. Victor was stretched out on the floor. He was naked except for his new jockstrap. A barbell was across his chest. He pressed it upward, then let his arms back with a grunt.

"Victor, aren't you listening?"

"I'm listening," he said. He took several loud breaths.

"Victor, it's one o'clock. Come to bed already and stop that."

He lifted the weight again, this time lowering it with a loud, drawn-out groan of finality. "I never realized how out of condition I was."

"Oh, come on," Jessica said, annoyed. "You're not out of condition. You've never lifted weights in your life."

Victor rolled the barbell to the wall, stood, inhaled deeply, then collapsed on the bed. "That was probably one of my biggest mistakes. You should see those guys at the gym. Healthiest sons of bitches I ever saw. Bulls."

"How about a little handball with bouncing Manny?" Jessica said sarcastically.

"It's no joke, Jess. I'm out of condition. I think most American men are out of condition—overweight, underexercised. Look at the facts. We die sooner than women, have more heart attacks. We're killing ourselves. The more I think about it the more I'm convinced the American male is an endangered species."

"Is that all you want to think about now?"

"Better now than later," Victor said. "I harken back to the blue whale."

"You always do."

"Jesus, Jess, where's your vision? You have to think beyond today."

"I'm trying to. I was telling you about Eleanore."

"I don't like her name," Victor said, peeved.

"That's absurd."

"More absurd than disregarding the continuation of our species? I hardly think so."

"Oh, stop that." Jessica was distressed to see that he was serious. "What's wrong with the name Eleanore?"

"Nothing—except every time I hear it I think of Eleanore Lupresky and I get depressed."

"Eleanore Lupresky? You've never even mentioned Eleanore Lupresky."

"Of course not—it would get me depressed."

"Victor! Who the hell is Eleanore Lupresky?"

Victor sat up. "Nice. Really nice. Why don't you say her name one more time and see if I'll crack? They could have used you at Auschwitz."

Jessica flung up her hands in disgust. "Forget it. I don't even want to know about Eleanore Lupresky."

Victor beseeched the ceiling. "Must I take this?"

Jessica clamped her hands against her head. "All I

wanted to do was tell you about the *possible* I met tonight."

"Then quit harping on Eleanore Lupresky," Victor said. "The next thing I know you'll bring up Milly Wolven."

"Who's Milly Wolven?"

"See!"

"Never mind!" Jessica lay down and wrenched the covers to her chin.

"Oh, by the way, a Bert Corley phoned." There was a suspicious tinge in his voice. "He wanted to know if you got home all right."

Jessica opened her eyes. "She," she said.

"She?"

"Yes, she," Jessica said. "Roberta. She, her, girl, woman, lady—" Jessica sat up angrily. The covers spilled into her lap. Victor's eyes dropped to her breasts, Jessica pretended not to notice. "Female," she said, bringing her face close to his.

"Male," he said, and tweaked her right nipple.

"Victor, please—"

"No need to beg," Victor said. He began to nuzzle. "You're a helluva woman, Jess."

Jessica was about to resist, then changed her mind. Horny men were like hungry animals and the only way to get them to pay attention to other things was to feed them first. She knew what she had to do. It was cold-blooded. It was the Movement's cardinal sin, but damn it all, it worked. She cleared her throat and began to moan softly.

"Hmmm," Victor said afterward. "That was good. Was it okay for you?"

"What do you think?" Jessica said warmly, righteously skirting a lie.

Victor sighed, content. "I hope you pick a wife who appreciates me."

"I met one tonight with a lot of potential. Likes kids, wants to settle down, very organized and bright. I thought if it were okay with you I'd call and invite her over sometime next week."

"Is that Eleanore?" Victor asked suspiciously.

"Lennie," Jessica said. "They call her Lennie." Or at least Jessica would.

"Fine with me," Victor said. His voice was vague.

Jessica kissed his head. She slipped out of bed and turned on the light.

"What are you doing?"

"I wrote her number on a piece of paper and I want to make sure that I still have it." She pulled several scraps from her purse. "Here it—no, that's Marilyn's." She riffled through her purse again. "Ah. El—" she caught herself—"Lennie, 230-6381." She turned to the bed. "Did Bert leave her number?"

"It's on the table in the hall."

"I know what I need," Jessica said. "I need a little black book."

Victor wriggled uncomfortably under the blankets. When Jessica got back into bed he told her he had pains in his chest. She told him it was probably gas and not to worry about it.

"I'm really out of condition," he said. "We weren't even doing anything fancy and I'll tell you, I was winded. I've got to start going to the gym regularly."

Jessica began to protest.

"No," Victor said. "That's the mistake American men are making. We keep assuring ourselves that we're all right, and the next thing you know it's a coronary. Believe me, Jess, we're an endangered species. Red-tagged. All the way."

Jessica didn't take Victor seriously, which was her most common marital mistake. Victor was serious. He was serious about everything. Frivolity for him was like cyclamates, something that could be indulged in, but with caution. Nothing upset him more than not being taken seriously—except perhaps being taken seriously when he was being frivolous.

After two weeks, Victor's concern about his body had become an obsession. Every Monday, Wednesday, and Friday night he went straight from the office to Buzzy's Gym. Buzzy's Gym was in the basement of a hooker hotel on West Forty-ninth Street. It was a hangout for boxer groupies and liberal New York businessmen. It featured a topless towel girl and an Ashanti masseur. Victor never spoke of the topless towel girl, but he said that the Ashanti masseur had once been privately employed by Aristotle Onassis. The Ashanti masseur's name was Osai Odoko, but everyone called him Jesus. Jesus told all his clients that Aristotle Onassis had liked his buttocks massaged with lemon butter. Jesus had asked Victor for the name of a literary agent because he said he had a lot to tell about Aristotle Onassis, enough to make a best seller. He was going to call his book *The Man Behind the Magnate*.

Victor's new physical fitness routine, despite its excess, intruded on the tenor of their perfect marriage in only one way: on Mondays, Wednesdays, and Fridays, sex was out. Victor would come home those evenings, eat his dinner, and go right to bed, crawling

under the covers with a groan that sounded like
Charles Atlas with a herina.

Jessica on those nights would do one of two things.
Or both.

One of the two things was rehearsing approaches to
possible wives. This was usually done before a mirror.
Jessica would face the glass and interrogate herself as
if she were another woman. She'd try out simple open-
ers like, "Do you really enjoy cooking?" and, "Aren't
kids great?" over and over again, inflecting different
words each time, speculating on what the other's an-
swers might be and evaluating them. It was sort of like
playing solitaire, and cheating. (Whenever Jessica
played solitaire and was stymied she'd turn up another
card and keep the game going. When her mirror an-
swers displeased her, she changed them. But no matter
how she tried, no matter how eager and willing she
imagined the other woman to be, when it came to
asking the ultimate question Jessica just couldn't seem
to push the fantasy to her desired end. The mirror person would either laugh or slash out sixteen devastating
put-downs. Jessica was forced to recognize that she
herself could never make it as her wife.

The other thing that Jessica would do on those
nights was read the April issue of *Home Handyman*.
This was a special distaff issue with a cover showing a
petite lady in a lounging robe standing next to floor-
to-ceiling bookcases. The feature article was: "Bookcases Even She Can Build." Jessica had bought the
magazine impulsively, thinking that she would give
Victor homemade bookcases for his birthday.

Home Handyman had opened up a whole new world
to Jessica, though even after extended perusal not one
that included a birthday present for Victor. There was

no way she could learn the difference between the fascia and ½-inch shims in four weeks. Probably not, she suspected, in four years. But the complete alienness of carpentry, its language and accoutrements, fascinated her. It fascinated her much the way, she imagined, aborigines fascinated Margaret Mead. Her discovery of the all ball-bearing, superpowered router was embarrassingly exciting. Here was a machine she'd never even seen that could do things she'd never even heard of. It would dado, rabbet, flute, joint, bead, and shape at 30,000 rpm's, all with a ¼-inch chuck! It looked as if it had been copied from the cover of a science fiction paperback. The thought that for some people this all ball-bearing, superpowered router was as commonplace as a coffeepot pummeled her mind; and the recognition that those people were male stunned her. Never had she realized the shocking insularity of the female world, a world in which such phrases as "six-spline floating spindle drive," and "self-lubricating graphite bronze bearings" had utterly no meaning. Some nights when she looked at the April issue of *Home Handyman* she felt as guiltily delighted as a pre-teener peeping into the boys' locker room. Other nights she felt lonely and excluded.

It was on one of the other nights that she phoned Bert Corley and asked her to come for dinner. Sharon was out of town. Bert was delighted.

Jessica decided to make moussaka.

Victor was not overly enthused about Bert's coming to dinner, and what little interest he had waned upon her arrival. Halfway through the meal he began to yawn. He apologized to Bert for his fatigue, and blamed it on Jesus. He explained that Jesus' massage could knead a rhinoceros into puree. Bert asked him for the address of Buzzy's Gym.

When Jessica went for coffee, Victor followed her into the kitchen.

"She's a dike," he whispered.

"You sound like Celia," Jessica said, unperturbed.

"But I thought. . . . Well, the moussaka, the wine you asked me to buy—"

"Your perceptions were correct," Jessica said.

"For christsakes, Jess."

"She's an excellent carpenter," Jessica said. "And a fabulous cook."

"So's my uncle Calvin, but I wouldn't want to—"

"Victor, we can't just leave her sitting out there." Jessica started for the living room. Victor stopped her.

"I think I'm going to bed," he said. "I'm really beat."

"Victor, you can't! What will I tell Bert?"

"I'll tell her." And before Jessica could protest he went back into the living room and told Bert that he was really beat and going to bed.

Bert said she understood and thought it was a great idea. And when Jessica handed her a cup of coffee, she winked.

"You sure you don't want any coffee?" Jessica asked Victor.

"Of course he doesn't," Bert said, not quite as fast as a speeding bullet, but close. "It'll keep him awake."

"It'll keep me awake," Victor said. He kissed Jessica, nodded to Bert, who rose and shook his hand, and went upstairs.

"Do you mind if I lie down on the floor?" Bert asked. "My back has been killing me."

"I'm sorry," Jessica said. "Sure, go right ahead."

Bert put her cup on the floor and stretched out beside it. Jessica sat down next to her.

Bert smiled and patted Jessica's knee. "I'm really glad you invited me over. I've been painting closets every night this week and this sure beats painting closets."

"I'm glad you could make it. How long is Sharon going to be away?"

"Till next weekend," Bert said. "She visiting her folks. I don't mind, though. We spend a lot of time away from each other, you know."

"No," Jessica said, "I didn't know."

"We have an understanding."

"An understanding?"

"We vary our diet, if you get what I mean. That's why we've been together as long as we have." She trailed her fingers along the rug to the tip of Jessica's shoe. "Different people have different needs and no one person can possibly fulfill all of another person's needs."

"I see."

"That's what I like about you," Bert said. "You're openminded." She patted Jessica's knee again. This time she left her hand there.

Jessica did not try to remove it.

"The one thing I loathe is a closed mind."

"Me too," Jessica said.

"I think people should have open minds about everything—politics, sex, everything."

"Absolutely!" Jessica sensed the fleeting propitiousness of opportunity. If she were going to move, it would have to be soon. It would have to be before Bert's hand traveled further up her thigh. Bert had a destination as clearly routed as an AAA triptick—

she'd have to be sold the detour Jessica had planned.

"I think anything done between consenting adults is okay," Bert said.

"Talk about coincidence," Jessica said. And without further elaboration she invited Bert to join her and Victor in bed.

"I think I'd better be going." Bert looked as if she were about to be sick.

Jessica ran a hand along Bert's arm, bolstering herself with the image of Vanessa Clyte. "Really, Bert, where's your open mind?"

"Listen," Bert said nervously, "You, yes—him, no."

Jessica tugged gently at the sleeve of Bert's workshirt. "He's a pussycat."

"He's a man!"

"Men understand women in bed. It'll be good for you."

"I don't know."

"And you won't until we get upstairs," Jessica brazened, knowing full well that if Bert didn't agree right then and there she would be unable to sustain the seduction.

"Well. . . ." Bert said slowly. "Okay. But this better not get back to Sharon."

"My lips are sealed." Jessica took Bert by the hand and led her upstairs. The door to the bedroom was closed. She thought about knocking, changed her mind, and pushed it open. Victor was sitting in bed reading a manuscript. He looked up, looked as if he had just been punched in the stomach.

"Surprise!" Jessica said.

"Holy shit," said Victor.

*

The next morning, over breakfast, Bert looked as shaken and pleased as a gourmet who'd finally tasted boiled goat testes. She kept repeating, "I don't believe it, I don't believe it." (Which, coincidentally, was all Victor could say about it for years to come.) Before Bert left, Jessica got her to agree to build the bookcases for Victor's study.

For the remainder of the week Jessica made a conscious effort to avoid all thoughts of wife hunting. She immersed herself in Rubicon work and Aaron's toilet training, but the latter usually interfered with the former and her spare-moment reveries almost consistently returned to finding the *Right* girl. She tried phoning Eleanore several times (when Victor wasn't around) but without success. When Celia extended an invitation for the weekend to her house in Woodstock, Jessica accepted without reservation. She needed a vacation from her life.

On Saturday morning Jessica and Victor had an argument in the Avis Rent-A-Car office about who was going to drive. Aaron began to cry and when Jessica picked him up to comfort him, Victor slipped behind the wheel. Jessica told him he'd taken advantage of her maternal instinct. Victor told her to fasten her seat belt.

Jessica counted red Volkswagens with Aaron until he fell asleep. "Are you going to be angry all the way up there?" Victor asked.

"I'm not angry," Jessica said. She began to hum "I Want A Girl" and then started to laugh.

"What's so funny?" asked Victor.

"I was thinking about Bert."

Victor said nothing.

"Those legs of hers were something else, weren't they?"

Silence.

"They looked like two baloneys squeezed in the middle," Jessica said. Victor's face was grim. "I'm sorry, hon," Jessica said. "I didn't think she'd be—I mean, she has a cute face." Jessica kissed Victor on the cheek. "You were noble. Truly noble."

"Ummm," Victor said.

"Ummmm what?" said Jessica.

"Isn't there a gun shop somewhere near the Remson's?" Victor asked.

"Yes. Why?"

"I've been thinking about buying a shotgun," Victor said. "Maybe do a little hunting this year."

"For what—taxicabs?"

"Funny. I mean up here."

Jessica made a face.

Victor ignored it. "Yeah," he said. "I think I'm going to get me a gun."

"What do you know about guns?" Jessica asked.

"My mother was almost killed by one, remember?"

"So what?" Jessica said.

"Oh. I see. Very nice. I suppose you'd feel the same if it were your mother."

"Victor! You know what I mean," Jessica said.

"Yes, I know what you mean, but I don't like the way you said it. I happen to know a lot about guns, believe it or not. And a lot about wives, too."

"What's that have to do with anything?" Jessica asked.

"Nothing."

Jessica waited with Aaron in the car while Victor was inside the shop. Aaron had wanted to go with

Victor, but Jessica forbade it. Guns, like wet dreams, entered a boy's life soon enough; there was no reason to encourage either prematurely.

When Victor came out of the store he lifted the shotgun above his head and grinned. He grinned like a boy in the midst of a wet dream.

On the mailbox at the entrance to the Remson's driveway was a colorfully lettered wooden sign; above the sign was a two-dimensional plywood sombrero. The sombrero had cost Dave Remson seventy-eight dollars. The way he broke it down was: twelve dollars for the X-Acto knife, three dollars for the paint, three dollars for the shellac, and sixty dollars for the stiches and tetanus shot at Kingston General Hospital. The colorfully lettered wooden sign said: EL RANCHO REMSON.

El Rancho Remson was a fine old Presbyterian barn that had been converted into an unextraordinary middle-class Jewish summer place. Its quaint, uneven windows had been replaced by Sears' storm-and-screen combinations; its massive doors nailed closed and usurped by a single, functional, framed one. The weathered siding on the exterior of the house had been preserved only by the fortunate limits of Dave's income.

The interior of El Rancho Remson bore a hardy resemblance to Celia and Dave's city apartment, except that it was roomier, sported a fireplace, and was accoutered with nothing that had cost more than twenty-five dollars. For some unfathomable reason, Celia and Dave used their summer place as a free port for bad taste. It was poxed with inelegance and cheap knick-knacks: ashtrays in the shape of toilet bowels and bidets, a cookie jar formed like a giant English muffin, coffee mugs that said "Peace" and "Love," glasses with decals of old automobiles. Nearly all the walls were mottled with a random assortment of old movie posters and original crayola sketches by the girls.

The upstairs suffered less from commercial detritus. It was closed off during the winter months with a trapdoor, a functional barrier which somehow had a sobering influence on Celia and Dave. When the trapdoor was opened it revealed an enormous loft living room with a twenty-foot-high ceiling and a balcony platform with three guest bedrooms. Jessica harbored a terror of somnambulism every time they stayed there.

Celia had arranged a party that evening with some of her Woodstock friends. She told Jessica that they were all creative, interesting people; told Jessica that she'd love them.

The first couple to arrive was Rhonda and Art. They were both in their late forties and wore faded blue jeans and denim jackets. They'd given up a costume jewelry business in Manhattan and moved to Woodstock "before the festival." She wrote poetry and he sculpted erotic candles.

"We're both creative," Rhonda explained to Jessica, in a nasal Bronx twang that neither time nor Woodstock would erase. "We're both Geminis."

"How interesting," Jessica said.

"You're from the city, aren't you?" Rhonda asked. Jessica nodded.

"How can you stand it? All that pollution and crime and dog shit. God, you poor thing." Rhonda looked truly concerned.

"I—"

"There are the theaters, of course, and the museums," Rhonda said, leaning toward second thoughts, "but all that crime and pollution and—"

"Dog shit," Jessica offered.

"Er, yes," Rhonda said uncomfortably. She looked up and appeared relieved to see new arrivals. She excused herself and went to the group at the door. She threw her arms around the neck of a chalk-faced man with a reddish, embarrassingly pubic goatee.

The man's name was Bernard Kadish. He was, as he explained to Victor, a neo-Rolphian unisexual therapist. He believed that the constant differentiation between the sexes was detrimental to the well-being of the individual. He ran his groups in a totally dark room and insisted that his patients wear *phoolyus*. A *phoolyu* was a disposable brown shroud with eye and nose holes that covered a patient from head to foot and rendered him indistinguishable from a large inverted paper bag.

"Once you eliminate sex as a factor," said Bernard, "you'd be amazed at the lessening tension, hostility, and depression. Even privately I never see patients without *phoolyus*. I wear one, they wear one. I'm not influenced by looks or facial expressions and neither are they. We just deal with human essentials. For all I know, my patient could be the most beautiful chick in the world, but to me she's just another paper bag with a problem."

"But once they begin talking about their problems, sexual problems, don't you—"

Bernard interrupted. "I forbid specific genital nomenclature in my therapy. If a patient wants to refer to a penis or a vagina it's called a 'thing.' This person's 'thing,' that person's 'thing.' No his or hers, he or she pronoun references either. Names are okay. Most of the time they're a giveaway, but at least there's not that relentless emphasis on *difference*." He glanced over his

135

shoulder and beckoned to a pinched-faced, wide-eyed woman wearing a caftan. "Honey, commere."

Honey was Julia. She was the organizer of the Woodstock Women's Collective and a macrobiotic zealot. The closest she had come to eating meat in the last two years had been an accidental bite of her tongue. There was an intense, troll-like quality about her that made Jessica thing she ought to like the woman yet forced her to recognize she didn't. Honey spoke quickly, defensively, punctuating her words with stubby little slashes of her hands. She was the person to whom Bernard had been relating physically for the past several months. Jessica wondered whether she wore a *phoolyu* when he did.

Celia brought out a platter of canapés, cheese and wine, Triscuits and smoked oysters, and put some rock records on the stereo. A man named Harvey, who limited his observations to "Really!" "Far out!" and "No shit!" passed around several joints of homegrown grass.

A young woman named Frankie asked Victor to dance; Victor was just high enough to comply. Afterward, Frankie told Jessica how lucky she was to have married a good dancer.

"God, you're lucky," Frankie said. "Do you dance too?"

Jessica was just high enough to answer with a quick demonstration. When she sat down again, Frankie said, "You don't know how rare it is for a good dancer to marry a good dancer. God, you're lucky."

Jessica asked Frankie if she were married.

"Not anymore," Frankie said. "My ex was a megalomaniacal stock broker. The worst. He thought he was the greatest thing that had happened to the exchange since ticker tape! He used to tell me how wonderful he was and follow up with the fact that no great men were monogamous. I could have overlooked his affairs if he hadn't had two left feet."

As Frankie went on about the way she used to single-handedly manage their house in Scarsdale, Jessica grew interested. And when Frankie casually mentioned that she designed and made clothes for a local boutique, and baked bread for the Health Food Store, Jessica's interest became instantly one-directional.

"Do you have any children?" Jessica asked.

"Hell, no. Too many of the little bastards running around as it is."

Someone put on a 78 recording of an old fifties favorite and instantly "ooh's" and "aahs" strafed the room. Such outbursts of nostalgia never failed to surprise Jessica. More, they mystified her. At virtually every party she'd attended since the close of that era, someone always put on an old favorite. The fifties were alive and well, had been alive and well, and would probably continue to thrive until the "DA," "Sockhop" generation was overtaken by senility or deafness. It was difficult for Jessica to work up nostalgia about something as ent as the fifties. It was like getting soft and mushy over Coca-Cola.

The record sparked a familiar outpouring of trivial reminiscences about semiformal dresses, Warner Merry Widows, crinolines, dyed-to-match shoes, and making out. Anecdotes abounded, and, aided by Harvey's homegrown, increased in hilarity. Bernard had just slicked back his hair with wine and was about to do an impersonation of Sal Mineo talking to James Dean when Celia swung her lamp of liberation into the room like a police spotlight flaring on teen-agers fumbling in a parked car.

In stentorian tones, she decried the era as the dark age of sexism. She ranted about the double standard, called the fifties ritual of dating as barbaric a sexual practice as priapic initiations. She denounced brasalettes and pantie girdles with equal vehemence, and drew a vivid, though specious, analogy between corsetoriums and concentration camps. And with frightening eloquence, she ground every last ounce of fun from the room by damning the fifties for being the age that had spawned the single and most malevolent sexist atrocity of all time: The *Playboy* Playmate.

No one argued. The room clouded with a flatulence of guilt. Honey applauded discreetly. Someone took "Earth Angel" from the record player. Harvey put his plastic bag of homegrown into his pocket. The party ended.

When the last guest left, Jessica sighed. Zero. Not a possible in the crowd.

She went to the kitchen to help Dave with the dishes.

CHAPTER 8

Ralph Asbell's apartment downstairs had just been re-painted.

The color was dusky mauve, which Ralph informed Jessica, was the hue of the year. He admitted that it was one of those colors you had to live with to get used to. Unfortunately the new-paint smell was driving him crazy and he couldn't stay in the place for more than ten-minute stretches. After a heroic half-hour attempt, he came upstairs to relive his watering eyes and tell Jessica a new joke he'd heard. Ralph Asbell prided himself more on being a raconteur than a hero.

He'd just finished the story when the phone rang, truncating Jessica's laugh. Ralph scowled and emitted a dauphin's snort.

Jessica apologized as she picked up the receiver. "Hello?"

"Jess? Is that you?" The voice at the other end quavered.

Jessica grew alarmed. "Mom? Of course it's me. What's the matter?"

Her mother wailed and began to cry. "It's awful. I still can't believe it."

"What's awful? What's happened?"

"Manny . . . Manny's gone."

"Gone—Where?"

"Gone," her mother said, gasping for breath between sobs. "Gone."

"Mom, you must calm down. I can't understand you. Tell me what happened?"

There was a long sniffling pause, then Florence said: "He went to Sheepshead Bay this morning to play handball with his old friends. There was some sort of tournament, I think. And . . . and. . . ."

"And what?"

"And—poof!"

"Poof?"

"Poof—a coronary." Florence began to cry softly.

"I'm sorry, Mom. I really am. Are you okay?"

"I'm all right, I guess," Florence said. "I just feel so bad for Manny. You know how proud he was of his heart."

"I know."

"If only he'd been hit by a car or something."

"What can I say, Mom?" Jessica said truthfully, hurting for her mother.

"What can you say?" Florence sighed. "That's life. Poof. The funeral's on Thursday. I'll go and I'll cry and then I'll try to stop crying and keep going."

"You have to."

"He was going to marry me, you know," Florence said.

"I know, Mom."

"Maybe I'll go to Kitchner's next weekend," Florence said, "and try to forget."

When Jessica hung up, Ralph Asbell had his coat on and was standing near the door.

"My mother's boyfriend died."

140

"I gathered it was bad news."

"He was going to marry her."

"That's too bad—I mean, that he died. You never know, I guess. That's life."

"That's life," Jessica said. "Poof!"

On Saturday, Victor went to New Jersey to kill rabbits. He'd received a flyer from the Conservation Department announcing an authorized one-day out-of-season hunt in a farm area that had become unhealthily overpopulated with the animals. All qualified hunters were to submit applications, and thirty-five would be chosen by lottery. Victor had one of his writers, the author of *Stalking Wild Dinners*—a guide to ecologically balanced hunting for food—use pull to get him in. Jessica thought it was detestable. Victor said it was just and harmless, and was euphoric when he learned he was one of the chosen.

Jessica had reluctantly packed two egg-salad sandwiches, a Hershey bar, and an apple into a small knapsack for him the night before, and pretended to be asleep when he kissed her good-bye at five thirty that morning. When Celia phoned later in the afternoon and happened to ask where Victor was, Jessica lied. She said he was at the barbershop.

At seven that evening Jessica began to seriously worry. Victor wasn't home, and her imagination working in conjunction with the safety booklet she'd found from the Conservation Department left scant hope that he'd return alive.

The booklet, modest in size, was a Civil Service *Psycho*; a terror-inducing masterstroke. Each page of helpful hints magnified fear. The photographs were devastating. One showed a man slumped and bloody upon barbed wire. He had tried to go over a fence with a loaded gun. Another showed a man bent over his steering wheel. He had been trying to get home to his wife and kiddies through an area unhealthily over-populated with hunters.

Jessica was distraught. She made the mistake of reading *The Flopsy Little Bunnies* to Aaron before he went to bed. When she kissed him goodnight, he looked up and said, "Da-da?" and she started to cry.

Before the first tear reached her chin, the downstairs door slammed.

"I'm HO—OME!" Victor shouted.

Her eyes dried instantly.

The anxiety that had buffeted her earlier was gone, replaced with a Nordic aloofness that gave her the relaxed look of a cyborg. She greeted Victor from the stairs with a wave of her pinky and ringfinger.

"Look!" He hoisted two very dead rabbits into the air.

"Ugh," said Jessica, feeling virtuous for restraining her distaste.

"You won't say 'Ugh' when they're cooked," Victor said. "Could you make me a drink while I clean them?"

Jessica poured two scotches, handed one to Victor, and took a gulp of her own. She watched Victor lay the rabbits on newspapers he'd spread across the kitchen table, then turned away.

"You're not the man I married," she said.

"What's that supposed to mean?" Victor said. He drained his drink and poured himself another.

"You were sweet, and gentle," Jessica said.

"What makes you think I've changed?" said Victor.

He took out a long knife and began drawing the blade rhythmically across a whetstone.

"That," Jessica said. She refilled both their glasses.

"Oh, come on," Victor said. "What do you think they did in the old days? Do you think pioneer wives thought their husbands crazed killers every time they brought home dinner? They saw them as heroes, great providers. A good husband was a good provider."

"It's not the old days," Jessica said. "Today a good provider doesn't mean a bunny butcher." Jessica turned her head. "Just last Easter you took pictures of Aaron at the children's zoo playing with them."

"These are different rabbits. They were devastating crops, becoming a health menace."

"Tell that to your son." Jessica refilled her glass vengefully and went into the living room. Weighted with self-righteousness and lightheaded with booze, she refused to think of what was happening in the kitchen. She blocked her mind with song. She sang "Here Comes Peter Cottontail."

"Cut that out!" Victor shouted from the kitchen.

"Bunny Butcher!" she shouted back, and sang even louder.

When Victor emerged from the kitchen he was pale. He listed against the door. Jessica, hands clasped behind her back, was making staccato jumps about the living room and chanting: "Hippity-hoppity, Easter's on its way...."

"They're in the freezer," Victor said. "Now stop it." He reached for her, but missed.

"Ooops, the rabbit's gone again!" Jessica giggled.

Victor resolutely ignored her. "You'll probably find some good recipes in that cookbook my mother gave you."

"I thought *real* hunters cooked their own kill. Isn't that true—*bunny butcher*?" Jessica hopped forward.

Victor's arm shot out. His fingers gripped her sleeve. Without thinking Jessica hopped back. There was a sharp tearing sound; twenty-three dollars' worth.

Jessica froze, stared at the rent fabric. "Look what you've done," she cried. "It's ruined."

"Are you sure?" Victor asked.

Jessica paused. She looked at the tear again. "Well, maybe I could—"

Before she could finish, Victor grabbed the front of her blouse with both hands and yanked. "Now are you sure?"

Jessica was too stunned to move. This, she realized, was her first mistake. Victor threw his arms around her waist and dragged her to the floor, pinning her with his weight. The reality of the carpet reversed her immobility. She began to move. This she soon realized was her second mistake.

Pushing hard at Victor's shoulders, she dug in with her nails, swung her hips to the side, and tried to wriggle free. Victor snaked his foot about her ankle, grasped both her hands, and locked them with his own above her head. He squeezed her wrists together painfully and held them. With his free hand he tore off the remainder of her blouse.

Jessica cursed. Her nipples scraped against his denim shirt, grew traitorously tauter with each abrasive shift of their bodies. She bucked against him and freed her leg, slamming her foot against the floor in an attempt to gain leverage. Before she could, Victor lifted her leg to his back and then rolled to the side, immobilizing it with his body.

Rage caromed through Jessica. She wasn't playing; she was really fighting.

And she was losing!

And it enraged her.

And it excited the hell out of her and she hated it.

"Let me go!" She jabbed Victor's side with her free foot.

Victor ignored her. He opened the zipper of her slacks with one hand. She bit into his shoulder. He opened the zipper of his Levi's with one hand. She bit his other shoulder. Then, in two impressive moves reminiscent of a bareback rider and no doubt facilitated by weekly workouts at Buzzy's gym, he had her naked and totally helpless.

The first impressive move had been a sudden lower-torso swing that set him backwards astride her chest and allowed him to remove her slacks and panties. The second impressive move was a reverse of the first. It implanted him firmly between her thighs.

"Bunny butcher, eh?"

"I take it back," Jessica murmured, and then she passed out.

When she opened her eyes sometime later she was alone on the living room floor. There seemed to be a pounding in her head. After a few moments she realized that the pounding was not in her head. It was the pounding of typewriter keys and it was coming from Victor's den.

Victor was hunched over his Olympia. The latest Rowena Westcott manuscript was scattered on the floor. Jessica came up behind Victor, looked over his shoulder. The paper in the machine was blank except for a title; an author, and a first line.

The title was: *The Naked Gun.* The author was Tony O'Sullivan. The first line was: "I hated to shoot her; she was my kind of slut."

"What are you doing?" Jessica asked. "Why's the Westcott manuscript on the floor?"

"That's where the simp belongs," Victor said.

"You're drunk," Jessica said. It was not an astute observation, but from a quick appraisal of Victor's condition it was conceivably one he might not have thought of.

"I'm Tony O'Sullivan. I always have a few before I begin a new book," Victor said, his words slurred, his voice surly.

"What's this Tony O'Sullivan business?" Jessica asked.

"Commercial," Victor said. "Tough, hard-boiled, and commercial. I've had it with pandering to menopausal markets. Rowena Wescott is out. Dick and Beverly can have her. Tony O'Sullivan's the new me."

"Oh," Jessica said.

"Figures," said Victor.

"What figures?"

"That you'd say something like that."

"All I said was 'Oh.' "

"It was a disapproving 'Oh.' "

"I'm going to bed," Jessica said. "You're drunk."

"C'est la vie, baby," said Victor.

CHAPTER 9

"Maybe I'm not going about it in the right way," Jessica said.

"About what?" Victor asked. He was sitting at the dinner table absorbed in a brochure from the International Wildlife Commission. He'd finished his dessert and was now abstractedly putting his spoon in the empty dish and bringing it regularly to his mouth.

"Do you want more chocolate pudding?" Jessica asked.

"Uh-uh." Victor continued to lick his spoon. "About what?"

"You know," Jessica said.

"Oh," Victor said. "I thought you'd given up."

"I don't give up that easily. What if Thomas Edison had said, 'Screw it! They can use candles—I'm going to bed?' "

"He would have gotten a good night's sleep. His wife would have been happy. Someone else would have invented electric light. Big deal."

"I don't want anyone else to get my wife," Jessica said.

"It's not a matter of being the first on the block to have one," Victor pointed out.

"You still think it's a good idea, don't you?"

"Terrific," Victor said. "Can I have some more chocolate pudding?"

"I really want you to meet El—Lennie, that girl who works for Hippolyte Green," Jessica said. "I can't seem to get hold of her. I left a message with someone who answered her phone yesterday, but she still hasn't called back."

"Maybe she's trying to tell you something."

"Ridiculous," Jessica scoffed.

"You're the one who told me that women know when someone's putting the make on them," Victor said.

"But I'm a woman," Jessica said. "A married woman. Why should she think anything like that?"

Victor shrugged. "I don't know. But if anyone I'd met casually suddenly began bombarding me with phone calls I wouldn't think they were after a fourth for bridge."

"She certainly doesn't suspect that I'm looking for a wife."

"I'll go along with that."

"Damn!" Jessica said.

"Chin up," said Victor.

From upstairs Aaron shouted: "Pee-pee! Pee-pee! Pee-pee!"

Jessica bolted from her chair, did the steps two at a time. There was a stitch in her side. (Did the Strategic Air Command stop to scratch itches?) She ignored it.

Aaron was standing in his crib. In the glow of the night light his smile was radiant.

"Are you Mommy's good boy?" Jessica asked.

Aaron bobbed his head delightedly and bounced up and down. The crib was soaked.

"Men," Jessica mumbled. "Damn liars, all of you."

When she came downstairs, Victor was stretched out on the living room couch.

"Your son's a creep," Jessica said. She flopped into a chair.

"You missed him again, huh?"

"That's right. *I* missed him again. It's *my* fault." Jessica slumped, went silent.

"Sorry," Victor said.

"I'm not giving up."

"Maybe you're trying too hard."

"I'm not talking about Aaron. I'm talking about a wife. It's a great idea and I know it. *You* don't care, Victor. That's the problem."

"Look, I've found two wives this life. Any additionals are up to you."

Jessica gave him a dirty look, which was something she rarely did. Jessica's dirty looks were unlike those given in movies, on TV, or on the street. In fact, they were not so much dirty as they were icily antiseptic. They were full-face confrontations. A beat. And then a tight-lipped smile that slashed across and sprung back like a rubber band. They were killers.

Victor softened. "You know I'm willing to help. Wasn't I there for you with Bert?"

"That one was a loser. She still hasn't finished the bookcases." Jessica sighed. "I must be doing something wrong. There are hundreds, thousands of girls dying to get married and I can't find one."

"You have to admit your requirements are rather special."

"What's so special about wanting someone who can cook, take care of a child, do—"

"Marrying a woman is not the same as marrying a man," Victor said. "Especially if you happen to be a woman."

"But you're part of the deal," Jessica protested.

"And another part of the problem."

"I disagree," Jessica said. "If only there were some way to meet a whole group of single girls so I could have more of a selection."

"Head for the Catskills. One of our salesmen, Irv Belder, goes every weekend and scores like crazy. He tells me he has to bat 'em off like flies."

"Irv Belder? The one with the big ears?" Jessica couldn't believe it. Irv Belder was one of those null human beings whose paucity of good looks was the embodiment of his intellect and wit. He'd never told a joke that didn't contain an elephantine pun or double entendre—that he didn't cap off with, "Get it?" He was about as romantic as a broken vibrator, and even that was going some.

"I don't believe it," Jessica said firmly.

"True. They think he's a doctor. He's even had phony cards printed."

"That's disgusting."

Victor shrugged. "Bats 'em off like flies, though."

"Disgusting." Jessica sat back down in the chair shaking her head. Then she stopped shaking her head. "You know," she began, "maybe you should go up to one of those hotels."

"What!"

"Oh, I don't mean to pull a repugnant stunt like Irv's. God, those poor girls." Jessica shivered. "I mean to just go up there and—meet them."

"Meet them?" Victor asked incredulously.

"Meet them and bring them home—or, you know—get their phone numbers. You could think of it as a hunting expedition," Jessica said.

"You can shove it up your ass," said Victor. And with that he poured himself a glass of scotch and stomped off to his den.

Guilt trailed Jessica like a puppy all the next day, yapping at her conscience. Victor had accused her of deprecating women, of using him. He'd accused her with such vehement accuracy, telling her that she was no better than Irv Belder, that she had broken into tears. It was the Irv Belder part that did it. She knew damn well if Victor had agreed to go she wouldn't have felt guilty at all.

Guilt! How she hated that erratic psychic guillotine.

When she arrived at Rubicon to deliver the appeal letters she'd written for Mike, she was relieved to find he wasn't there. If he had been he'd have only made her feel good and loved and talented—and more guilty.

Guilt! How she reviled that parasite of pleasure.

She spoke awhile with Abby, who'd just broken up with her therapist bedmate. Abby told her that the sex had been okay, but the morning vomiting had worn her out. She was now living at a yoga commune on 130th Street and was in the throes of discovering her third eye and celibacy.

"The way Guru Bowmou gets you into celibacy, it's the greatest fucking thing in the world."

Jessica told her that she'd try it sometime—and felt guilty about that too.

On the way home, Jessica stopped at Ernshweiger's

for some éclairs. Lilly Ernshweiger gave her a half-nod of recognition. It was the nod you gave someone you met on the bus every morning but never spoke to, never cared to speak to.

Jessica retaliated with her warmest smile.

"Any éclairs today?"

"Nope. Not today. Not any day. Not anymore."

"Oh. How come?"

Lilly cocked her head to the side. "You eat éclairs?" she asked.

"Not usually, but—"

Lilly Enshweiger held out her palm. "Does your mother eat éclairs?"

"Well, she's usually dieting, but—"

Lilly Ernshweiger palm pressed forward. "How many women that you know eat éclairs?"

"Well, I don't know anyone who doesn't like them, but—"

"BUT!" Lilly Ernshweiger shouted. "There it is. *But.* But they buy them and if they eat them they hate themselves. I refuse to encourage such masochism among my sisters. The female self-image has suffered enough. No more éclairs."

"But I'm buying them for my husband."

"Let him eat cake."

Victor had two slices of mocha butter-cream cake for dessert that evening. He said they were delicious and that he was going to have to watch his cholesterol. He also said that he would have preferred an éclair.

Jessica said nothing.

Victor scraped the icing from his plate with his finger. "I think I've got Wiffet this time."

"What do you mean?"

"The *Labroides Dimidatus* is going to do it. I feel it. It's going to go all the way." He stood and began to pace the kitchen.

"Go where?" Jessica asked. "What is it?"

"It's a fish."

"A fish?"

"Found off Australia's Great Barrier Reef." Victor's eyes widened. His lips curled in a funny way that made Jessica apprehensive. "it's going to get me a raise," he said slowly, "and pin Wiffet's feathered page proofs to a dusty shelf."

"A fish?"

"*Labroides Dimidatus*," Victor said reverently. "I'm going to make it a household word."

"Good luck."

"Mock, go ahead. I'm telling you I'm going to turn an ordinary manuscript about an interesting fish into an explosive best seller that will have as many sociological, anthropological, and psychological reverberations as *On the Origin of Species*." He slapped the table. "*Labroides Dimidatus*."

"Sounds like a fungus infection," Jessica said, though not unkindly.

"It's a species of fish whose females cannot abide the absence of a dominating male. When the male is lost—disappears or dies—a female physically turns male to replace him. First she simply adopts his behavior, then slowly her organs change and she actually becomes a male." Victor socked his palm. "And if we handle it right we can enrage feminists enough to cash in on a lot of free publicity. I told the author we'd need a provocative title, and he came up with *Girls Will Be*

Boys, subtitled: *Labroides Dimidatus—A True Fish Story.* How do you like it?"

"I hate it."

"You don't like it?" Victor asked, stunned.

"I hate it," Jessica said. "Talk about Irv Belder."

"Who's talking about Irv Belder?"

"You're talking about exploiting women to get what you want, a best seller. It's no different from Irv's using phony cards to get laid. Women are human beings. We're not 'things' with a hundred and one handy uses."

"Look who's talking? What about you and your wife?"

"Let's leave my wife out of this," Jessica said angrily. She narrowed her eyes. "You've changed, Victor. I don't think I like it."

"Oh, for Christ's sake." Victor ran his fingers through his hair.

"How come," Jessica asked slowly, "you've suddenly become more interested in a little transsexual fish than the mighty blue whale?"

Victor didn't answer. He got his coat.

"Where are you going?" Jessica asked.

"Bowling," Victor said. "Want to make something of it?"

The door slammed.

Bowling? Victor had never bowled in all the years she'd known him. Bowling? Now, really. . . .

Jessica cleaned up the kitchen and bitched to herself. She bitched about Victor going bowling while she scrubbed pots. She bitched about the pots, which were Teflon and shouldn't have needed scrubbing. She bitched about the leftovers that needed wrapping, about the grease that had to go down the toilet. She bitched, bitched, bitched until she told herself to shut up already.

She dried her hands and phoned Eleanore again. There was no answer. Annoyed, she snatched an old copy of *Ladies' Home Journal* from the pile she'd prepared for the recycling drive and collapsed on the living room sofa. She forced herself to read.

She objectively considered the *Journal*'s Notes from the Editor, seriously perused the Table of Contents, and dutifully read how a marriage in which the wife was an alcoholic and the husband a philanderer could be saved. She learned the warning signs of vaginitis.

She was about to put the magazine down when an article caught her eye. It was: "How I Met My Husband." It consisted of interviews with wives of fairly well-known politicians, actors, scientists, and businessmen. It was a revelation. One woman, the wife of a handsome Democratic Senator from Minnesota, said she met her husband by accidentally ramming her Volkswagen into his teaberry bushes; another, the new missus of an up-and-coming young actor named Pete Moss, told how she'd spilled yogurt on him in the UA commissary. (They were married, she said, three weeks later.) Except for one woman, the wife of a New York psychoanalyst, who confessed to premeditated seduction (she deliberately made up dreams to entice her husband), and a couple of bland executive wives who admitted to being prosaically introduced to their future mates at parties by mutual friends, the general tenor of the romantic first meetings was one of farcical cataclysm.

The implications were fascinating. Were minor disasters the most erotic catalysts? (If someone splashed yogurt on the Queen of England, would her Royal Highness tumble?) Jessica began to think.

She thought about seducing famous women. This reminded her in many ways of her teen-age daydreams of seducing famous men. One of the famous men she'd wanted to seduce then was Marlon Brando. She'd read somewhere that he liked exotic women. Her fantasy was that she'd be so outrageously plain that he'd find her unique. He was supposed to be hooked on exotic foods, too. The meal she'd prepared for him when they were alone was turtle soup, made from a Galapagos turtle. It was a nice fantasy. They always did the dishes together afterward. Naked. She'd come a long way.

She thought about seducing ... Jane Fonda? (Uh-uh, too feisty) ... Mia Farrow? (Hmmmm, too prissy) ... and then it hit her. She closed her eyes and thought about seducing Brigitte Bardot. She saw herself in a small green sports car on the French Riviera ...

A playful wind brushes Jessica's hair from her face. She carefully slows the car behind the sleek Jaguar at the intersection. She checks her reflection in the rearview mirror. Suddenly there's a bang. She's thrown forward. The front of her small green sports car has impudently nudged the rear bumper of the Jaguar.

The woman driving the Jaguar jumps out.

It's her! She's wearing dark glasses and a kerchief over her long blond hair. She walks angrily toward Jessica and curses in French.

Jessica says, "Je ne parle pas français," *and smiles, pretending not to recognize her.*

BB points to the dent in the Jaguar's rear bumper. "Look what you have done," she says in English.

"It's in the back," Jessica says. "No one will notice."

BB is about to say something, but hesitates. Suddenly she laughs.

Jessica laughs.

They go to a small café for wine and laugh some more. BB invites Jessica back to her villa. Jessica goes. It is the servants' day off. They are alone. They drink a lot of wine and giggle like schoolgirls.

It is warm. As the sun dips below the horizon, BB suggests a swim. Jessica agrees. They leave their clothes in a careless heap at the side of the pool. The pool is warm and azure. It is shaped like the letter B. They frolic like porpoises. They drink more wine and play waterball. Jessica wins: 21–6.

They emerge from the pool. Their bodies glisten in the new moon and the night air provokes their nipples. They are suddenly aware of a tension. The silence throbs about them. They say nothing. They know.

Jessica follows BB into her bedroom. It is all pillows and mirrors and white satin and softness. She lies down on the bed, opens her arms to Jessica. "Ici," she murmurs.

Jessica understands.

They lose themselves in forbidden ecstasies. Then, entwined in each other, they sleep.

When they wake they are ravenously hungry. They go to the kitchen. BB scavenges for fruit and cheese as Jessica makes omelettes.

Afterward they do the dishes together. Naked.

*

Jessica opened her eyes slowly. Reluctantly. She pitched the magazine back on the recycling pile and went upstairs to bed.

A while later she heard the front door open. "Is that you, Victor?" she called.

"No," he said sarcastically. "It's Marlon Brando."

CHAPTER 10

Jessica developed an itch.

She suspected the worst. She suspected Marilyn Kantor. She phoned her gynecologist immediately.

Dr. Glemmings, the nurse informed her, was in Port-au-Prince on vacation for three weeks. It didn't surprise Jessica. Dr. Glemmings charged women forty dollars to take off their clothes, lie on his table, and spread their legs. He was fiftyish and charmingly aloof. He had family money and a clientele that spent as much for the perfume they dabbed on their pussies as they did for the office visit. He had also written a book about the women who took off their clothes, lay on his table, and spread their legs. Dr. Glemmings could afford to be in Port-au-Prince on vacation for a year.

The nurse gave Jessica the name of another gynecologist. "Toutter," she said. "With two t's."

Jessica phoned Dr. Toutter and made an appointment for Friday morning. She always made her gynecologist appointments in the morning, arranged them so that they would never be more than three hours after her shower. It gave her confidence when she took off her clothes, lay down on the table, and spread her legs.

Dr. Toutter's office was on Park Avenue and

Eighty-first Street. The waiting room was small and aseptically cozy. There were two numbered Picasso prints on the wall. The magazines were all encased in thick plastic covers.

A middle-aged woman in a beige pants suit was the only other patient in the waiting room. She was surreptitiously tearing something from one of the magazines. She slapped the magazine closed when she saw Jessica and looked quickly toward the window.

Jessica hung up her coat and sat down. She picked up a copy of *Town & Country* and began leafing through it. She felt the woman in the pants suit staring at her and glanced up. The woman again closed the magazine on her lap quickly and looked away. A half-torn page dangled from the thick plastic cover.

The nurse entered, looked at the clipboard in her hand. "Mrs. Waxman?" she asked.

The woman in the beige pants suit pushed the frayed magazine under the pile stacked on the table, then stood.

"Right this way," the nurse said. She looked at her clipboard. "The doctor will be with you shortly, Mrs. Prior." She led Mrs. Waxman down the corridor. A few minutes later, she returned. "Mrs. Prior?" she asked.

Jessica nodded.

"Right this way, please."

Jessica followed the nurse into one of Dr. Toutter's four examining rooms. On the medicine cabinet, alongside a box of disposable plastic gloves, stood a large pink plastic model of the uterus. It was split down the center like a giant halved pear. It was unnerving.

The nurse handed Jessica a white paper robe. "Take

everything off except your shoes," she said. "Dr. Toutter will be with you shortly."

"Thank you," Jessica said.

The nurse left and Jessica undressed quickly; actually, as fast as she could. Not that she was unduly modest, but there was something embarrassing about being caught seminude by the doctor. She put on the paper robe and inadvertently tore the sleeve. It flapped annoyingly as she hoisted herself onto the table. The table faced the pink plastic uterus.

The door opened and Dr. Toutter walked in. He had a clipboard in his hand and was studying it so intently Jessica wondered if he knew she was there. She coughed.

Dr. Toutter looked up, nodded, then returned to studying the clipboard. His eyebrows arched and straightened as he read. When he was through reading, he put the clipboard on the cabinet. He clasped his hands behind him and addressed Jessica directly. "Having problems with the machinery, eh. What seems to be the trouble?"

"I've had some discharge lately and—" Jessica began.

"Leaky valve problems, eh? Well, let's get your chassis up on the lift and have a look." He told Jessica to slide back and adjusted her feet in the stirrups. Then he draped her with a sheet.

"Any difficulties with the hose connection?" he asked, thrusting his fingers into a disposable plastic glove.

"Beg pardon?"

"Voiding," he said grudgingly.

"Oh. No," Jessica said.

"Stalling in traffic?"

"Excuse me?"

"Difficulties with intercourse," he said.

"No," Jessica said.

He made two quick marks on the clipboard. "Better check under the hood." He raised the sheet slightly and pushed his fingers inside Jessica, pressing down on her abdomen with his other hand. "Right bearing o—kay. Left bearing o—kay." He withdrew his fingers and removed the glove. "Front end seems to be pretty much in line." He put a condom over one of his fingers. "Now we'll check out the rear axle—just breath deeply."

Jessica began to fume.

"All righty. Everything in order there." Dr. Toutter pulled over a stool and sat down. He turned on a light and inserted a speculum. "Hmmm. A little sludge in the tank, but nothing serious." He removed the speculum, stood, and eased her feet from the stirrups. "I'll write a prescription."

Jessica was enraged. "Where do I get it filled," she muttered acidly, "at a gas station?"

"Hm?" Dr. Toutter looked up. "What's that?"

Jessica held out her hand for the prescription.

"There you go," Dr. Toutter said as he tore the paper from the pad. "That'll get your engine purring again."

"Listen—" Jessica began.

Dr. Toutter ignored her, headed for the door. "Oh, by the way," he said as he left, "no pleasure driving for about a week."

Abby and Aaron were on the living room floor. Aaron's toy trucks were parked on alternate sides of the couch. Abby was making *Vroom, Vroom* noises. Aaron was laughing.

"We've been playing speedway," Abby said. "Aaron won the Indy 500 three times and made bubbles in the bathroom twice."

"Bubbles?" Jessica said.

"Pissed," Abby said.

"Really?" Jessica was amazed. "That's fantastic. How did you do it?"

Abby shrugged. "I asked him if he wanted to make bubbles. He said yes, so I took him to the bathroom and—he made bubbles."

"That's all?"

"Uh-huh."

"That's fantastic," Jessica said.

"Not really," Abby said. "He wet his pants twice, too."

Jessica plummeted. "Oh."

Abby picked up Aaron's trucks and put them back in the toy chest. "I wouldn't worry about it," Jess," she said with the confident wisdom of a nineteen-year-old nullipara. "He won't walk down the aisle in diapers."

"Don't bet on it," Jessica said.

"I wouldn't put money on it," Victor said that evening, "but just between you and me I'm willing to wager that Wiffet's planning to put the kaibosh on my *Labroides Dimidatus* book. He was hovering around Faraday with his own new project all day."

"Now, really," Jessica said. Victor's paranoia about George Wiffet had taken on a disturbing intensity over the past several days. Wiffet's wiles, according to Victor, were invidious. Even though Jessica opposed the

Labroides Dimidatus book from the sexist promotion angle, she did want it to succeed for Victor's sake. The psychic misery he'd endured from the postponement of the blue whale made Ahab's torment from Moby Dick seem like a tension headache.

"You think I'm exaggerating," Victor said. "I'm telling you that featherheaded Iago is out to cut the balls off my book. He's evil."

"Victor, please."

"I hate him."

"You don't hate him."

"I do. Once, just once, I want to beat that bastard out of a leader."

"It's only a book," Jessica said.

"Ah. There it is, your all-purpose assuager—'It's only.' It's only a book, only money, only a car, only a broken leg, only, only. What do you care. It's only my career."

"Victor!"

"What's important to you? Isn't anything in this world that's a cut below cataclysm worthy of concern?"

"Of course, but—"

"Don't but me. Faraday *buts* me all the time. It's a good book, Victor, *but* Wiffet's got something here that we can sell the hell out of."

"But George Wiffet doesn't have anything better than *Girls Will Be Boys*," Jessica protested.

"Oh, no?" Victor sneered. "Are you ready for this? *Boo Who-Whoo: The End of the Wise Old Owl*. A scare book with academic sales appeal that can't miss."

"You're being unreasonable," Jessica said softly.

"Sure," Victor snapped. "What do you care. I'm only your husband."

*

Over the next few days, Jessica forced herself to recognize that a film of distrust, like wispy spores on aging marmalade, had begun to cloud her perfect marriage. At first she recoiled from the thought. Anything that tested the mettle of a Jessica Truth of Life was to be recoiled from. But the more Victor questioned her concern and affection for him, the more suspicious she became of his doubts. It was a savage cycle and she didn't like it. She didn't like it a bit.

She submerged herself in Aaron's toilet training.

A friend of Celia's, named Missy, a dropout wife from Lake Hopatcong, New Jersey, whose consciousness had been raised just enough to recognize that she no longer had to stand for beatings by her husband every time she lost one of his socks, gave Jessica her old family formula for toilet training. According to Missy, no girl in her family wore diapers after eight months, no boy after nine.

"All you need," Missy said, "are gumdrops and lollipops. You use the reward system. A gumdrop for a piddle and a lollipop for a plop. Never fails." She gave Jessica her phone number and told her to call and tell her how it worked out.

Jessica bought the candy. At the end of the week, most of the lollipops were gone, but the gumdrops hadn't been touched. She flushed them down the toilet along with Missy's phone number.

One night Victor was three scotches into *Naked Gun*, and Jessica (usually a shower person) was treating herself to a long warm bath, when the doorbell rang.

She heard Victor go to the door, then heard him exclaim "Well, I'll be a muddy mule!" Which pushed her to pull the plug immediately and step from the tub. The only time Victor used old Elcho, Wisconsin, expressions like "muddy mule" or "dingbat's daddy" was when he was totally nonplussed, and a little nervous. She dried herself quickly, threw on her robe, and went downstairs.

"Paula!" Jessica cried delightedly.

The girl next to Victor smiled shyly. "Hi," she said.

Jessica ran to her. "You're back! It's been years!"

Paula kept her arms rigidly at her sides as Jessica hugged her, nervous but pleased at the greeting. "Eleven and a half months," she said.

"You have to tell us everything. Come in and sit down. You look marvelous," Jessica said, though it wasn't quite true.

Paula Kramer would never look marvelous, but Jessica noticed someone had finally done the right thing with her hair. It was shoulder-length and cut to flip coyly at the ends. Paula was the type of girl who never struck you as attractive until you'd known her a couple of months or longer. Jessica and Victor had befriended her when they lived on the East Side; the common ground being the abutment of their apartments. She was plaintively introverted; a Barnard graduate who played the violin and did woodcuts of cats. (She was also the victim of a neurotic mother who phoned frantically to see if she were alive whenever an unidentified female body was found within a fifty-mile radius of the city.) Shy and quiet as Paula was, she rarely wanted for dates, though her relationships with men mysteriously went nowhere. After her last breakup she'd quit her job in the Metropolitan Museum gift shop and obtained a grant that enabled her to go to Europe and to complete her thesis on seventeenth-century Italian woodcuts.

"Can I get you a drink?" Jessica asked.

"If you have a little club soda," Paula said.

That's no way to celebrate a homecoming," Victor said. "How about some wine?"

"Please, no. I've been living on wine and pasta for a year." She stood up and patted her hips. "Look at the weight I've gained."

Victor was looking. So was Jessica. Paula's figure had never been better. It was, in fact, terrific. She'd put on just enough to round her curves—just enough to turn Victor's paternal tone *basso voce* and Jessica's thoughts away from club soda.

"Three cheers for wine and pasta," Victor said admiringly.

Paula blushed.

"Would you like to smoke?" asked Jessica. She avoided Victor's eyes.

"No, really," Paula said. "A little club soda would be fine. I'm still trying to shake jet lag and acclimate to being home. I feel as if I've been gone for centuries. So much has changed. I guess I'm shook. That's why I came over tonight without calling or anything. I just needed to touch something solid."

Jessica and Victor looked concerned.

Paula fluttered her hands. "Oh, it's nothing terrible or anything. It's just—remember my friends Judy and Kevin?"

"She's the one you made the baby shower for," Jessica said.

"Right," Paula said. "Well they've split. I couldn't believe it when Judy told me. I mean, they'd done everything right. They lived together for two years before

167

they got married, they waited to have the baby, and they loved each other. They really loved each other. It just dropped me when I heard they were getting divorced." Paula shuddered, rubbed her arms. "I never thought it could happen with them. I get this awful feeling that I'm skating through life and there's no warning signs for thin ice. All of a sudden—crack."

"Nobody gets any guarantees," Victor said.

"I know," Paula sighed. "But I thought of them the way I think of you and Jessica. Rock-solid, the perfect couple." She reached impulsively and grabbed their hands. "I can't tell you how good it is to be here."

Jessica patted Paula's head. "Let me get you your soda," she said. "I want to hear all about Europe."

"A scotch for me," Victor said.

Jessica frowned, but Victor ignored it. He'd had several drinks before Paula arrived, and his voice was getting louder. Ordinarily, Jessica wouldn't have cared, but the new developments, especially Paula's, made her anxious to keep him sober. She diluted his drink with water and poured soda in Paula's glass.

Paula Kramer, Jessica thought. *What an ideal wife.* The girl's apartment had always been spotless. She used to go as far as taking down hundreds of books to wax the shelves once a week. And was she an organizer! Her Christmas card list was on file cards, with addresses kept current; every plastic container of leftovers in her refrigerator was labeled and dated; she was never without extra light bulbs, Scotch tape, Band-Aids, aspirin, or sugar. She was the only person Jessica had ever known who had never received a "Have You Forgotten?" notice for unpaid bills.

Jessica thrummed her fingers quitely on the counter. Paula Kramer was definitely worth a concerted effort.

Her pot roast and dumplings were out of this world. And kids—she loved them. In fact, she was a high scorer on almost every point—except perhaps for a sense of humor. Not that she didn't have one; it was just slightly off. Paula Kramer. Hmmm, Jessica thought, but how?

"Where are the drinks?" Victor called.

"Coming," Jessica said.

Her mind was a freeway jammed with potentialities, each one futilely vying for an opening. How was she going to proposition a girl who deep in her heart still believed in Crunchy Granola and Khalil Gibran? Then Jessica remembered the article in *Ladies' Home Journal* about women who had bumped and splashed their way to the altar. It was worth a try.

She handed Victor his drink, then stretched her arm out toward Paula. As Paula reached for the glass, Jessica tipped it.

"Oh, Paula, I'm sorry," Jessica said. "I'll get a towel."

Paula had a bewildered look. "I'm soaked," she said.

"Here." Jessica handed her a towel, and began sponging up the soda that spilled on the rug.

Paula dried herself awkwardly. "I'm still sopping wet."

"I'm really sorry," Jessica said. "Why don't you take those off and I'll put them in the machine."

"Well. . . ."

"Let me get you a robe." Before Paula could protest Jessica went upstairs and returned with a pink terrycloth bathrobe. "Here. Get out of that stuff and we'll have it dried in no time." Jessica aimed her in the direction of the bathroom. "Watch out for the begonia plant when you turn on the light," she said.

"What are you up to?" Victor asked suspiciously.

Jessica winked.

"Holy shit, you've gone off the deep end." Victor gupled his drink.

"Honorable intentions, remember?" Jessica said. "She's wife material."

"I don't know, Jess." Victor shook his head. "I don't know."

"Are you with me?"

"There's something . . . incestuous about it."

"Are you with me?"

Victor raised his glass, grinned. "What the hell, why not?"

Jessica glared. "There's no need to get vulgar about it."

"Is something wrong?" Paula asked. She had Jessica's bathrobe draped around her and was clutching it closed.

"Slight headache," Victor mumbled.

"There doesn't seem to be a sash," Paula said. "Have you a pin or something?"

Jessica nodded and got a diaper pin from a drawer. Paula closed the robe as best she could, but looked ill at ease nonetheless.

"Relax," Jessica said. "You're among friends."

"I really am relaxed," Paula said. "You truly don't know how much you two mean to me. I thought about you a lot when I was in Europe. Everytime I'd read about what was going on back here, the way things were changing, I'd get upset. Then I'd remember you and tell myself that some things do abide."

"Sun in the morning and the moon at night," Victor said. "Period."

"I knew you'd make a remark like that," Paula said

happily. "I told myself before I came here tonight, Victor will have some marvelously cynical comment for everything."

"That was hardly marvelously cynical," Victor said.

"Oh, you know what I mean," Paula said. "And I knew that Jessica would be just as sweet and enthusiastic as ever."

Jessica smiled weakly and said nothing. Guilt was sneaking up like calories; so was frustration. The "How I Met My Husband" splash approach might have worked in the UA commissary, but it wasn't working on West Eighty-seventh Street. Maybe she was being too direct. A more subliminal advance could possibly be more effective with someone like Paula. Something like . . . "the dream" come-on.

Jessica coughed. "You know," she said, attempting to look mischievous, seductive, and reticent at the same time, "I had the strangest dream about you the other night. I'm sort of embarrassed to tell it, but—"

"Dreams!" Paula laughed. "That reminds me of the nut I met in Rome." And without a smidgin of curiosity or (what Jessica found off-putting) courtesy, Paula proceeded to relate a series of plenary anecdotes with uncharacteristic zest.

After a seemingly endless story about a lost valise, Jessica yawned.

"My god, what time is it?" Paula asked.

"About one thirty," Victor said.

"I feel awful. Here I've been babbling away and both of you have to get up early. I'd better leave." She leaned over for her purse and there was a flash of skin as the robe parted. She clutched it closed and said, "Excuse me."

The flash had activated Victor. He moved attentively

to the edge of his chair. Paula drew the robe tighter around herself.

"Are my clothes ready?" she asked.

"Damn!" Jessica said. "I forgot to put them in the dryer."

"Do you have an extra pair of slacks and a sweater I could wear home?"

"Sure," Jessica said. "But say, why don't you stay here tonight? It's late, and we'd really love to have you."

"Oh, I couldn't. It would be an imposition."

Jessica put her arm around Paula's shoulder. "It wouldn't be at all."

"But you have Aaron in the morning and Victor has to go to work. I'd just be in your way."

Victor stood and put his arm around Paula's shoulder too. "Don't be silly."

"Well . . . If you're really sure that it's all right."

"Really sure," Victor said.

"Positive," said Jessica.

"Okay. You've convinced me. Where do I sleep?"

Ready or not, here I come. "With us?" Jessica said hesitantly.

"Huh?"

"With us," Victor said. "We've got a huge king-sized bed, and neither of us snore."

Paula stiffened. "Ha ha."

"Seriously," Jessica said.

"Honestly," said Victor.

Paula began to cry.

"Paula, what's the matter? There's nothing to get upset about."

"Not you and Victor. I don't believe it," she wailed.

"You were my Gibraltar, and now . . . and now—" She covered her face with her hand and sobbed quietly.

"Now, now, you're taking this all wrong." Victor flashed a warning look at Jessica. Jessica rolled her eyes upward.

"I am?" Paula sniffled.

"Of course," said Jessica. Win some, lose some, as her brother would say.

"Definitely," said Victor. "What sort of people do you think we are?"

"I was beginning to wonder," said Paula.

"I'm ashamed of you for even thinking that way," Victor admonished gently.

Paula lowered her head. "I'm sorry. I guess I don't know when people are joking anymore."

"Well, we weren't joking," said Jessica.

The wariness came back into Paula's voice. "You weren't?"

"But we didn't mean what you thought we meant," Victor said quickly. "Sleeping together is a warm, wonderful social experience. Wolves do it all the time."

"We thought it would be a nice thing," Jessica said.

Paula nodded dumbly. "A nice thing."

"Of course if you don't *want* to—" Jessica removed her arm from Paula's shoulder.

"It's not that—" Paula began, and then she blushed. "It seems so—so sort of unnatural, I guess."

"Wolves do it all the time," Victor reminded her.

Paula forced a smile. "I know I must sound ridiculous. I'm sorry." She took a deep breath. "Well, then, what are we waiting for?"

When they got to the bedroom, Victor began unbuttoning his shirt. Paula excused herself and went to the bathroom.

"Listen," Victor whispered. "No funny stuff."

"What do you mean no funny stuff," Jessica whispered back.

"No hanky-panky," Victor said. "We gave her our word."

"You must think I'm Lucretia Borgia," Jessica said. "Don't you trust me?"

"No."

"You prick!"

"I'm being honest."

"Sorry. No medals. But to be quite honest I don't trust *you*, either."

"You do too."

"Not when you're horny."

"What makes you think I'm horny?"

"Randolph."

Victor looked down. "Oh, that," he said. "Hell, it's just nerves."

"Well, hurry up and relax because here she comes," Jessica said.

"No funny stuff," Victor said.

"No funny stuff," Jessica said.

Paula entered the room. Still clutching Jessica's pink robe around her. "I used your dental floss. Was that all right?"

"Sure," Jessica said. She stood and shrugged off her housecoat.

Paula averted her eyes. "That's a terrific clock. Is it an antique?"

Jessica walked naked to the bureau. "That's not, but this jewel box is." She held the box out to Paula.

"Very nice," Paula said, studying the box as if she'd never seen anything like it in her life.

"How about some sleep?" Victor said.

Jessica went back to the bed and crawled under the covers. Paula remained in the center of the room.

"Paula?" Jessica called.

Paula fingered the terrycloth, started to open the robe, then stopped. "Er ... do I get a top or anything?"

"There's a bottom—or a nightgown in the left bureau drawer," Jessica said.

Paula seemed relieved. Keeping the nightgown tight in her hand, she took off the robe.

Victor raised himself casually on one elbow.

"Nerves, my foot!" Jessica muttered. As she followed Victor's unswerving gaze she found herself caught in a cloudburst of envy. She tried to think sisterhood, but it didn't help. Paula's breasts were the ones she'd always wanted. They were rounded and firm, with uppity pink nipples that boasted an impudent confidence Paula herself would never possess. They were the sort of breasts young men jerked off to in fantasy; the sort that young women fantasized Mark Eden could give them. They fired in Jessica a covetousness unequaled since that long-ago day when Sondra Katz closed the door of her bedroom and exhibited her first pubic hair.

As Paula pulled the gown over her head, Victor murmured: "Lovely." It was the *coup de grace*.

Paula stood awkwardly at the side of the bed. Waited.

"Well?" Victor said.

"Er. Which side?" Paula asked.

"I always sleep on the left," Victor said, adding, "even in motels," to ensure his sovereignty of the side.

"I get nightmares if I'm not on the right," Jessica said.

"I see," Paula said. "That sort of leaves me in the middle, doesn't it?"

"Plenty of room," Victor assured her.

"Do you think I could have a cigarette first?" Paula asked.

"Sure." Victor handed her one from the pack on the night table. She sat on the edge of the bed and smoked in silence.

When there was nothing left but the filter, she dropped it into the ashtray and climbed in between Jessica and Victor. She lay flat on her back, her arms locked against her sides.

Victor flipped off the light.

The darkness magnified the tension. A dozen invisible drills ground away at Jessica's temples. She wished she were in Mallorca, in Cleveland; she wished she had a night light.

The quiet was overpowering. It sounded as if no one in the bed was breathing. It was so still that Jessica could hear the hum of the refrigerator downstairs. She wanted to cough, but didn't dare. She forced herself to close her eyes. As she did, Paula screamed.

"What the—" Victor bolted upright and turned on the light.

Paula scrambled from the bed.

Jessica glared. "I thought we agreed no funny stuff," she whispered angrily.

"That's what I thought," he shot back through clenched teeth. "What did you do?"

"Nothing," Jessica said. "And don't play that game with me."

"I didn't touch her."

"Owww. Oooh," Paula moaned.

They looked up. Paula was in the center of the room hopping on one foot.

"Cramp in my leg," she said. "It's killing me, but it'll be all right in a few minutes. I've had them before. I'm really sorry to disturb you like this. Oh, there." She stopped hopping. "See it's gone. Isn't that the craziest thing?" She came back to bed.

Jessica took three aspirins.

Victor switched off the light and knocked the ashtray to the floor. They all went uneasily to sleep.

CHAPTER 11

Jessica felt like shit.

The fiasco with Paula had sullied her conscience. It made her snippish with Aaron and screwed up her Rubicon releases. Even though nothing had happened, she felt like a dirty old lady. She had to find a wife and settle down.

It was taking longer than she'd anticipated—though, when she stopped to consider it, she actually had more opportunities than a man to find a compatible female. She had entrée to such distaff bastions as beauty parlors, powder rooms and dressing rooms, lingerie shops, Tupperware parties. There were a lot of advantages to being a woman in search of a woman.

But there were also disadvantages. Women weren't conditioned to having other women proposition them. A man could wolf whistle, say something obscene, even make an overt pass, and the average female would ignore it, respond, or forget the whole thing right after it happened. If another woman tried it, the average female could freak out for months, years, life.

Eleanore was not an average female. Jessica tried phoning her again and learned that she was out of town, wouldn't be back for weeks.

Damn. It was time for organization. For action.

Jessica made a note to check out the girls in her exercise class. She'd have to begin trying harder. Columbus didn't discover America by sitting on his ass in Grenada.

"Don't you ever sit down?" Ralph Asbell asked as Jessica gathered up the detritus of Aaron's day which cluttered the living room floor.

"Never," she said. "Ask Victor."

Victor was sprawled on the sofa. He was slightly drunk and totally exhausted. He'd worked out at Buzzy's that evening, and then had gone bowling with two of the men he'd met there, Al Sterly and Marty Pellicone. Al Sterly was a one-armed amputee who worked for the phone company. According to Victor, Sterly had more muscles in his one arm than most men had in their entire body. Marty Pellicone worked for the Department of Sanitation, drove one of the bulldozers out at the dumps. The rumor at Buzzy's was that he was a narc. Victor referred to them as "the guys." On Monday mornings, when he left for work, he prided in saying, "I'm bowling with the guys tonight."

"Hey, Victor." Ralph poked his arm. "Does she?"

"Huh?" Victor turned lazily. "Does she what?"

"Ever sit down?"

"Never." Victor put his glass on the coffee table, then stretched. His right arm hit the lamp, nearly knocking it over.

Jessica caught the lamp. She looked disapprovingly at Victor. He grabbed her arm and pulled her down over the back of the sofa and kissed her.

"Next time you won't get off so easy, baby. So watch it," Victor said.

Jessica shook her head, sighed.

Ralph picked up a copy of *Scientific American* and flipped pages. It could have been the light, but it looked as if he were blushing.

"Pssst," Victor hissed loudly.

Ralph looked up. Victor swung his hand in the air, a beckoning motion more appropriate to swatting away flies. Ralph leaned forward.

"They like that," Victor said, thumbing toward Jessica.

Ralph looked confused.

"The rough treatment." Victor winked. "Just put it to them regularly and they're yours for life."

"That's not funny, Victor," Jessica said.

Victor dropped back on the sofa. "Aw, come on. I'm only kidding." He turned to Ralph. "You've got to be in condition for it too. You know that fifty thousand men under forty suffer heart attacks every year?"

Unconsciously Ralph touched his chest.

"We've got to fight to stay in shape," Victor said.

"Jessica's told me that you've been going to the gym four nights a week."

"Three," Victor corrected. "Thursday I go to the Police Academy and use the target range. Friday's karate."

"Well, well, aren't we getting macho," Ralph chided. "It sounds as if you're going for the John Wayne award."

"What's that supposed to mean?" Victor sat up unsteadily.

"Nothing." Ralph backed into his chair, crossed his legs.

"Where the hell do *you* come off telling me about machismo?" Victor snapped.

"Victor!" Jessica said, glaring.

Ralph looked stricken; looked as if he'd just seen his mother flash her crotch from the steps of the Hall of Justice.

"I used to be a Golden Gloves boxer, you know. See—" He pulled a yellowed newsclip from his wallet. It showed a picture of a blond skinny young boy in shorts, gloved fists raised. The caption said, "Kid Asbell Readies for Golden Gloves Bout." There was a story beneath it. He extended the clipping toward Victor.

Victor waved it away and covered his eyes. "Christ, Ralph, I'm sorry. You know I didn't mean that. I'm sorry. I really am. I'm drunk and—"

"It's all right. I understand," Ralph said. He stood. "I guess I'd better be going." He folded the newsclip and carefully put it back into his wallet.

"Ralph, I'm really sorry," Victor said, now painfully sober.

"Forget it." Ralph nodded good-bye to Jessica and put on his coat. "By the way," he said. "I won that match."

Jessica picked the remainder of Aaron's toys up in silence.

Victor grabbed his glass from the table and hurled it to the floor. It broke, leaving tiny shards lost forever in the weave of the carpet.

On Thursday night, when Victor returned from target shooting, Jessica told him that there was something wrong with their bedroom.

"What's wrong with our bedroom?"

"It's too middle-class married."

"We *are* middle-class and married."

"I know, but our bedroom doesn't have to be that way. It should be younger, more seductive."

"We'll hang up pictures of rock stars and burn incense, how about that?"

Jessica gave him a look.

"It was only a suggestion," Victor said.

Jessica bit her thumb and concentrated. Then she whipped her thumb out and said excitedly, "I've got it!"

"I'm afraid."

"We can buy fabric and drape it from the ceiling. It would make the room look like a sheikh's tent. How much more seductive can you get?"

"Beats me," said Victor. He started back down the stairs.

"Where are you going?" Jessica asked.

"To clean my gun," said Victor.

Jessica was washing Aaron's sweaters in the kitchen sink, trying to think up a new fund-raising slogan for Rubicon, when something cold and wet pressed up against her leg.

It was a nose. It was Mauser's nose, and Mauser was with it.

Jessica froze. "Victor," she rasped, her voice barely audible.

"Rick's here," Victor called cheerily from the hall.

The dog licked Jessica's knee appreciatively. Jessica cringed. Victor had told her he'd invited Mauser's owner to stop by. He hadn't told her that he would come armed. It wasn't that she was afraid of dogs, but meeting Mauser knee to nose was like taking tea with the Boston Strangler. A cautious encounter.

"Mauser's in here," Jessica called back.

Victor and Rick came into the kitchen. Rick snapped his fingers and the dog turned, tail wagging, and sat down at Rick's side.

"He was licking my knee," Jessica said.

"He likes you," Rick said. He scruffled the dog's chest.

"I thought he was tasting me," Jessica said.

Rick laughed. It was a nice laugh, plump and real, which surprised Jessica. Rick was a consumptively thin twenty-seven-year-old. His cheeks bore the hollows of six years of canned food and TV dinners. He was handsome in an intense sort of way, and one suspected that his destiny was dark and tragic. No matter what season, his shoulders were always slightly hunched. He gave the impression of someone who lived in a world where chill factors never ended. "He's usually pretty good with people in their own homes," Rick said.

It was a tenuous assurance. Jessica flashed a full-toothed smile. It was the smile she'd flash if Martians landed and she wanted to show them that she was friendly too.

"He's territorial and very protective of his turf," Rick said. "Of course, anyplace he stays for more than an hour or two becomes his turf, and then he behaves more or less the way he does in my apartment."

Jessica looked quickly at the clock. "How's that?"

"Protective," Rick said. It had to be euphemism. "But once you're in the apartment, he's okay—as long as you don't move too fast, shout, or put your face near his."

"You can count on me," Jessica said. She made an okay sign.

Mauser growled.

"NO!" Rick shouted. The dog lowered his head contritely.

Jessica was impressed. Mauser outsavaged every animal she'd ever seen uncaged, and the fact that he obeyed this slim young man, who couldn't have bested him by more than ten pounds, was a mystery matched in her mind only by the inexplicable magic properties of aspirin and the aerodynamics that kept 747's aloft.

Rick explained that he had to run the dog through his training every day in order to keep him under control. He said he's always had tough dogs, but this one was the toughest. He confessed that he liked the feeling of mastery and respected Mauser's hostile indifference to the world. "He's a potential killer," Rick said.

Victor was fascinated. Jessica took a cherry pie out of the refrigerator and put it on the table. Slowly.

Rick sat, and gave Mauser a command to lie at his feet. The dog obeyed. Rick told Jessica it was the first homemade pie he'd had since Christmas.

Jessica felt pleased and told him to take the remainder home, but he refused.

"It would only intensify the void," he said. "I find it easier to live without something than to lose it."

"But eating it isn't losing it," Jessica protested.

Rick cocked his head to the side. "When you have something and then you don't have it, you've lost it—whether you eat it or it moves out of your apartment. Chicks or cherry pie, same thing."

Jessica bristled. "That's offensively sexist," she said. "There's a big difference between cherry pie and—"

There was a snarl from somewhere around Rick's boots.

Jessica lowered her voice. "Between cherry pie and chi—women."

Rick shrugged easily. "I have nothing against either, and enjoy both equally when they're offered."

"That's awful—" Jessica began loudly, then halted, hearing Mauser stir. "That's a very shitty attitude," Jessica said. "Don't you believe in love?"

"Love's cool," he said. "But I take a much more anthropological view of things. When I find a chick who's good company, a good cook, and a good lay, I'll probably team up. I want my own cave, my own clan. You can call me sexist, whatever you want, but I know my own nature and the nature of the male animal."

"We've been out of the jungle a long time," Jessica said icily.

"Have we?" said Rick. His eyes leaned hard on Jessica as he cut himself another piece of pie.

"The more I think about it," Victor said later, "the more I'm convinced we should get a guard dog."

"I hope it'll be able to wash your socks," Jessica said, "because I won't be around if you do."

"A good guard dog is nothing like Mauser," Victor assured her.

"I don't need a guard dog," Jessica said. "I need wife."

"But a well-trained guard dog is gentle and loving. He works on command."

"Big deal," Jessica said. "So does a wife. Oh, shit, now who's that?" The doorbell hawked noisily. She tossed down the socks she was pairing and went to the door.

Florence Siskand stood on the stoop holding a bell-shaped plastic umbrella and the hand of a short wet man. The short wet man was holding a small damp cake box.

"Mom!" Jessica said. "What on earth are you doing here at this hour? Come on in."

Florence Siskand towed the short wet man into the hall. "Arnold and I were at the movies. We were so close—and I've been telling him all about you—I thought we'd just pop in. Oh—excuse me. Arnold, this is my daughter, Jessica. Jess, this is Arnold Fisher."

"Nice to meet you." Jessica nodded.

"We were at the movies," Arnold said. "Your mother's been telling me all about you. We were so close we thought we'd just pop in." He handed Jessica the soggy cake box.

"We tried to get éclairs," Florence Siskand said, "But they didn't have any. I know how Victor loves them."

"Damn good thing, too," Arnold said. "These cookies cost enough."

"Mrs. Ernshweiger makes all her own pastries," Jessica said.

"Damn well better, at those prices."

"Victor," Jessica said. "This is Arnold Fisher, My husband, Victor."

The two men shook hands.

"We were at the movies," Arnold said. "Your mother-in-law's been telling me all about you. Since we were so close, we thought we'd just pop in."

"Can I take your coat?" Victor asked. "You look as if you've gotten a little wet."

"Fuckin' soaked." He handed Victor his coat, then walked into the living room.

"Isn't he cute?" Florence whispered to Jessica.

Jessica didn't answer and was relieved that her mother didn't press. Arnold Fisher was a stoop-shouldered badger. His nose, cheeks, lips, and chin all puckered forward like a fleshy muzzle. When he spoke, it sounded as if he had Kleenex wadded between his teeth. He was about as cute as a hemorrhoid.

Arnold stood in front of the bookcase and nodded. "You two must be readers, huh? I do a little myself, now and then."

"Victor is an editor."

"That so? Well, you and I have a lot in common, Vince."

"Victor," corrected Victor.

"Arnold used to be in the music business," Florence said.

"Oh."

"Novelty records," Arnold said. "You probably remember the Fangs' recording of 'I'm Dreaming of a Red Christmas.' "

"I don't think I ever—"

Arnold coughed, began to sing: *"I'm dreaming of a red Christmas, just like the ones I used to know. Where blood drops glisten and children listen to shrieks of terror in the snow. I'm—"*

"I know the tune," Victor said.

"Everyone was singing it in fifty-two. My brother-in-law and I could have built Firo, that was our corporation, into an empire if that *putz* hadn't gone into politics."

"Your brother-in-law's in politics?"

"Ran for Congressman twice," Arnold said proudly. "Poor sonofabitch didn't stand a chance, though. Not with Rocky badmouthing him all over the place." He lowered his voice. "My brother-in-law used to ball Happy."

"Happy Rockefeller?"

"You didn't hear it from me," Arnold said. "But let

me tell you, Vince, if I ever turned stoolie I'd have one helluva book for that company of yours. Right, Flossie?" He pinched Florence's waist.

Florence giggled. "Arnie's brother-in-law had quite an adventurous life."

"His shtick was political pussy, if you get what I mean. Senators' wives, comptrollers' mistresses, district representatives. It was sort of an obsession with him." Arnold cupped a hand by his mouth. "He used to jerk off to pictures of Bella Abzug."

"Would you like some coffee?" Jessica asked.

"Ethel Kennedy, too," Arnold said. "Did you say coffee?"

"Did you say Kennedy?"

"You didn't hear it from me," Arnold said. "Black, two sugars."

Florence Siskand followed her daughter into the kitchen. "What do you think of him?" she asked anxiously.

"I don't know, Mom. You haven't even been here ten minutes."

"I met him last weekend and I feel as if I've known him all my life."

"Is he divorced?" Jessica asked.

"Widowed. His wife's unveiling is next Sunday. How's that for timing?"

"Well—" Jessica began.

"Hey, Flossie!" Arnold shouted. "Bring in some of those cookies, will ya."

"Coming!" Florence nudged Jessica's arm. "Just his voice gives me goosebumps."

She sighed inwardly as her mother put the cookies on a plate.

Arnold was telling Victor a joke about a drunken

husband and a frigid wife when Jessica returned with the coffee. He whispered the punch line into Victor's ear, then broke into gastrointestinal laughter.

"No. I never heard that one before," Victor confessed.

"I got a million of 'em," Arnold said, and proceeded to eradicate any skepticism by telling one after another until Florence interceded in her children's behalf.

"Save some for next time, Arnie," she said.

Victor helped Arnold on with his coat. "You do know a lot of jokes," Victor said.

"Got a million of 'em," Arnie said.

"Worms, for Christ's sake," Victor said, slamming down the manuscript he was reading. "You'd think a marine biologist would write about something more interesting. She's probably a homely Ph.D who hates sex."

"What makes you say that?" Jessica asked.

"Look what she's devoted two years of research to." Victor flapped the manuscript. "A species of green marine worm where the female is about the size of a fat thumb and the male is microscopic. When this fat green thing has her young they swim around like all aquatic worms. If they settle down anywhere on the sea floor they grow into more fat female worms. But if they fall upon their mother's back, which is covered with a protective poisonous film to ward off marine predators, they mature into the microscopic and retiring male of the species."

"Quite a worm," Jessica said. "The study sounds interesting to me."

Victor pushed the manuscript back inside a manila folder and scrawled *Reject* on the top. "It sucks," he said.

*

The following Wednesday, when Victor returned from Buzzy's gym, Jessica was combing her hair and smiling. "Guess who'll be here any second?"

"Say it's your mother and I'll cut your tongue out."

"Marjorie Shierer," Jessica said.

"Oh, God, Jess, I'm in no mood for Bob's bitching about his salesmen."

"They've split," Jessica said brightly.

"No kidding." Victor pursed his lips contemplatively. Then he caught the gleam in Jessica's eye and shook his head. "Uh-uh."

"You always said you thought she was pretty. And you used to bug me about ironing your shirts the way she did Bob's."

"True. But those puns of hers drive me up the wall. I still remember walking into the one about the Chinese food named after a shrink—Egg Foo Jung. Argggh."

"I like a sense of humor," Jessica said.

"So do I," Victor said. "That's the point."

"You haven't seen her in a while," Jessica protested. "Give her a chance."

The doorbell rang.

"I should have been a priest," Victor said, and went to pour himself a drink.

"Marjorie! Come on in!"

Marjorie Shierer was an ample but trim woman in her early thirties with an obsession for thin metallic bracelets. Whenever she entered a room it sounded like the Prisoner of Zenda being dragged from the dungeon. Jessica braced for the clatter as Marjorie hugged her.

"Like the cat said, 'You can't keep meow-t!' " Marjorie laughed.

Jessica hoped that Victor was safely out of earshot.

"I feel so strange being here without Bob," Marjorie said when they were seated in the living room. "Ten years is a long time, you know."

"I didn't realize you were married that long."

"It seems longer to me," Marjorie said. "He's being a bastard about everything. You should have seen him when we were dividing up the records. He got really nasty when I refused to let him have our Beatle collection. God, am I happy he's out of my life. No more waiting for the bathroom—he used to read the whole goddam sports section in there! No more tugs-of-war for the covers. I can't believe I don't have a shirt to iron when I get up in the morning. Do you know what a pleasure it is to have a tube of toothpaste that isn't scrunched in the middle?"

"You always seemed so happy."

"Façade. Oh, sure, Bob could tune in to my moods. He always knew what would make me happy or sad or angry and sometimes he'd even know what I wanted before I did. But let's face it, he never really knew me as a person. I finally realized he never would."

Victor excused himself and went into the kitchen.

"Being single again is really great. I can go to any movie I want whenever I want to, watch what I want on TV, blast the radio on Sunday morning, have my girlfriends over anytime at all. And it's nice to be— well, you know—a woman again. To be able to go out with different interesting men."

"Have you met many?" Jessica asked.

Marjorie hesitated. "Frankly—no. Actually, the guys I've been meeting have been drips. Not even my cooking puts any life in them. I used to think a little oven went a long way—hell, Bob just about got erections from my *gnocchi*—but the guys I've had over recently don't know the difference between béchamel sauce and bicarbonate of soda. No wonder they're single. All the good ones are married. Not that I want to get married again right away—I want my freedom and fun—but I would like to meet someone viable." She leaned toward Jessica. "Just between you and me, I'm horny. I haven't found one guy yet who's good in bed. The other night I got so drunk and depressed that I almost called Bob. I hate to admit it, but I've bought a vibrator."

"I imagine you do have to make a lot of adjustments," Jessica said tactfully. "Bob's probably got his problems, too."

"God, yes. He's down to taking out flighty little twenty-year-olds, I hear. I mean girls with all the depth of a saucer. I don't know how he does it. If I were a man I'd be bored silly." She told Jessica she wouldn't want to be twenty again if they paid her, and spent the remainder of the evening justifying the statement, raptly quoting Simone de Beauvoir and Princess Grace of Monaco.

As she was leaving, Marjorie thanked Jessica for letting her unburden herself, admitting with some sadness that many of her married girlfriends had cut down on their invitations now that she was single again.

"Ridiculous," said Jessica, and with the magnanimity of inspired forethought invited Marjorie to join her and Victor for a night on the town the following week.

It was going to be a big night on the town. Expensive. It was a long shot but it could work. It used to work on Jessica. She and Victor would spend so much money on Marjorie that she wouldn't have the nerve to say no to them.

*

Dinner at Lutèce was more successful than Jessica had hoped it would be, and more expensive than Victor had feared it could be. Marjorie, who never could handle wine, was knotting napkins into phalluses by the time they were ready to leave for the theater.

The show was an off-Broadway farce called *Crock*. According to the critics, its only noteworthy feature was a particularly erotic third act where a baptism turns into an orgy, which was enough for Jessica.

Marjorie was enthralled.

By the time the three of them left the theater, Marjorie was snuggling playfully against Victor, joking about borrowing him for the night.

Jessica suggested a nightcap.

"Why that's the nicest proposition I've had all night," Marjorie said.

"The night's young," Victor said.

Marjorie giggled.

While Victor walked Abby, who'd babysat, to the bus, Jessica, imbued with confidence and goaded by high hopes, lured Marjorie into a discussion of act three of *Crock* and erogenous zones.

"I personally don't believe in erogenous zones," Marjorie said, trying to look serious and stand at the same time.

Jessica handed her a brandy.

"It's who's stroking you, not what's being stroked, that does it," she said. "Before I met Bob, I used to go out with this guy, Winkie. His father was Miss Tress bras?"

Jessica shrugged. The name meant nothing to her.

"You've seen their ads: 'From A to triple E, Miss

Tress makes you a special she? I still have a drawerful from Winkie. Anyway, where were we?"

"Erogenous zones," Jessica said.

"Oh—yes. Well, Winkie was one of those pseudo-sophisticated Casanovas who learned how to make love from paperback novels. His idea of foreplay was to use his tongue like a roto-rooter in your ears and then slip a finger between your legs. But his big target was nipples. He was convinced that they were the most erogenous zones and that biting a girl's nipple would throw her into orgasmic frenzy. He used to tell me that there was something, psychologically wrong with me every time I screamed."

"You really screamed?" Jessica asked.

"Goddamn right I screamed," Marjorie said. "Once—actually the last time I saw him—I kneed him in the balls. It wasn't until I met Bob that I realized what Winkie obviously didn't—that there was a difference between biting a nipple and biting the cap off a beer bottle. In other words, it's not what's being bitten, but who's doing the biting that counts."

When Victor returned, Marjorie was on her third brandy and half off the living room couch.

"We were discussing erogenous zones," Jessica told him.

"My favorite subject," Victor said.

"If I really stop to think about it," Marjorie said, "I guess I do have one or two." She covered her mouth with her hand. "But I'm embarrassed."

"Come on," Victor chided. "You're among friends."

Marjorie tittered. "I'm embarrassed because they're so silly. One, believe it or not, is the tip of my nose."

Victor moved forward wagging his finger.

"No, no," Marjorie squealed. "I mean it." She buried her face in her hands as Victor approached.

"Come on, Marjorie," Victor said. "Just a little touch—for an old friend?"

Marjorie laughed, scrambled up on all fours, and pushed her face into the couch pillows like a dog sniffing for a bone.

"Okay, truce," Victor said. He sat down on the end of the couch.

Marjorie raised her head slowly, suspiciously. Then she sat up and laughed until tears rolled down her cheeks. Jessica brought her another brandy.

Marjorie chugged it down. "Boy, would Bob have a fit if he could see me drinking like this. I really shouldn't have any more." She turned to Jessica. "I have to leave, but it was a fabulous evening. I don't know how to thank you."

Jessica smiled benignly.

Marjorie rose unsteadily to her feet, keeping one hand on Victor's shoulder to retain her balance. "It was just grand. You'll have to come to my place for dinner soon. Okay?"

Victor nodded.

"Those snails tonight were great. The whole dinner was great. God, it must have cost you a fortune. I feel wonderful and awful at the same time. All that money! I haven't done much entertaining since Bob and I split, but I really would like to reciprocate."

"Don't you worry about it," Victor said. And with that, he placed his finger very gently on the tip of Marjorie's nose.

"Er—um . . . oh, my." She looked from Victor to Jessica. "I—um—I've never done this before, you know."

"Neither have we," Jessica lied.

"Gee, I don't know if we should—"

"Of course we should," Jessica said, knowing that Victor had shelled out $150 to insure that they did. She gave Marjorie's nose a tap, for luck, and led her to the stairs.

When they reached the bedroom, Marjorie said: "Wouldn't Bob just die if he knew?"

Victor looked as if someone had just sprayed him with a garden hose. He seemed to recover quickly, but Jessica suddenly grew uneasy. Randolph, usually a bulwark of solidarity, had been getting temperamental lately. Jessica had attributed it to Victor's heavy gym schedule, and had ignored it with a courtesan's delicacy. Damn that Marjorie. She might just be too much of a wife.

They undressed with the light on and, except for mild sexual anticipation, with the locker-room ease of old swimming-team buddies.

Marjorie was bouncier than Jessica had expected. She whipped off her clothes like a weekender at a nudist camp and jumped onto the bed. She had an uninspired though not unattractive body. Rubenesque. Her longish and piquantly melancholy breasts were emblazoned with large brown soulful nipples, and her auburn pubic hair was manicured into a perfectly contained triangle. Divested of all embarrassment by alcohol and the sheer novelty of the situation, Marjorie stared brightly at Jessica and Victor.

Jessica threw an anxious glance at Victor and was pleasantly relieved. It was not unlike the relief she felt as a hostess when everything was ready by the time the guests arrived. Ever since that first time with Marilyn, she'd become increasingly aware of a certain obligatory protocol. There were, after all, amenities to be observed.

"I never realized how similarly you and Bob were built," Marjorie said, her gaze now a relentless appraisal. "It's remarkable."

Victor coughed, mumbled something, and went to the bed.

Jessica clutched, felt the sinking sensation of opening-night amnesia. She dared not look at Victor, and her apprehension mounted when he flipped out the light before she'd even gotten on the bed.

"Ooo, it's scary-dirty," Marjorie said, giggling. "Oh . . . oooo . . . whose hand is this?"

"Mine," Victor said tightly. "You're squeezing my ring against my fingers."

"Is that really you, Victor? I always thought you were hairier . . . oooo . . . no, not there, it tickles . . . ha-ha-ha. . . ." Marjorie's laugh churned the darkness like a boat propeller caught in the mud. "Oh, Victor, you devil . . . oh, Oh, ha, ha, ha . . . I'm going to get you for that. . . . Gotcha!"

There was a muffled grunt from Victor.

"Oh, I'm sorry." Marjorie laughed. "I didn't mean—oh, wow, Jessica, that feels terrific . . . a little to the right, though . . . no, down a little . . . mmmmmm, yes. Christ, I wish that Bob and I had thought of something like this . . . oh, Victor, don't stop—or is that you, Jess? . . . Oooo . . . I feel like a ping-pong ball . . . ha-ha-ha."

Jessica felt as sensuous as a dead eel. She dared not even speculate about Victor. There was nothing to do but press on and hope for the best.

"Mmmm . . . well, *now* we're getting somewhere . . . Mmmmm," Marjorie said huskily.

Jessica filled with new respect for Victor. She couldn't see exactly what was going on, but Marjorie was growing quieter and breathing heavier.

Then the phone rang.

Marjorie jumped up. "Oh, my God!"

"It's only the phone," Jessica said.

Victor fumbled for the light switch, cursing.

"But it's so late," Marjorie said. "It has to be bad news."

Victor picked up the receiver, said hello, and then groaned. "No, no, I won't," he said tiredly. "I understand. Good-bye." He hung up the phone and got out of bed and put on his trousers.

"What is it?" Marjorie asked.

"Beverly Davis," Victor said, putting on his socks.

"Not again?" Jessica said.

"What's this all about?" Marjorie asked nervously.

"Beverly Davis is a friend of ours," Jessica said. "She's just swallowed six tins of Midol. Is there a match over there?"

"How can you be so calm?" Marjorie fairly shrieked. "She could . . . she could die."

Marjorie was starting to panic. "Aren't you going to do something?"

"Victor's going to take her to St. Vincent's."

"Where's my green sweater?" Victor asked.

"Look in the bottom drawer, or maybe in the closet."

"My God," Marjorie said. "A girl's life is at stake. How can you worry about what to wear?" She began to pull nervously on her lip.

"I think we might as well call it a night," Jessica said. Marjorie was obviously useless in a crisis. If she couldn't even deal with a remote emergency, how could

Jessica be confident that she'd be able to cope if something, God forbid, should happen to Aaron? No. Marjorie Shierer was not going to be their wife.

"Victor's going downtown, Marge. He'll be able to drop you off."

Marjorie was out of the bed and dressed before Victor had his shoes on. "Hurry," she urged.

"I'll be back as soon as I can," Victor said. He leaned over and kissed Jessica on the forehead. "A hundred and fifty fucking dollars," he whispered sweetly.

"I love you," said Jessica.

CHAPTER 12

Lilly Ernshweiger had been arrested.

The New York Times gave the story a small factual paragraph on page forty-three; it was a headliner in the *Daily News.*

BLUE BOYS BUST LIBBERS ARSENAL

There was a photo of Lilly, her crullerlike braid askew, handcuffed between two policemen. She was sneering at the camera. The caption beneath the photographs said: "THAT'S THE WAY THE COOKIE CRUMBLES: Sixty-four-year-old femnist baker and Congressional hopeful, Lilly Ernshweiger, being taken into custody after discovery of arms cache in oven." The story was on page three.

BUNS AND GUNS

THAT TAKES THE CAKE

An anonymous phone call from a man who identified himself as a women's lib widower led to a raid on Ernshweiger's Bakery at 2466 Broadway early this morning. Ms. Ernshweiger, described by her neighbors as "nice, but a big mouth," was alone in the shop when the police arrived. She is alleged to have hurled a tray of apple turnovers at the officers, injuring one of them, Sgt. George Schlegal, who was taken to Roosevelt Hospital for treatment.

A search of the bakery revealed a cache of arms concealed in an inoperative open. "I've never seen anything like it," said one of the officers, referring to the hidden arsenal, which included 2 Uzi 9mm submachine guns, a Stoner gun which was described as a "military pinch-hitter for a bomb", three shotguns, two .22 caliber pistols, six Daisy air rifles, a gross of 5-inch hatpins, and six hundred rounds of ammunition. Also discovered in the bakery was a raft of radical feminist literature from a group calling themselves the C——ts, and the outline for a proposed kidnapping of the Mayor's wife, with diagrams of bus and subway stations near Gracie Mansion. Ms. Ernshweiger, the sixty-four-year-old estranged wife of a telephone lineman and mother of two, who announced her candidacy for Congress last week, is being held on $50,000 bail.

When Celia stopped by Jessica's house later that afternoon she looked wilted. "Damn Cunts," she said. "How they managed to get hold of Lilly I'll never know. I've been on the phone all morning. Sharon finally reached Hippolyte about an hour ago and she's agreed to help. We're thinking of a demonstration to raise the bail money."

"I thought Hippolyte opposed the Cunts," Jessica said.

"Well . . . she does. We all do, *in practice*, but let's

not get into that. Lilly's been used. It was a setup. She's a political prisoner and we can't let her down. We're going to need some good press, strong advance publicity, slogans. That's where you come in."

"Me?"

"We need hard-core appeals, ones that will make women feel they can't live with themselves if they don't give—and give generously."

"I don't know if I can do it, Celia. I'm overloaded with Rubicon work now."

"Screw it," Celia said hotly. "Lilly Ernshweiger's worth a dozen junkies. She's not just any woman— she's all women. If she's in jail, we're all prisoners." Celia rose and laid a hand on Jessica's shoulder. "Remember, Jess, no matter what happens to you in this life, you'll always be a woman."

Mike Halprin leaned back in his chair and put his feet up on the desk. He was wearing a paisley shirt open to the waist; a copper mandala on a chain, which he wore often, nestled enticingly in the faintly silvering black thatch on his chest. Whenever he'd say something sexually suggestive, even mildly flirtatious, his finger flicked the mandala. It had not gone unnoticed by Jessica that he'd been flicking the mandala for the past five minutes.

"My approach on the letters to the committee was all right, then?" Jessica asked.

"Your approach to everything is all right," Mike said.

"I'll remind you of that next time you wield your red pencil," Jessica said. She picked up the folder on the desk. "When do you need this? Wait, don't tell me, I know. Tomorrow."

"Hey, that's really strange," Mike said. He flicked the mandala.

"What's strange?"

"You said the same thing in my dream last night." He smiled. "It was quite a dream. You delivered some work to my apartment wearing nothing but a see-through dress. You told me your back hurt, and I, uh, gave you a massage, and, uh, well one thing led to another. I, um, hated to wake up."

Jessica felt the flush take her cheeks and cringed inwardly. Mike was using the same approach she'd read in "How I Met My Husband," the same approach she'd used on poor Paula Kramer!

She looked at her watch, quickly mumbled something about being late. Mike was still fiddling with his mandala.

Victor phoned around two to say that he had tickets for a concert that night at Lincoln Center. Jessica had no desire to hear a thirteen-year-old prodigy play the complete Brandenburg concerti on a flute, but she and Victor had spent very little time together since his physical fitness regimen began, and it seemed like a good idea. If he was willing to give up a night at Buzzy's, it was the least she could do.

She spent the remainder of the afternoon winding up Aaron's putt-putt train and outlining the Free Lilly Ernshweiger campaign. Neither activity pleased her, and around four o'clock she found herself drifting into fantasies of appearing at Mike Halprin's apartment with a backache.

She wondered if Mike fingered his mandala in bed.

She was frustrated, guilty, and late with dinner when Victor came home.

Victor was euphoric. Faraday was beginning to show strong interest in the *Labroides Dimidatus* book.

"I think he's considering it seriously as a list leader," Victor said as he changed his shirt.

"Either he is or he isn't."

"You don't understand Faraday. He's not an is or isn't person. You have to read him between the lines. He stopped at my desk twice today and mentioned the book. That's a damn good indication."

The bell rang. "That's Abby," Jessica said. "Can you get the door? I'll be ready in about three minutes."

"Minutes?" said Victor.

Jessica bridled at the implication, but said nothing, since she knew it was true. All she ever accomplished successfully in three minutes was a soft-boiled egg and self-induced orgasm, and sometimes even the latter ran a bit over, depending on circumstances. She hurried her makeup, smudging her mascara, which left a shadowy, racoonlike circle beneath her left eye.

"Fuck it," she said softly, and went downstairs.

The concert bored Jessica painfully. Victor was enjoying it, so she forced herself to stay awake and appear entertained. She did this by tilting her head to the side and staring hard into empty space. It was a trick she'd learned in college lecture halls, perfected in front rows.

Victor leaned over and whispered, "Do you have a headache?"

"No. Do you?" Jessica asked—hopefully.

"No," Victor said. "But you look funny."

It had been a long time since college. Jessica added a smile to her tilted head and hard stare. This placated Victor, and he ignored her for the remainder of the performance, which for Jessica was an Herculean ordeal. She retreated into her head and began to work on Free Lilly Ernshweiger slogans. All she could come up with was: Don't geld our Lilly! It lacked something. In the middle of the second concerto she launched an affair with Mike Halprin. By the end of the concert she was a sheaf of ganglia braided with raw guilt. She hated herself for not having enjoyed the performance, for pretending that she had enjoyed it, for letting Mike Halprin go down on her while she held Victor's hand.

Abby was curled up asleep on the couch when they returned. Jessica touched her shoulder gently and she opened her eyes and smiled.

"I must have fallen out a second ago," Abby said. "Sorry about that."

"Aaron has a healthy pair of lungs," Jessica said. "If he needed you, you'd know it. How did everything go?"

Abby sat up. "Perfect. As usual."

"I'm going to have a drink," Jessica said. "Victor? Abby?"

Victor nodded.

"Alcohol changes your natural chemistry," Abby said. "It's bad for your liver."

"Salt's bad for my kidneys. Smoking's bad for my lungs. Cholesterol's bad for my heart. I'm tired of living for my organs," Jessica said. "I want a drink." She went to the kitchen.

"There are some cookies on the stove," Abby called after her. "I got into a real baking thing. Hope you don't mind."

"Mind? You've got to be kidding—Abby! What have you done?"

The kitchen, which had been a wreck when Jessica

had left earlier, was immaculate. Not only had all the dishes been washed and put away, but the chrome on the cabinet handles and faucets shone, and Aaron's silver baby cup, which Jessica used as a receptacle for rubber bands, baggie ties, and pennies, had been polished to Cartier luster.

Abby came up behind her. "I wasn't into watching the tube. Besides, it's fun playing house. I like it. I cleaned your sugar bowl and refilled it, too." She took one of the cookies from the tray and bit into it. "Good cookies, if I say so myself."

Jessica tried one. "Delicious. Victor! Come in here."

Victor entered and blinked. "Wow! What happened here?"

"I'm basically a very oral Gemini," Abby said. "But I have an anal-retentive streak that betters me sometimes."

Victor took his glass. "Here's to your anal-retentive streak."

"I second that," Jessica said.

Abby lifted the hair at the sides of her face with her thumbs and flipped it back. "I'm on kitchen detail at the commune a lot, but it's not as much fun. I enjoy doing it here. Like, you've got a real house, if you know what I mean."

"I don't," Jessica confessed, "but I'll take your word for it."

Abby leaned back against the counter, scratched her stomach. She wore jeans and a skimpy blue pullover that hiked up and exposed a wide band of mocha-smooth skin every time she raised her arm. Jessica was suddenly conscious of herself waiting for Abby to raise her arm again.

"You know," Abby said, "a *real* house, with electric

mixers and Wonder Bread and shit food like Fritos. That's what I mean. Don't get me wrong. I dig the commune. It's just not a home." She yawned and raised her hand to cover her mouth. Jessica noticed that Victor had become aware of the discrepancy between Abby's jeans and pullover.

The idea sprang into Jessica's head. She bounced it back. Abby? *Abby?* Out of the question!

Abby stretched and yawned again. "I'd better start moving or I'll fall asleep right here. It's past my bedtime."

"It's only twelve," Victor said. "When do you usually go to sleep?"

"I'm a day person. Once the sun goes down, my natural rhythms start drumming me toward the nearest bed."

"There's one right upstairs," Victor said.

"I'll take it."

"Uh"—Victor stammered—"are you serious?"

Abby raised an eyebrow and lowered her lids. "Are you?"

Victor turned to Jessica. "Am I serious?"

"Victor's always serious," Jessica said blankly.

"I'm always serious," Victor said.

"Groovy," said Abby. "You lead the way."

It all happened as naturally and amazingly as photosynthesis. Abby had an easy confidence in her being, in her body. She walked to the bed, sat, and kicked off her shoes with the happy comfort of a traveler returning after weeks of Holiday Inns.

Jessica and Victor were too overwhelmed to be self-conscious. Victor's eyes had the glaze of a three-year-old seeing Santa Claus for the first time and Jessica was hung on the brink of saying something that refused to come forth. An unsophisticate viewing the scene would have been convinced the man with the glazed eyes and the woman with the frozen, slightly parted lips were the victims of mild botulism.

Abby stood, stretched, and began to peel off her clothes. As she ducked out from under her pullover, revealing two wholesome and perky cheerleader breasts, she laughed happily.

"Hey, no fair," she said. "What about you two?"

Jessica realized that neither she nor Victor had moved since Abby's first shoe had hit the floor. They both flushed and started undressing. Jessica yanked the zipper at the back of her dress too quickly and snagged it, though it wasn't until Abby asked if she were having trouble that she realized she'd been tugging at it for several minutes.

"I know how to talk to zippers," Abby said. "Let me." She crossed to Jessica, her breasts jogging with a pre-game bounce, her jeans unsnapped and exposing a flawlessly creamy belly. As she pulled at the zipper, her nipples brushed against Jessica's back. For the first time in years, Jessica was frightened by her own feelings.

"There," Abby said, pleased. "Free at last." She looked at Victor, grinned mischievously. "You're pretty slow. Having trouble with your zipper, too?" She started for him and he unconsciously gripped the front of his pants. This seemed to delight her. She raised arms. "No zipper problem for me. Watch." She whirled around and wriggled her jeans to the floor. "Ta-ta!" She stepped from them and tossed them on a chair. "Betcha a dollar you can't beat that," she said.

"Oh, yeah?" said Victor, and he released his hold on the trousers. They shot to the floor, weighted by keys and change and a breath spray called Sudden Action that rolled across the carpet and under the bureau before he could stop it.

"Not bad," Abby said. She turned to Jessica. "What about you?"

Jessica stepped between Abby and Victor and bowed her head. "Gypsy Rose Prior is here," she said. She lowered one shoulder and then the other, shrugging until the top of the dress fell to her waist; then, clasping her hands behind her head, she bumped her hips until the dress lay at her feet.

Abby clapped, then jumped up onto the bed. Standing there, shifting her weight, she took off her bikini panties and pitched them to Victor.

He reached out and caught them without looking. His eyes didn't leave Abby. She stood with her legs apart, her hands on her boyishly slim hips and her long black hair trailing down over her shoulders and breasts. "Well?" she said, and thrust her diminutive dark triangle forward with the sassiness of a schoolgirl's tongue.

Victor whipped off his shorts. The weeks at Buzzy's had paid off handsomely, and he knew it. His stomach was trim and hard and his chest and biceps had burgeoned with unmistakable power. Randolph himself extended with new ramrod surety.

Jessica was impressed. Proud. She slipped from her panties and joined Abby on the bed.

Victor stood at the foot of the bed and looked from Abby to Jessica and then back again.

"Thank God," he said. "Thank God."

"Thank God—what?" Jessica asked.

"Thank God that I don't have to choose," he said. And with that he flung himself upon them. Hooking Jessica with one arm and Abby with the other, he said,

"I knew that not walking under ladders would pay off someday."

And then the three of them were kissing.

Jessica was overwhelmed by the trio of mouths, by the utterly pleasurable sensual dynamics of it all. Abby hugged Jessica with the same youthful fervor with which she clasped Victor, and Victor stroked and fondled both women as if they were halves of a wondrous female whole.

The tripartite foreplay seemed to go on for hours. And when Victor made love to Abby, they both held Jessica so closely to them that the fact that he was actually inside one and not the other was only a technicality.

They reveled in each other until dawn clouded the darkness, and then slept dreamlessly burrowed together like exhausted puppies.

Jessica smelled bacon and fresh coffee. She opened her eyes and saw that Victor was still asleep. Smiling. Abby was gone. The digital clock said that it was Thursday, that Victor was a half hour late for work.

"Wake up." She nudged him.

He mumbled something and reached out for her breast.

Jessica gently brushed his hand away. "We've overslept. You're late."

"Huh, what?" Victor shook his head and sat up. "Holy Christ! Nine thirty. How did that happen? What about Aaron?"

"I don't know," Jessica said. She hadn't heard a "pee-pee."

"Good morning." Abby stood in the doorway, smiling, holding two glasses of orange juice. Her hair was drawn back in a ponytail that gave her a regal, equine sleekness.

She handed Jessica and Victor their juice. "Aaron and I have been playing trains in the living room. The bacon's done. Just tell me how you like your eggs."

"Abby—" Victor began.

She interrupted. "I called your office and told them that you wouldn't be in until eleven, so how do you want your eggs?"

Victor blinked repeatedly.

"Over easy?" Abby suggested.

Victor nodded.

"Jess?"

Jessica gaped. She could not coordinate thought and speech. Her mind balked at every attempt to force it into functioning. The only thing she could think to say was, "Will you marry me?"

Abby's cheeks dimpled. She leaned over, kissed Jessica and Victor. "I thought you'd never ask."

CHAPTER 13

Abby was the perfect wife.

No matter when Jessica arrived home, cocktail glasses were chilled, dinner was ready, and Aaron was bathed and happy. Never having had any domestic role model, Abby emulated the cheerful prototypes she saw on TV commercials. She wore an apron whenever she was in the kitchen, served even soup and sandwiches on a table set with crystal and tall tapers. So dedicated was she to perfecting her wifely image that once, when Jessica spilled something, Abby actually said, "Oh, my! Lucky I waxed with Mirrorcoat," and whipped out a superabsorbent paper towel to wipe it up with. Smiling.

She seemed to joy in learning Jessica's habits and tastes as well as Victor's and thrived on catering to them. The butter for Jessica's toast was always just soft enought for spreading, Victor's grapefruit was never too cold. She arranged gourmet meals so inexpensively that Jessica suspected she was shoplifting until Abby showed her the prices of the items on paper. She loved taking Aaron to the park, loved sex, loved Sloan's. Heaven.

Freed from housewifely shackles, Jessica moved easily into her new routine at Rubicon. Mike Halprin's initial distress at losing Abby was quickly obliterated by his delight at having Jessica full-time. Jessica had explained that she'd hired Abby as an *au pair*, and Mike had no reason to doubt it. Despite Jessica's basic Honesty-In-Living credo, which was as ingrained a part of her as Jessica Truths of Life, she felt it wiser to omit details.

Her only difficulty in readjusting to a career was coping with Mike's libido. Somehow her constant presence seemed to stoke his loins. It was impossible, the first two weeks, to sustain a fifteen-minute conversation without his tossing in a least one double entendre or a suggestive remark. Jessica countered by pretending not to understand them. When Mike finally eased off, she found herself wondering if he'd given up because he thought she was too stupid to bother with. This disturbed her, and every so often after that she'd inject small sexual references just to keep things interesting.

One Thursday night, after Abby had been living with them for three weeks, Jessica returned home and was surprised to find Victor sitting on the floor playing with Aaron.

"Don't you have bowling tonight?" Jessica asked.

"I've decided to drop it," Victor said. "Too much of a hassle. Besides, with Faraday getting ready to put everything behind *Girls Will Be Boys*, I don't want to spread myself too thin."

"Isn't that great?" Abby said. "About Faraday, I mean." She kissed Jessica.

"Uh—sure," Jessica dropped a manila folder of papers on the coffee table and sat down next to Aaron.

"How was work today?" Abby asked.

"We're getting the allotment from the mayor's committee." Aaron crawled onto her lap and reached for her earrings.

"No-no," Abby said, gently taking Aaron's hands and drawing them down. She handed him a toy. "Are you hungry?" she asked Jessica.

"Not really."

"Dinner will be ready in five minutes."

"Oh—I guess I can work up an appetite."

Aaron threw the toy on the floor and reached again for his mother's earrings. Abby picked him up and sat him in front of his putt-putt trains. "Now don't bother Mommy. Play nicely."

"That's all right, Ab."

"He shouldn't be allowed to do things like that. If he gets away with it, he'll keep doing it. It's the sort of thing kids do that annoys people."

"I'm not people," Jessica said, more seriously than she'd intended. "I'm his mother."

"I'm famished," said Victor.

"Jess, why don't you get Aaron into his pajamas and read him a story while I set the table." Abby hoisted Aaron into the air and handed him to Jessica.

"But it's not his bedtime yet," Jessica said.

"I've cut his nap down to an hour so he can get more sleep at night. It's really better for him."

"But that won't give me much time to play with him when I get home."

"Too much excitement before bedtime is no good for a child. Even Spock says so."

"She's right, you know," Victor said, gently.

"I suppose." Jessica kissed Aaron's head. "Do you want Mommy to read you a book?"

Aaron bounced excitedly. "Mommy read you a book. Mommy read you a book."

"Mommy read *me* a book," Jessica corrected, pointing his finger at his chest. Aaron could not comprehend the dichotomy of pronouns used in reference to himself. His mother called him "you" and herself "me," why shouldn't he? This was particularly upsetting when a surprise that was supposed to delight him would end up as a catalyst for a tantrum. If he'd say, "Give to you," and Jessica corrected him, he'd start wailing with plaintive incomprehension. Toilets and pronouns anathematized Aaron's life.

The corners of Aaron's mouth began to quiver.

"Forget it." Jessica lifted him in her arms and went upstairs. He could always point.

Abby made tacos for dinner. It was one of Victor's favorite meals, despite the fact that he was allergic to chili; allergic to any spice more exotic than pepper. Victor's reaction was profuse perspiration. Once, in an East Indian restaurant, he perspired so heavily that the waiter, a pre-med student at Columbia, was convinced Victor was having a heart attack and lunged to loosen his belt buckle. Not realizing the youth's good intentions, Victor had slugged him in the stomach. Explanations afterward were of little consolation to the youth and his father, who owned the restaurant, and Victor was asked not to return. After that, Victor always laughingly explained his allergy to waiters or others at the table before he took a bite. He still looked as if he'd just run the three-minute mile when he ate, but at least no one was upset about it.

As his forehead beaded, Victor explained his allergy to Abby. She felt terrible even though he repeated how much he loved Mexican food and kept apologizing for his sweat throughout the meal.

After dinner the three played Scrabble. The game

broke up when Abby added *ing* to Jessica's *screw* and Victor thought it was a great idea.

Jessica followed them up to the bedroom, secretly miffed. It was rare that she beat Victor in Scrabble and she'd been winning. Also, difficult as it was to admit, she was tired of nightly three-way sex.

Working at Rubicon was exhausting both emotionally and physically. Before Abby had come to live with them, there had been many nights when either she or Victor didn't feel like making love and told the other so. But Abby had changed all that. She was lusty and eager and seemed to inspire equivalent feelings in Victor. Though Jessica several times had felt like saying, "You two go on without me," she just couldn't. No matter how she rationalized, she was indeed guilty of the two cardinal lib sins: competitiveness and faking it. Though the latter was rarer than the former, it was nonetheless a fact. Jessica was determined to match Abby orgasm for orgasm, and God, it was draining her.

It was draining her more and more every night. Abby liked prolonged foreplay, prolonged enough for her to have at least three orgasms *before* intercourse. And after the first week she'd said so. Not demandingly, but in such a way that both Jessica and Victor were conscious of it being incumbent upon them to fulfill the precoital quota. Abby said the first three were just throwaways.

Their wife, they'd soon discovered, was a talker. Everything she experienced in bed was promptly and clearly vocalized, as if it were all being recorded for science: "Ooooh, you're licking my nipple," "Wow, I'm rubbing your cunt," "Now I'm on top of Victor and he's throbbing inside me, and you're touching me."

Most disconcerting was her verbal countdown to orgasm: "I'm getting there . . . I'm shifting into stage two . . . I'm past the point of no return . . . It's going to go . . . Any minute now . . . I'm going to make it . . . Here it comes . . . I'm coming . . . NOW!"

And every orgasm was evaluated immediately afterward in, oddly enough, terms of food. Abby had "ham sandwich" orgasms and "prime porterhouse steak" orgasms, even "marshmallow sundae with hot fudge, whipped cream, sprinkles and cherries" orgasms. The "marshmallow sundae" ones invariably made Jessica jealous and Victor too cocky for his own good.

When they climbed into bed, Jessica found herself wishing that she were enough of a sexist to make love on *her* terms, wishing that she'd have a "marshmallow sundae" orgasm too.

Jessica awoke early the next morning and tiptoed downstairs, so as not to wake Aaron. She wanted to sit alone with a cup of coffee, not have to smile, not have to respond in any way. The pot wasn't on the counter, and when she looked in the cabinet where it was usually kept, it wasn't there. She was annoyed. Where the hell— She opened the other cabinets and found that Abby had reorganized everything: glasses in the dish cabinet, dishes where she usually kept the canned foods.

"Whatcha looking for?" Abby asked sleepily. She was holding Aaron and trying with one hand to tie the housecoat she was wearing.

Florence Siskand had brought the housecoat back from Hawaii for Jessica two years ago. It was an expensive kimono, silk with a delicate floral pattern, slits on the side, and very sexy. It was the most intimate gift Florence had ever bought her daughter. Usually

Jessica's mother's benevolence was utilitarian: warm jackets, thermal socks, ashtrays. Jessica prized the wrap and wore it only on special occasions. Seeing Abby draw it around herself so casually, Jessica felt a stab of resentment but said nothing. She took Aaron and hugged him.

"Where's the coffeepot?" Jessica asked.

Abby went to the cabinet beside the stove, where Jessica usually kept the frying pans and took out the coffeepot. "I rearranged the closets so things would be easier to find. You had the glasses and cups way over there. See"—she opened a cabinet and took out two mugs—"Isn't it easier this way?"

"I guess it is."

"Want toast?" Abby asked.

"Love it."

Abby made the toast, Aaron's egg, and poured Jessica's coffee while Jessica sat at the table and played with Aaron.

"It's seven thirty," Abby said. "I'd better wake Victor."

"Don't bother. I'll do it when I finish my coffee."

"No bother. You relax." She kissed Jessica's cheek. "He likes my backrubs. He told me yesterday that I was better than Jesus."

"Huh? Oh, at the gym."

"I'm really getting good at it."

"I'll bet," Jessica said, and was instantly chagrined at the frost she heard in her own words. She came back quickly with effusive praise for the coffee and was exonerated by Abby's smile.

As Jessica was leaving, the phone rang. Abby answered it.

"Just a second. I'll see if she's left yet."

Jessica walked back into the kitchen. Abby handed her the phone. Abby shrugged.

"Hello?"

"Jess? Is this you?" Florence Siskand asked.

"It's me, Mom. How's everything?"

"Who was that before?"

"Abby. She's—um—taking care of Aaron. She's living with us."

"Living with you? Where? Since when?"

"Few weeks. I've gone back to working full-time."

Florence's voice grew serious. "Things are bad with Victor's job?"

"No, of course not. I just couldn't sit home anymore."

"I see," Florence said, in the tone that Jessica knew meant she didn't understand at all. "So who's the girl?"

"She's very nice. Young, capable, I knew her from Rubicon."

"Pretty?"

"Yes."

"Jess—" Florence drew out the name. "Is that smart? I know Victor is a good man and he loves you a lot, but he's only a man, if you know what I mean."

"I know what you mean, Mom," Jessica said curtly, "and I'm ashamed of you even thinking things like that about Victor."

"Don't get upset. But looking at pretty young girls and living with them are two different things. Just because you're not afraid of lightning doesn't mean you should stand out in a field and wave spears at it. You're over thirty, Jess."

"I'm going to be late for work, Mom."

"All right. I won't keep you. I was just calling to say

that Arnold and I were going to be in your neighborhood tonight and I wanted to know if you'd be home."

"No," Jessica said quickly. "I—er—we're going to the Remson's for dinner." Jessica didn't like to lie, but the thought of Arnold made it easier. "Maybe another time. How are you going with Arnold?"

Florence grew girlish. "You could say we're more than just friends. I don't think it's right to say anything yet, but I might be calling in a week or two with some surprising news."

"That's great."

"We'll see, we'll see," Florence said. "Speaking of calling, have you spoken to your brother lately?"

"No. Is anything wrong?"

"Does something have to be wrong for a sister to call her brother? It would be nice, that's all."

"I have nothing to say to Howard. Besides, he could call me, too, you know."

"Sylvia told me that he's been so busy this past month that he hasn't even been playing golf."

"I'm working now too, Mom."

"That's different."

"I really have to go, Mom. I'll give you a call next week."

"All right. Go, go. Kiss the little one for me."

"Take care, Mom. Bye." Jessica hung up the receiver. She leaned against the wall and shook her head.

Abby looked at her questioningly.

"Every time I speak to my mother I'm keenly aware that there are definite advantages to being an orphan." Jessica picked up her manila folder. "See you tonight." She gave Aaron a big hug and started for the door.

"Hey!" Abby called. "You forgot to kiss me goodbye."

Celia rang Jessica at Rubicon to tell her that the Free Lilly Ernshweiger demonstration was set for Friday in front of Gracie Mansion. When Jessica hedged, said she didn't know if she could attend, Celia told her she had to.

"You have to," Celia said, "if you call yourself a woman." Jessica was too tired to argue; besides, Ernshweiger's was the only good bakery in the neighborhood.

Mike Halprin was uptown at the clinic most of the day, and without any help handling inquiries, Jessica couldn't get any of her work done.

When Mike returned, it was nearly five thirty. Jessica was ready to leave, and snippish. Before Mike removed his jacket she began to list all the things that had gone wrong.

"Now hold it," Mike said. "I don't know what's got into you, but you're too young to be menopausal."

"What does being pissed off have to do with my reproductive system?" Jessica said.

Mike gripped her shoulders. "Whoa, girl. Loosen it, will you? What you need is a drink or a joint. I can offer you both at my place, or we can go across the street to Billy's."

Jessica's head fell to her chest. "I'm sorry. It was a hairy day."

"How about a drink?"

"I have to get home," Jessica said. "Abby'll be expecting me."

"Call and tell her you'll be a little late."

Jessica hesitated.

Mike laughed. "You're acting like a pussy-whipped husband."

Jessica dialed Abby and told her she had some work

to finish up, that she'd be home in an hour or so. Not that there was anything wrong with having a drink with Mike, but somehow Jessica felt that Abby's feelings would be hurt. When she hung up the phone, Mike clapped his hands.

"Done like a businessman missing the five fifteen for Westport," he said.

"I usually help with the dinner," Jessica lied. "I'd feel too guilty saying I'm stopping off for a drink."

Mike tossed Jessica her coat. "Your guilt amazes me. Never has one woman paid so much for so little. Are you sure you won't cab it to my place?"

Jessica shook her head. "Billy's."

Mike sighed. "Billy's it is. Come on."

Billy's was an old ice cream parlor that had been converted into a bar and grill. The long formica soda fountain had been retained, along with padded stools that raised and lowered as they spun around. A large splayed ceiling fan, remnant of hot summers and cold phosphates, hung in the center of the room, its blades now painted in dayglo colors. The place was owned by Billy Dewes, a masochistic ex-alcoholic who ate his heart out every time he served a drink, and loved it. It had become a big weekend hangout for Columbia students who respected the place for not having a TV set and enjoyed drinking their beer through straws. They also enjoyed Dana Shapiro, a six-foot-tall waiter turned waitress with major silicone endowments that she'd exhibit regularly at ten and twelve on Saturday nights.

Mike and Jessica sat down at a booth in the corner. Billy's mother, who helped out during the week, and was known as a colorful character, took their order.

When she returned with the drinks she plunked a wooden bowl down on the table.

"Nuts," she said.

"Thank you," said Jessica taking one.

"To the whole mutherin' world," she said, and shuffled back behind the bar to her son.

"Drink up," Mike said. "If you were any tighter, your spine would splinter."

Jessica took a great gulp of her drink and coughed.

"I said 'drink' not drown." Mike leaned over the table and patted her on the back. "Okay?"

She nodded. Then she leaned her head back against the upholstery.

"So—" Mike cocked his head to the side. "What's bugging you?"

"Nothing," Jessica said quickly. "Shitty day, that's all."

"You look pretty."

"You're a master of non sequitur."

"But I know where I'm going," Mike said.

"So do I, but we can spare each other grief if you get off that path right now."

"Sica, Sica, Sica. It's so right. Our vibes are in tune."

"Sorry. Mine are all played out."

"I give up." He drained his glass.

"Now you're talking," Jessica said, and drained hers.

They ordered another round. Doubles.

"Hmmm. I was just wondering," Mike said.

"Wondering what?"

"If Victor makes love to you the way you ought to be made love to."

"If that means eloquently, inventively, and often, the answer is yes."

"Hopeless," Mike said.

"Hopeless," concurred Jessica.

They ordered another round.

And another.

"I have to leave after this," Jessica said.

"Should of known." Mike was now noticeably experiencing the effect of the alcohol.

"Known what?" asked Jessica.

"That you were the sort of chick who'd talk about nothing but sex for an hour and a half, get a guy all worked up, and then split."

"You're drunk," Jessica said, and knew from the way the floor swayed as she stood up that she was none too sober herself. "Thanks for the drinks." She held out her hand.

Mike brought it to his lips, and then slowly took her fingers into his mouth and began to suck them.

An unruly sexual thrill mixed with embarrassment streaked through her. "Mike!" she said, acutely aware of his agressive tongue circling her knuckles.

He took her hand from his mouth. "Sica—" he began.

"I have to go," she said.

"Cock tease," he muttered.

Jessica stood on the stoop for several minutes convincing herself that she'd done nothing to be ashamed of and trying to look sober. When she was sure she was in perfect control and free of guilt, she climbed the steps. She opened the door with a minimum of difficulty, and felt quite pleased with herself until she realized she'd left her keys in the lock. She reached round to retrieve them.

"Is that you, Jess?" Abby called.

"Me," Jessica answered cheerily, and slammed her fingers in the door. She screamed.

Victor came running from his den. "Honey, are you all right? What happened?"

Her eyes clenched shut, Jessica flapped her bruised hand in the air and pointed at the door.

"What happened?" Abby asked.

"Slammed her fingers," Victor said. He put his arm around Jessica. "You'd better run them under cold water."

She nodded. Hot pain numbed her forearm. *Why, God, why? I've been good.* She put her fingers under the faucet. They were already beginning to swell. *Christ! All he did was suck them.*

"Feel better?" Abby asked.

"I'm fine," Jessica said. "I like dramatic entrances." She kissed Victor and Abby. "Aaron asleep already?"

"I expected you half an hour ago," Abby said. "I would've kept him awake, but I didn't know when you'd be in and he was getting cranky."

"I ended up having a quick drink with Mike," Jessica said, as off-handedly as she could manage. "He was—uh—depressed."

Victor reached for her hand and she jerked it back.

"I just want to see if anything's broken," he said.

"Don't be silly—hey, what are you doing home? No karate?" Jessica's head began to clear.

"I've decided to drop out. It was just too much."

"Dinner's ready," said Abby. She waved a wooden spoon in the air. She'd seen a young bride do it on a Buitoni Spaghetti commercial.

"Great," said Victor with real enthusiasm.

"Swell," said Jessica without it.

Dinner was, as usual, perfect. Abby never undercooked the potatoes, never overcooked the vegetables, never even burned a pot. Not once had she forgotten to defrost the meat for the evening meal, or run out of a key ingredient. She whipped up her own mayonnaise, made pancakes and pie crusts without mixes, and, what Jessica found most incredible, she even made chocolate pudding from scratch. She followed recipes with an exactness that would shame a chemical engineer. Her culinary flair was limited only by Jessica's cookbook library, but eating the way Julia Child, Dionne Lucas, and *The New York Times* intended wasn't bad.

Except, as much as Jessica tried to deny it, it irritated her. She couldn't even explain why to herself, or rather didn't want to, but Abby's consistently flawless performance in the kitchen had in the last week grown on her like hives.

"Is something the matter?" Victor asked Jessica.

"No. Why?"

"You haven't said a word through the entire meal."

"I'm sorry. I was thinking about a new appeal letter," Jessica said.

Victor shook his head, placated, and went back to his discussion with Abby about why her utopian vision of absolute equality couldn't work.

"As Durant says, 'Freedom and equality are mutual and foresworn enemies, and men of superior ability will always choose freedom.' So you see—"

Abby interrupted him. "Just a minute. Jess, come on, what's wrong?"

"Nothing, really. I told you. It's this letter I have to write."

"You can't fool me," Abby said, now obligating Victor to renew concern.

"You really are quiet," Victor said. "Did something happen at the office?"

Damn Abby and her solicitation. "No. Do I have to talk all the time?" Jessica asked hotly.

"Wow. Something sure is bugging you," Abby said. "But"—she held up her hands—"if you don't want to talk about it, that's okay."

"I'm glad I have your permission to remain silent," Jessica said, her sudden acrimony causing Victor to choke on his pudding.

Abby got up and put her arms around Jessica. "You've been working too hard. Don't get upset. I love you."

There they were. The three talismanic words. The adult equivalents of "fins" and "no backs." Uttered as an explanation, they conferred upon the speaker absolute immunity from all further aggression. "I love you," the wifely ace in the hole. Jessica knew, when she had been beaten, and she didn't like it. Especially when she had been beaten at her own game.

"How about a nice warm bath," Abby suggested.

"A cup of coffee and two aspirins will be fine. I really—" she stopped when she heard the doorbell. "Oh, God. I hope it's not mother."

"It's probably Beverly or Dick," Victor said as he went to answer it. "I forgot to tell you. I've put Rowena Westcott back in business."

"You mean Tony O'Sullivan's no more?"

"Dead," Victor said.

"Why?"

Victor shrugged. "*C'est la vie.*"

CHAPTER 14

The morning of the Free Lilly Ernshweiger demonstration was auspiciously dismal. A slick film of late spring mist dampened streets and spirits. Jessica had taken her umbrella to work at Abby's insistence and was annoyed that, wet as the air was, it wasn't enough to warrant using an umbrella without embarrassment, except perhaps as a weapon. And on this particular morning Jessica had a strong urge to use it in just such a capacity. On anything that moved.

Abby had been distinctly cool at breakfast because Jessica couldn't tell her what time she'd be home. Abby planned the weekly meals on Monday and had scheduled roast beef for that night.

"Timing is everything with roast beef," she'd said. "If you would have told me about the demonstration, even yesterday, I could have switched the meals around."

"I'm sorry," Jessica said. "I forgot."

"Well, you'll certainly be home by seven, won't you?"

"It depends. I don't know what's going to happen at this thing. I might even be home before five. I'd just prefer not having a deadline."

"Or roast beef."

"I love your roast beef," Jessica protested.

"It'll taste like shit if the timing's off."

"Look. Make it for Victor and yourself. I'll have it cold whenever I get home. How's that?"

"Whatever you say." Abby began scraping the dishes.

Jessica came up behind her and kissed her cheek. "See you later."

You're forgetting something," Abby said. She dried her hands and went up to the hall closet, pulled out the umbrella. She thrust it at Jessica.

"It's hardly raining," Jessica had protested. "I don't need it."

"You don't need pneumonia either," Abby said. "Here."

Jessica kicked the umbrella under her desk and phoned Celia to find out when they were meeting. She hadn't yet told Mike that she was leaving early, and she wasn't looking forward to it. She knew his sentiments on women in politics. They were summed in a derisive flick of his mandala.

"Why don't you come by at two and pick me up," Celia said. "I can't carry all this stuff myself."

"What stuff?"

"Liberate Our Lilly posters. Lisa's sure that ABC, CBS, and NBC are going to be there." Celia's voice dropped. "You know, Jess, I'm a little disappointed that you didn't do more with your contacts."

"For god sake, Celia, I had Harvey do that piece for the *Times*, and believe me it's not easy to get space for lib these days. It's not hot copy."

"What about *The Ernshweiger Papers?*" Cella demanded. "Talk about 'hot copy.' "

"I don't know what you're talking about."

"If you'd been at the last few raps, you'd know."

"Don't start, Celia," Jessica warned.

"Okay. Okay. Lilly's notes from jail. They've been bought by Harper & Row. The editor over there told Bert that the book's going to be hotter than *Soul On Ice, Sexual Politics,* and *The Feministo* combined. I've got a Xerox of the manuscript. It's terrific. You'll love it. I've based my new marriage contract on it. Wait'll you see it. It's a beaut. You know, Jess, you ought to—"

"See you at two," Jessica said, and hung up. Marriage contract. Ha! She had a big picture of that. If she were any more liberated she'd be single and paying alimony and child support to Victor as well as Abby. No contracts for her, thank you.

Then the thought struck her: What if Celia enticed Abby into the Movement? There indeed was a chilling double bind. If Abby were just any ordinary twenty-year-old slaving away at being a homemaker, Jessica herself would urge her into a rap group. But with Abby being her own wife, it was different. Besides, Abby was happy just the way she was. Why shouldn't she be? She could lounge around the house, read, rap with the girls in the park. She didn't have to rush out for work in the morning or worry about a boss, and she had Jessica's charge cards for Bloomingdale's and Saks to use whenever she wanted. A girl like Abby wouldn't know what to do with liberation, Jessica told herself—but with not quite enough conviction to make it a Jessica Truth of Life.

She snapped a pencil in half and tossed it in the wastebasket. "Shit!" she said softly.

"Dock that woman two cents," Mike said, walking toward Jessica from the doorway.

"I didn't hear you come in. Hi."

"Obviously. You were too busy muttering obscenities and destroying public property." He took off his trench coat and hung it on the coat stand in the corner. "Trouble?"

"Depends how nasty you're going to get when I tell you that I won't be here this afternoon." Jessica twirled a lock of her hair around her finger, slowly. Deliberately.

"Why the hell—er—" He cleared his throat. "Why not?"

"I have an appointment," Jessica said.

"Doctor?"

"No. Personal matter."

"Personal matter?" Mike said suspiciously.

Jessica held her ground. "That's right."

"You're not screwing around on Victor, are you?" He asked the question with the look of someone about to witness a disemboweling.

"Of course not!" Jessica said. "Do you think I'm like that?"

"I've learned that it's the innocent ones who fool you."

Jessica stared at him with exaggerated disbelief.

"Victor's a nice guy." He shook his head as if the thought had just come to him. "Good man. I'd hate to see him get the shaft."

"There it is." Celia proudly flourished the three neatly typed pages of her new marriage contract.

"Looks signed last night." "Looks impressive," Jessica said.

"Is," Celia said emphatically. "Is impressive. Read."

Jessica took the papers. The newly revised Remson marriage agreement went like this:

1. PRINCIPLES

We fully adhere to the Ernshweiger principle of marital love as the hole in the doughnut of life. Marital love, like the hole in the doughnut, is nothing if not defined by its framework: the marriage. Doughnuts, unlike other foods which are often deep-fried, cannot be cooked by any other method; marriage, unlike other partnerships which are often contracted, cannot work with any other method. We believe that each partner has an equal right to her/his own thoughts, ideas, opinions, anxieties, socks, toothbrush, pillow.

As parents we believe in the Ernshweiger alternate-side-of-the-bed principle. Monday, Wednesday, and Friday husband gets up to care for children. Tuesday, Thursday, and Saturday wife gets up to care for children. Sunday children remain untended. In the event of an emergency, a coin will be tossed and the loser of the toss will take charge.

Celia was responsible for combing, cutting, and untangling the girls' hair, but Dave was responsible for washing it. Dave, on the other hand, was to get the children in bed and read to them, but Celia would tuck them in and kiss them goodnight. As far as the housework went, Celia would make all breakfasts requiring the use of at least one frying pan and Dave would prepare all others for a two-week period, after which the jobs would be reversed. On months with thirty-one days, Celia would do the meat marketing and Dave would buy the groceries, and vice versa for the other months. From January to June Celia was responsible for cleaning the oven every three weeks and from July to December it was Dave's job. From 3 to 6 P.M. on alternating Saturdays, Dave would do all the housework and Celia would entertain the girls, and from 4 to 7 P.M on alternating Sundays Celia would handle all chores while Dave entertained the kids. Contraception was Celia's responsibility on odd days; Dave's on even.

"Well?" Celia asked as Jessica handed the sheets back. "Is that a contract or is that a contract?"

It's a contract, all right." Jessica suggested that they leave for the demonstration.

Celia dragged a sheaf of large, hand-lettered oaktag posters from the closet.

"We're not taking all of those, are we?"

"Have to. You never know where the TV cameras are going to aim, so we have to spread them through the crowd." Celia glanced at the window. "Damn. You'd think Mother Nature would have some consideration."

On the cab ride over to Gracie Mansion, Celia asked Jessica how Abby was working out as an *au pair*, asked with detectable smugness that intimated a knowledge of something Jessica was unaware of.

"Swell," Jessica said warily. "Why?"

"Just curious," Celia said too easily.

Jessica wondered if Celia could possibly have any idea of the arrangement. It wasn't likely. Celia's perceptions of people and situations were fairly predictable, and if she'd had any suspicions she would certainly have voice them by now.

"I doubt that," Jessica said. "What aren't you telling me?"

"Jess, you're pleased with the way she's working out, so why should I say anything?" She paused. "If she were watching my kids it would be different."

"What do you mean?"

"I'd take a more directorial attitude. I wouldn't, for example, let her cavalierly jeopardize my children's safety or inculcate warped values. Really, Jess, I've seen her park Aaron's stroller right next to Mauser. Well, maybe not right next to him, but certainly within striking distance. And when I was standing behind her at the toy rack in Sloan's the other day, I saw her let Aaron pick out a water gun!"

Jessica looked confused.

"A gun, Jess. She happily let him have a gun," Celia said with horrified incredulity.

"My god, Celia. It was a water gun, not a Luger." She felt virtuous in her connubial defense. "He plays with it in the bathtub. He gets a kick out of it. Besides, it gives his penis a rest."

"Masturbation is normal," Celia said, lifting her chin. "I'd rather see a child jerk off than learn to become a killer."

"I don't feel confined to those alternatives," Jessica said, and dropped the subject.

The cab pulled up to the police barriers that cordoned off East End Avenue. When the driver gave Jessica her change he asked what was going on. Jessica told him about the demonstration for Lilly.

"She's a captive of the chauvinist state," Celia added.

"Say," the driver said, "that wouldn't be the dame who owned that bakery on Broadway?"

"The same," said Celia.

"Christ. I used to go into that bakery all the time," the driver said, "until the old broad went bananas."

"What do you mean, 'bananas?' " Celia growled.

"Bananas. You know, crazy. Last time I went there I asked for some éclairs and she got vicious. I'd tell you what she said, but you look like nice girls to me. Take it from me, she's better off behind bars. That one's a certifiable nut."

"Cocksucker!" Celia snarled.

Jessica gripped Celia's arm before she could swing and hauled her from the cab. "Come on. Watch the posters."

"He can't say that about *Her* and get away with it," Celia said.

Someone shouted Celia's name and her anger disappeared. She squinted into the swelling crowd. Women of assorted ages and varying dress, from blue jeans to minks, streamed out of the mist into the gathering throng. Many carried homemade placards demanding Lilly's freedom. A few were carrying candles, obviously unaware that the proposed torch parade had been canceled. Sharon was coming toward them.

"Celia. This way." Sharon waved.

"Our group must be over there," Celia said. "Come on."

A small platform, no larger than six seltzer crates, was set up on a truck parked in front of the mansion's gates. A microphone shrouded with someone's plastic raincoat stood on it. Hippolyte Green's storm troopers guarded the platform. Jessica craned to see if Eleanore was among them, and felt a twinge of adulterine guilt. She had to assure herself that she merely wanted to say "hello" before the guilt would disappear.

Sharon gave Jessica a cool nod as she took some of

the posters from her. Bert waited until Sharon had moved away, then sidled up to Jessica.

"How are the bookcases working out?" she asked. Then she winked.

Jessica's eyes darted. She had an irrational panic that someone had noticed Bert's wink. She wondered how men handled the winks and private nudges of girls they'd one-shotted in bed?

"Er . . . great." Jessica eased to the right.

Bert pinched her thigh, leaned forward. "Sharon's going to Puerto Rico next week," she whispered.

"I hear the weather's terrific," Jessica said. "Oh. I wanted to ask Lisa something. Excuse me." Jessica moved forward blindly; one of the posters she was carrying fell. Before she could retrieve it there was no longer any point in trying. The poster was soaked. Two young women in denim jackets glanced down, then marched right over it as if it were Sir Walter Raleigh's cape.

"Hi!" Lisa Lee said. "Isn't this absolutely the crummiest weather? I don't know if these things are going to be seen." She took one of the posters from Jessica. "I'm just going to hide my face with it anyway. My hair looks yecchy. I can't take dampness. I get the frizzies."

"You look fine."

"Thanks," Lisa Lee said, with the confidence of someone who never doubted that she looked any other way. "Usually I do a scarf number. Drape and tie, pull a few strands here and there. But I was in such a hurry today, I forgot."

There was a murmur from the crowd.

"Here comes Hippolyte." Lisa patted her hair.

"Where are those damn camermen?" She began swiveling her head.

Followed by four thin tall girls in green military-styled outfits that made them look like praying mantises, Hippolyte Green wended her way to the platform, smiling, waving, occasionally raising a clenched fist or making a peace sign with two fingers. There were loud cheers. Hippolyte Green demurred regally.

She grasped the microphone and there was an ear-splitting whine, the silence. Shouts of "Louder . . . *louder!*" rose from the gathering. The praying mantises stepped in front of Hippolyte and raised their hands for quiet while the microphone was adjusted.

Then Hippolyte began. She opened with a brief history of injustices performed against women. She spoke of Medea ("viciously maligned by men because she refused to be trapped in the humdrum of marriage"), Jezebel ("unfairly condemned by Biblical chauvinist pigs for asserting her female sexuality"), and Salome ("spuriously damned for getting ahead in a man's world"). She called Lucretia Borgia "a victim of misogynistic bad-mouthing," and said that Lizzie Borden was "merely an aware innocent who saw her life being sexistly forged by her parents and fought back the only way she knew how."

Jessica listened in rapt dismay. How could Eleanore have written such a speech?

"—and Lilly Ernshweiger is yet another victim of the poisonous patriarchy that persists in vilifying our vital female essence," Hippolyte went on. "Every day that we allow her to remain under the boot heel of the male Reich costs all of us a pint of pride and a pound of integrity as women. Are we going to let her remain a political prisoner? Are we going to let this happen? Are we going to let the most shining among us be snuffed out by—*them?*"

The women shouted, "No! Never!" Placards were waved wildly and one young woman leaped to the gates of the mayor's mansion and tugged on them, screaming: "Let our Lilly free!" until the police pulled her off.

"We will have justice," Hippolyte shouted, "for all sisters. If we don't get it, then we must take it. We must seize the courts, seize the lawmakers—seize the genetic code if necessary. But it will be done!"

Jessica could listen no longer. She had to get away. She signaled Celia that she was leaving. Celia looked stricken.

"You're not leaving?" Lisa Lee said. "We're making history!"

"My wife's making roast beef," Jessica said.

"Huh?" Lisa Lee looked intensely blank.

Jessica elbowed through the crowd without looking back. Toward the rear she saw one of Hippolyte's retinue in a raincoat and dark glasses standing alone. Every so often she'd glance at an index card, then let out a loud: "Clout now!" A *plant?* God, had Eleanore engineered all of this?

"Excuse me." Jessica tapped the girl on the shoulder.

The girl stuffed the index card in her pocket.

"Do you know if Eleanore is here?" Jessica asked.

"Eleanore Frimmer?"

Jessica nodded.

"Are you a friend of hers?" the girl asked suspiciously.

"An acquaintance," Jessica hedged. The way the girl had asked the question made her wary.

"You haven't heard then."

"No," Jessica said, suddenly concerned. "What's happened?"

"She committed matrimony," the girl said solemnly. "The worst possible way. She married a doctor from Scarsdale in a double-ring ceremony. Hippolyte got the details from Eleanore's sister and was sick for a week. They even had matchbooks at the wedding with their names imprinted."

Jessica saw a taxi, excused herself, and ran for it. She wanted to go home, but gave the driver Rubicon's address instead. She hunched in the corner of the back seat and hugged her arms around herself. She felt abandoned, alone. She felt foolish. She wanted to read Aaron *Peter Cottontail*, wanted to rub Victor's back while they watched the late movie on TV. She wanted an office with an intercom, a view of the East River, two secretaries. She wanted to have her own chicken soup—on an expense account lunch at Lutèce.

Mike was on his way out when she arrived.

"You're an angel," he said. He handed her a large overstuffed folder. "I was just about to drop this off at your house. I have to go up to the clinic."

"What is it?"

"Budget time, love. We're going before the committee next week and I want both of us to be prepared."

"Why do I have to go?"

"Because you have a persuasive ass."

Jessica slammed the folder back into his hands. "Shove it."

"Hey. I was only kidding." He followed her to her desk. "Come on. You know those guys, Harrison and Gellert, much better than I do."

239

She took the folder and dropped it on the desk. "Why didn't you say that in the first place?"

"Because I thought you had enough of a sense of humor to know it." His voice was cold and vaguely hostile. "You know I didn't mean that."

"About my ass? Oh, yes, you did." She didn't look at him. "Besides, even I know that it's true," she said tiredly.

Jessica sat at her desk for a long time after Mike left, staring at a crack in the wall.

Walking home down Broadway, she passed Ernshweiger's Bakery. The door was padlocked and there was a large CLOSED sign on the window. A furtive teen-aged hand had incorporated the letters in the sign into a gutter acrostic. It looked like this:

CLOSED
u   h   i
n   i   c
t   t   k

When Jessica arrived home, the aroma of Abby's roast beef flaunted its savoriness in the air, greeting her at the door like an insolent mistress. She suddenly reviled herself for being hungry.

"We're in here," Victor called. There was a bouyant lilt to his voice.

Abby and Victor were on the couch in the living room. They were beaming. They were drinking champagne from the good crystal.

"Party?" Jessica asked coolly.

"Bacchanal," Victor said. He stood, put his arms around Jess, and whirled her.

"Don't say anything until I get her champagne," Abby said. She brought in another glass, filled it.

"What's going on?"

"Faraday's backing the *Labroides Dimidatus* book all the way," Abby said excitedly. "And ..." She grinned mischievously.

"And?" Jessica asked, trying not to look annoyed.

"And Abby has toilet trained Aaron," Victor said.

Jessica felt as if she'd just been kicked in the stomach by her mother. She opened her mouth to speak and couldn't.

"Well?" said Victor. His smile wavered.

"I—I'm speechless."

"We thought you'd be thrilled," Abby said.

"I am. I am." Jessica swigged her champagne with the gusto of a soldier awaiting an amputation. "This calls for a celebration." She poured another glass.

"That's what we're having," said Abby. "I'll see if the roast beef's ready."

Jessica stopped her. "No, no, no. You stay right here. You're the guest of honor tonight." Jessica pushed her gently back onto the couch and headed for the kitchen.

"But I want to make gravy," Abby protested. "And Yorkshire pudding."

"Leave it to me," Jessica called back gaily. *Yorkshire pudding*? She pulled a cookbook from the shelf and quickly thumbed to Y.

"Jess? You sure you don't want me to help?" Abby called.

"Positive!" Jessica muttered silent obscenities as she rummaged through her rearranged closets looking for a baking pan. When she found it, she chortled. She was suddenly a housewife possessed. She beat the eggs, milk, flour, and drippings with dervish enthusiasm, pouring the batter into the dish with a sense of triumph marred only by the searing of her knuckles on the oven door.

She washed and dried the lettuce for the salad, ignoring her stinging fingers, and set the table like a Vegas sharpie dealing cards. She had worked herself into a domestic frenzy and her carving of the roast beef without mutilating herself broached the miraculous. When everything was ready, she took a deep breath and walked slowly back into the living room.

She smiled at Abby and Victor and stretched lazily. "Ready."

Abby blinked. "Wow," she said as she approached the table. "How'd you do it so fast?"

"Fast?" Jessica looked sincerely surprised, which was not easy considering she felt thoroughly rotten, confused, and on the verge of tears.

They drank two more bottles of champagne with dinner, and despite Abby's and Victor's protests, Jessica left the table while they were still eating to make zabaglione for dessert.

She refused to let either Abby or Victor help her with the dishes, and when she finally rejoined them in the living room, they were watching TV. She held out a bowl of freshly popped popcorn.

"Really, Jess—" Abby began uncertainly.

"It's a party." Jessica tossed a piece of popcorn in the air and caught it in her mouth.

"I think you're drunk," Victor said.

"Goddamn right," Jessica said. "And I want to get laid."

"Er . . . now? Laid?"

"Laid. Screwed. Balled," Jessica said, adding "Fucked" as an afterthought.

"But *Love Story*'s on right after this," Abby said.

Jessica backed up to the television and bumped her hip against the Off button. "Haven't either of you heard of conjugal rights?"

In bed she made wild loveless love to Abby, substituting erotic experimentation for sexual passion, then straddled a reluctantly aroused Victor, virtually raping him to climax. When it was over, she flung her face into the pillows and began to weep hysterically.

"Honey, honey," Victor murmured. "What is it?"

Jessica continued to wail.

Abby stroked her hair. "Jess, tell us. What's the matter?"

"Leave me alone," Jessica sobbed. "I'm always this way when I'm getting my period."

CHAPTER 15

"That's finished," Florence Siskand said.

Jessica cradled the phone on her shoulder and lit a cigarette. "I can't say that I'm unhappy to hear it."

"Arnold had a lot of problems. A lot of problems."

"You're better off without him, Mom."

"Don't you think I know it?" Florence's embarrassment for not knowing lay detectably under her indignation.

"You'll find someone else." There was always another Arnold.

"I know. I know." There was just the slightest sound of a sigh. "Anyway, what I really called to tell you was that I'm going away next weekend. I don't know if you happened to notice in the *Times* last week Goldie Kitchner—Abe's wife, Kitchner's Castle—passed away."

"No. I usually skip the obits," Jessica said.

"Oh. Well, I always turn to them first to see if there's anyone I know. And sure enough, last Tuesday, there was Goldie Kitchner. She had a special column, too. Not just a listing." Florence said this with some envy. "Anyway, I'm going up. Abe and I always

244

had fun together. It'll be good for him to see a friendly face."

Jessica smiled, shook her head. Her mother was dauntless. "Good luck. Call me when you get back." She hung up the phone and reluctantly returned to opening the mail on her desk. She could not concentrate. On anything. The simplest inquiry seemed open to as many interpretations as the *I Ching*.

Mike was busy showing Abby's replacement the filing system. She was the third in four months. Her name was Linda. She'd recently recovered from a near-lethal case of the clap and hadn't worked for half a year. Before that she'd been a social worker. She was enthused about everything, objected to nothing. When Mike would ask her if she cared to do this or that, her response would be an unequivocal, "I want to help."

Jessica phoned Victor. He seemed surprised.

"Anything wrong?" he asked.

"I was wondering if you were free for lunch," Jessica asked.

"Uh—sure. Why?"

"It's sunny and Tuesday and I thought it would be fun," Jessica said. "Tell me where and I'll meet you."

"Le Manoir?" Victor said uneasily. "Are you sure nothing's—"

"At twelve thirty," Jessica said and rang off. She began to hum.

She hummed for the remainder of the morning. When she left the office at noon, she told Mike she'd probably be late returning from lunch and was out of the office before he could question her.

Victor was already at the restaurant when she arrived. She slid in beside him on the banquette and kissed his cheek.

"Now what's this all about?" Victor asked, after she'd ordered a drink.

"I just wanted to have lunch with you," Jessica said. She brushed a hair back from his forehead, let her fingers trail slowly down around his ear. "Pretend I'm an author."

Victor's eyes narrowed, softened. "Tell me about your book."

"It's very sexy," Jessica said conspiratorially. "It's about this pond, see, and all kinds of damp and erotic things happen there. I call it *Deep Moat*." Jessica laid her hand on his knee. "I think you'll like it."

"I like it already. Tell me more."

Jessica moved her hand up to his thigh. "Well, there's this frog with a really, really long tongue, and he likes to—" She stopped and put the tip of her finger to her lips. "Maybe I shouldn't give it all away."

"You're not going to stop now."

Jessica wriggled discreetly, nudging her leg against Victor's. "I can be coaxed with mussels and a glass of Chablis."

Victor ordered their lunch, then stared suspiciously at Jessica. "You're up to something. What is it?"

"Me?" Jessica went wide-eyed. She reached across the table for his cigarettes and pressed her breast against his arm. "What ever gave you that idea?"

"Um . . . I think we'd better cool this game," Victor said. "You're rousing Randolph."

"Really?" Jessica batted her eyes. She slipped her foot from her shoe and scratched her toes against Victor's ankle.

"Jess, no kidding. It's getting uncomfortable."

"I have an old family remedy for that."

"At Le Manoir at high noon?"

"The St. Regis isn't too far away," Jessica suggested.

Victor smiled and tousled her hair. "You're a funny lady."

The waiter brought their lunch and Victor began to eat. Jessica didn't move.

"Aren't you hungry?" Victor asked.

"I was serious—about the St. Regis."

"Uh—you were?"

"Was—still am." She waited for him to say something. When he didn't, she said, "Well?"

"I don't know. I'd love it, but I think we'd both feel rotten when we went home tonight. Abby's so—trusting."

"And I'm not. Right?" Jessica snapped. She turned away. Victor reached for her arm, but she jerked it back. "Forget it. I wouldn't want to be the one to make you unfaithful."

"That does it." Victor put his napkin on the table, hailed the waiter. "We're going to the St. Regis right now."

Jessica's eyes rimmed with tears. She looked down. "No."

"Why not?"

Jessica snorted. "Why else? Abby."

"Is something wrong?" the waiter asked.

Victor took Jessica's hand. "How about a hot dog in Central Park?"

She nodded without looking up.

The waiter was acutely distressed when Victor requested the check, and when they got up to leave the maitre d' stopped Victor at the door. He fairly demanded to know what was wrong. Was it the service? The food? Victor explained that it was neither, that they simply wanted some fresh air.

The maitre d' refused to accept the explanation, pointed to an air conditioner. "Up there," he said.

"Up yours," said Victor. He hailed a cab and they rode in silence to the park. They bought two hot dogs from a Sabrett wagon and then walked to an empty bench and sat down.

"Talk to me," Victor said. He put his arm around Jessica.

"I can't handle it," Jessica said. "I don't know who I am, who I'm supposed to be—your wife? Abby's husband? A mutual friend? I'm being smothered by alternatives I don't want. Identity is everybody's problem, but at thirty do I need a gender crisis?"

"Do you love me?" Victor asked.

"Of course I do. But that doesn't solve anything. I love being your wife and Aaron's mother. And—ha—surprise, I even like doing things that define me that way."

"That's good enough for me."

"But not for *me*. I can't accept the strictures of that role anymore." She dug the toe of her shoe into the dirt. "I obviously can't relinquish them either. I'm going nuts. My consciousness has been raised so high I can't even reach it. I thought I had the perfect solution with Abby, but it's gotten all screwed up. I'm jealous, I'm guilty, and I've sacrificed the only freedom that means anything—the freedom to just be me—for an equality that can't, *doesn't* exist. I'm a martyr without a cause . . . and it's crucifying me." Jessica broke into tears.

"Crying won't help."

Jessica sniffed. "It's one of the few things that doesn't hurt, either." She threw her arms around Victor and squeezed him tightly. "I feel awful. What are we going to do?"

"We'll have to tell Abby," Victor said.

"Tell her? Tell her what?"

"That she has to leave. She'll have to understand."

"Have to understand! How can you say that when even I don't understand?"

"Yes, you do," Victor said.

"All right. What gives?" Abby said, pushing her chair back from the dinner table.

"Uh—nothing," Jessica pretended not to see Victor's frown. "This pie is delicious."

"You've been pushing it around your plate for the last ten minutes. Would one of you please tell me what's going on? I've been talking to myself all evening."

"Abby—" Jessica began, and could not continue.

"Abby," Victor said. "Let's go in the living room."

There was just the smallest flash in Abby's eyes, a tiny flicker of her lids, an infinitesmal dilation of her pupils. There was no measure minute enough to gauge it, but in that instant Jessica saw Abby hearing what they had not yet told her. And as they walked into the living room, Jessica knew that no matter what happened, the worst was over.

Abby sat down on the couch and Victor and Jessica sat on either side of her. They each clasped one of her hands simultaneously.

"Uh-uh," Abby said. "It's a heavy, isn't it?"

"A heavy." Victor patted her hand.

"Abby," Jessica said, "there's something we—oh, shit!" She turned away and started to cry.

"Jess, don't." Abby put her arms around Jessica and

held her. "It's okay. I understand. I really do. And it's all right."

She reached back and grabbed Victor's hand and squeezed. "It's even better than all right, it's perfect."

Victor winced. "Abby—"

"I know. You want me to leave."

Victor stared at her. Jessica lifted her head slowly.

"Before you say anything," Abby said, "let me. I've never been happier than I have been living here. You've both given me something that I never had before, never even knew I wanted. I didn't think that home and family trip really existed. I believe it now. And when I said that I understand . . . that it's perfect, I meant it. Like I've been feeling guilty for a while now, on a lot of counts. I didn't want to hurt you and I didn't know what to do but . . . oh, I might as well get it out." She took a deep breath. "Rick and I are in love and he wants me to move in with him."

"Rick?" Victor said.

"Mauser?" said Jessica.

Abby nodded.

"How?" asked Victor.

"When—" asked Jessica.

"I—I lied about my afternoons with the girls."

Victor sat in bed reading a manuscript and Jessica lay beside him staring at the ceiling. "It looks different, doesn't it?" she asked.

"What?"

"The ceiling, everything—without Abby, I mean." She remembered having the same perception of unfamiliarity when she'd brought Aaron home from the hospital. It was an ending-cum-beginning parallax, and she liked the view.

Victor put the manuscript aside, leaned back with his hands behind his head, and stretched his legs wide across the bed.

"Oh, Victor." Jessica sat up, distressed. "I just realized that we don't have any pictures."

"Pictures?"

"Photos. Of Abby." Jessica smacked the blanket. "Damn!"

"If it's any consolation, I don't have any pictures of my ex-wife, either."

"That's different. You threw them out."

"I don't have them, do I?"

"It's still different," Jessica said, "and don't try to reason me out of it."

Victor raised his palms. "Why, God?" Why women?"

Jessica punched him affectionately in the ribs.

"I wonder if it's too late for me to become a monk," Victor said.

"I don't know," Jessica said, "it's only twelve thirty."

Victor pulled her down and held her.

"I think Mrs. Williams is going to work out fine," Jessica said. "Aaron seemed to like her."

"Ummm."

"I hope there won't be any problems. I'm going to have my hands full preparing for those FDC hearings."

"Is Mike going to Washington, too?" Victor asked.

"He's not sure. Maybe. Why, are you jealous?" asked Jessica.

"Of course," said Victor. "You're going to be away for a week."

"Two nights!"

"I'll still wonder what you're up to."

"My usual standards. I promise."

"Bitch!"

Jessica kissed him.

"What was that for?" Victor asked.

"I'd forgotten how nice it was to have someone feel possessive about me."

"As long as that's all you've forgotten."

"That's all." Jessica reached across for the cigarettes. "Matches?"

"There are some on your bureau."

Jessica went to get them, and coming back stubbed her toe on Victor's barbells. "Victor! When are you going to get these things out of here?"

"Soon, I think. Beverly Davis wants to buy them."

"Good God, why?"

"With Beverly, who knows? Wants bigger tits, I suppose."

"Sexist," Jessica said.

"Okay. Maybe she doesn't want bigger tits. Maybe she wants to beat up her father. Better?"

"Stop right there. I'll believe the tits." Jessica nestled her head against Victor's shoulder. "Are they coming over tomorrow night? Beverly and Dick?"

"Oh, shit, yes. I forgot." He sighed. "I'll be glad when this one is finished."

"Rowena Westcott getting writer's cramp?" Jessica asked.

"I am," Victor said. "How many times can you write the same book? I'm ready for a change."

"Tony O'Sullivan?"

"I've been thinking about Victor Prior."

"I'm impressed," Jessica said sleepily.

"Nonfiction. Maybe the Boer War. I think it would be interesting from the Boer point of view."

"As long as it has a happy ending."

"You're incorrigible." Victor rolled over and began to nibble her neck.

The phone rang when Victor was somewhere around Jessica's navel. He answered it grudgingly.

"Oh—*Oh*, hi. Sure. How've you been?"

Jessica wrinkled her forehead, mouthed, Who is it?

Victor held up his palm. "I—uh—um—I—er no, no I don't think so. It's a—well, Jess is working and um—hang on, let me get her." He covered the mouthpiece with his hand. "It's Marilyn Kantor and she's 'dying' to see us again. Why don't *you* tell her no. I think it would be more tactful."

Jessica heistated, then a slow, playful smile crept across her face.

It was as playful as Eve's at the onset of her reptilian encounter, and imbued with as much wisdom and courage. It had spunk.

It was a perfect prelude.

Jessica covered Victor's hand with her own. "Why no?" she whispered.

Victor blinked. "Beats me," he said.

"Friday night?"

"Friday night."

Jessica took the phone. As she did, Victor's lips brushed her ear.

"You're a helluva a woman, Jess," he said.

THE SWEEPING ROMANTIC EPIC
OF A PROUD WOMAN
IN A GOLDEN AMERICAN ERA!

PATRICIA GALLAGHER

Beginning at the close of the Civil War, and sweeping forward to the end of the last century, CASTLES IN THE AIR tells of the relentless rise of beautiful, spirited Devon Marshall from a war-ravaged Virginia landscape to the glittering stratospheres of New York society and the upper reaches of power in Washington.

In this American epic of surging power, there unfolds a brilliant, luminous tapestry of human ambition, success, lust, and our nation's vibrant past. And in the tempestuous romance of Devon and the dynamic millionaire Keith Curtis, Patricia Gallagher creates an unforgettable love story of rare power and rich human scope.

AVON   27649 $1.95

CIA 5-76

"BASIC AMMUNITION FOR THE WORKING WOMAN"

Library Journal

getting yours
LETTY COTTIN POGREBIN

HOW TO MAKE THE SYSTEM WORK FOR THE WORKING WOMAN

The most important and informative guidebook you can read on the pitfalls and possibilities of the workaday world, GETTING YOURS is absolutely indispensable for the career-minded woman who is looking for a job opportunity that suits both her skills and her spirit.

From handling on-the-job sexism to dealing with conflicts between career and family, GETTING YOURS is filled with the facts and understanding you need to get your future moving.

"COGENT ADVICE, SOLID INFORMATION... POGREBIN'S SPIRITED ADVICE SHOULD STIFFEN THE RESOLVE OF WOMEN ON THE WAY UP AS WELL AS THOSE TOTTERING AT NEST'S EDGE."
—The New York Times

THE BIG BESTSELLERS
ARE AVON BOOKS